UNDER THE SKELETON FLAG

RUSSELL JAMES

SEVEREDPRESS

UNDER THE SKELETON FLAG

WWW.SEVEREDPRESS.COM

ISBN: 978-1-922861-91-7

Other books by Russell James

Rick and Rose Sinclair Adventures
Quest for the Queen's Temple
Voyage to Blackbeard's Island

Grant Coleman Adventures
Cavern of the Damned
Monsters in the Clouds
Curse of the Viper King
Forest of Fire
Mammoth Island
Atoll X
Desolation Canyon

Ranger Kathy West National Park Adventures
Claws
Dragons of Kilauea
Ravens of Yellowstone

Horror/Thrillers
Demon Dagger
The Portal
The Playing Card Killer
Q Island
Dreamwalker
Dark Inspiration

Dedication

For Christy,

On to more adventures. Always.

CHAPTER ONE

I'm going to tell you a story that you won't believe. I can say that because I scarcely have confidence in its veracity myself, and I lived through it. Am I writing it down to try and make you believe it, or to help me do so? I can't say for certain. Perhaps I will know by the time I pen the last page.

Most stories start at the beginning, but I will begin this tale earlier than that, because it is important that you know my background. My name is Baxter Whitcomb, and I am a rational man. That attribute led me to become a man of science in the profession of a medical doctor, trained at one of the finer London universities in all the latest techniques. I graduated in 1714 at the top of my class. I mention this not to brag, but to demonstrate that I have a history of exercising studious diligence. I am not one taken to flights of fancy nor a belief in that which I cannot see or touch. I will confess those attributes led me to scoff at anything claimed to be supernatural, at least until I'd experienced what I've recorded on these pages for you.

Part and parcel to my skepticism, my religious dedication had dwindled to just a bit more than lip service to the Church of England. That put me squarely at odds with the faith of my younger sister. Elizabeth had a strong belief in the Almighty, in fact in the entire Holy Trinity. She'd married a Catholic man and converted to his faith. This religious affiliation placed her in a minority in England, where the Church of England was almost universally attended, and nominally headed by the king himself. Feisty Elizabeth's position of being in an oppressed minority may have made her more determined to be a papist. She had a tendency to be contrary like that. She raised her daughter Mary within all the Roman sacraments.

How ironic that her religious fervor would change the life path of an irreligious person like myself.

Elizabeth's husband Franklin yearned to be out from under the religious restrictions of British rule, and the New World seemed like the place to do that. The eleven colonies along the American coast were reported to be havens for religious freedom, harboring Quakers and Calvinists and all manner of strange sects. A plan was made for him to travel there two years after I graduated university. I would look after Elizabeth and Mary in his absence. He would make a home ready for his family when they followed.

For eighteen months I did just that. Elizabeth and Mary resided under my roof. Some may think this was a burden to me, but it was instead a sheer delight, as I had always adored my little sister and her cherubic daughter was her diminutive likeness.

At the same time, in the four years since graduating, my practice and my reputation grew. The London populace had no shortage of maladies, to be sure. Between appointments with my wealthier private patients, I spent hours at the hospital, treating the lower classes, believing that a person's circumstances should not preclude them from treatment.

Now and again, letters from Elizabeth's husband made it back to London. His skills as a cooper had served him well, and he'd established a prosperous shop in Boston. After he'd purchased a house suitable for his family, a final letter arrived inviting Elizabeth and Mary to join him. To repay me for caring for his family, he offered to pay for my passage as well. He promised that the colonies had a keen need for doctors.

I appreciated, but had no need for his largess. I could have easily kept growing my London practice and lived a comfortable life there until the end of my days. But the idea of a new continent and unlimited possibilities intrigued me. I will confess that the chance for adventure was also alluring. My life thus far had been almost exclusively academic and occurred within fifty miles of London proper. Stories of a vast wilderness populated by strange and savage natives sent an anticipatory chill up my spine. What medical mysteries might I be the first to solve?

Last, and perhaps most importantly, the year and a half with my sister and niece under my roof had been quite pleasant. In fact, I'd grown quite close to little Mary, and seen in her the daughter I might one day have for myself. If I relocated with them to this New England in America, I could avoid the loneliness such a separation from them would engender.

So the three of us booked passage on a ship sailing for America. My excitement about my first sea voyage ran unchecked. I could never have imagined that only months later, I would vow to never set foot upon a ship's deck again.

***

I undertook this maritime journey with little understanding of what rigors lay ahead. I must confess that my lifetime had been spent in England's higher social class, a place of civilized teas, personal servants, and table settings placed just-so upon white linen. I'd dined on friends' personal yachts and assumed the sea voyage would be strikingly similar.

I was quite wrong.

On a cold, drizzly day, we arrived at the London docks for our departure. I'd dressed in what I'd thought was proper travel attire befitting my station in life; a long coat over knee breeches and a tri-corner hat hosting an ostrich feather. We entrusted our luggage with crew members, including my personal medical bag. The instruments within were precious to me, and I'd also brought with me a limited number of cutting-edge medical treatments to introduce to the New World.

Mary wore several layers of clothes, her mother being fastidious about her daughter's warmth and health. Elizabeth wore a simple, practical blue dress, with long sleeves against the chill air. Even covered so completely, she could not help but attract male attention. Her fair skin and red hair had done that since we were children.

Our vessel, the *Maureen Lavelle,* resembled my friends' yachts in no other way than it floated, and it seemed to do that poorly. All manner of aquatic life clung to the waterline. In my estimation, the two-masted brigantine seemed much smaller than a vessel crossing the Atlantic Ocean should have been. When we boarded the ship, I was immediately assaulted by a horrid stench that combined rotten food, human waste, body odor, and algae. Even bobbing at the dock, a constant chorus of creaks emanated from the deck and rigging, convincing me that the ship was prepared to disassemble itself at the least provocation.

The crew inspired as little confidence as the sad excuse for a ship. My expectations had been set by the splendid Royal Navy crews I'd seen at parades and ship commissionings, resplendent in their bright uniforms, exchanging salutes as sharp as the creases in their trousers. The disheveled men crewing the *Maureen Lavelle* were the opposite. Poorly clothed, randomly shod, and decidedly ungroomed, the crew were more reminiscent of a chain gang than a ship's complement.

My sister shared my disappointment at our vessel. "May heaven preserve us," Elizabeth said as we stood on the deck. She gathered Mary closer to her side.

It fell to me to present a brave face. "It won't be so bad. We shall stay in our quarters and have our meals served there."

Captain Montgomery approached from the stern. At least I assumed the small man was the Captain by the faded and frayed Royal Navy officer's coat he wore. His bloodshot eyes and unshaven face certainly would not have made me assume he was an officer at all.

"I say, Captain, I'm Dr. Baxter Whitcomb and family. Could you direct us to our quarters?"

Without a verbal response, and without breaking stride, he pointed to a hatch in the center of the deck and a set of steps that descended into the ship.

"He seems quite busy," Elizabeth said.

"One should never be too busy to be civil," I said.

We went below decks. My first thought was that the rude captain had misdirected us. There were no cabins here. Just an open deck, crowded with passengers standing about. To my right, a crewman was lashing closed the ports along the bulkhead. I asked him where the passenger cabins were.

He laughed. "Right here, your Lordship. Cabin Number One. The one and only. Enjoy the trip."

It was then that I realized my brother-in-law Franklin had booked our passage upon a ship that carried cargo and additionally passengers, not the other way around. And passengers were to be treated little better than cargo.

"Franklin could not have known the kind of vessel he bought us passage on," Elizabeth said.

"I'm sure he didn't." I wasn't sure of that at all. But I was certainly going to find out as soon as we set foot in Boston. His magnanimous offer of a ticket seemed far less magnanimous now.

We took up a spot against the bulkhead. I began to worry about the luggage we'd foolishly entrusted to the ship's crew for loading and that we'd seen the last of those trunks. To my relief, they were delivered, quite unceremoniously, to the hold a few minutes later. I immediately inspected my medical bag, and was pleased to find my instruments and medicines had remained untouched.

The ship left the dock and I took stock of the people around us. They were uniformly of the lower classes, sitting on bundles that may have been all they owned in the world. Dirty and forlorn, I got the impression that these were people with nothing to lose and everything to gain by a fresh start, however penniless, in the American colonies.

The medical practitioner within me came to the forefront. With quick spot assessments I diagnosed malady after malady: arthritic joints, poorly healed broken bones, wheezing congestion, boils, tumors. These were people who could not afford my services, and their maladies were the result. If this was a fair sampling of the New World residents, then indeed, Franklin had been correct. My services would be in great demand.

The discussions among my fellow travelers were filled with nightmarish tales of the sea. They shared horror stories of failed passages, with the next teller seemingly determined to top the tragedy told by the preceding person. Listening to them increased my own anxiety. You see, so many people had made this passage that I thought it rather a routine thing, an English Channel crossing on a larger scale. But these conversations were about dangers I hadn't considered.

I was already concerned about the seeming unseaworthiness of the vessel, and the haphazard look of the crew. To that I now added the potential of raging storms with gale force winds, of calamitous waves that towered over the masts, of shoals that tore the bottom off the sturdiest ship. Some mentioned sea monsters with such authority that I almost deemed them credible. The rolling of the ship and the creak of the timbers amplified every fear the passenger conversations birthed.

Then someone mentioned pirates.

With all the potential natural disasters that could befall the ship, I'd not even contemplated the humans who might do us harm. Tales of pirate raiders stalking the western Atlantic were rife throughout London. Several pirates had enough notoriety that their names were well-known. It was said they practiced a level of savagery that was inhuman.

This threat of piracy I placed last upon my list of concerns for the trip. In a few days, I would find that I should have placed it at the top.

CHAPTER TWO

As a doctor, I can attest to a strange phenomenon about women. The process of giving birth is almost uniformly arduous. There is tremendous pain, times of panic, stretches of exhaustion. Directly afterwards, most women assert that they shall never do it again. But somehow over time, their memories of the experience soften, and they come to believe that having another child would be a good experience.

I believe the same thing happens to people who travel the seas. All the softened memories of an oceangoing voyage they'd related to me were nothing like what we experienced aboard the *Maureen Lavelle.*

Unsettled weather paced our progress. We were subjected to constant motion, constant cold, and an inescapable dampness. Silence wasn't to be found amid the constant noise of the passengers, whether it be chatter when awake or snoring when asleep. We were served miserable and frequently wormy meals. Knowing the crew suffered the same fare did not make swallowing it any easier. Often I questioned whether there could be a new beginning worth this interminable voyage.

After many days, the weather changed. The ship-consuming waves of the deep Atlantic transformed into more gentle swells. A sun stronger than I'd ever experienced shined down from the blue heavens and the temperature became decidedly warmer. Our first port of call in the New World before sailing north with the currents to Boston was in Charleston in the Carolina colony. Everyone had told us that the weather would be a warm, but humid, change from what we'd left in dreary England. The crew took our change of weather as confirmation that we were approaching our destination, and that buoyed all our spirits. What we'd come to see as the worst portion of our journey would soon be at an end.

About noon one day, from our home in the hold, I heard a crewman sing out from high in the rigging that he'd sighted something off the port bow, though I could not make out his specifics. An officer barked out orders and then a great commotion among the crew followed, including the pounding of feet across the deck and the trimming of sails.

This raised everyone's hopes that at last we'd sighted land and would soon be free to leave this floating prison. I took my telescope from my medical bag, left Elizabeth and Mary beside the bulkhead, and rushed with others to an open hatch. I was giddy at the thought of seeing the green shores of the New World instead of the monotonous grays and blues of the open sea.

But from my vantage point, I could see no sign of land. The seemingly limitless horizon looked no different than it had since we'd departed. A collective sigh of disappointment rose from the group.

One of the boys had a keener eye than the rest. "Look there! It's a ship."

I'd purchased a spyglass for our journey and took it from my medical bag. I followed the direction his finger pointed and with my spyglass could see it quite well. Sails billowed from three masts and the ship was coming in our direction. As the distance between us closed, I could make out more of the vessel. She was a frigate, with the aft two masts more closely spaced together than the forward. The vessel was longer and wider than the merchantman we were aboard. My heart skipped a beat as sunlight set alight the black metal muzzles of the line of cannons that bristled from ports along the side. I was heartened that our war with France and Spain had ended two years ago, as our defenseless boat would be no match for this warship. I hoped that it was one of His Majesty's vessels, welcoming us to the colonial shores.

With the spyglass to my eye, I focused my attention on the ship's stern and tried to discern the colors that flew from the jack there. It flapped in the shadow of the aft sails and in that dusky light, I could not make out the design. As the ship shifted course and let more sunlight shine upon the flag, I realized why it was so hard to distinguish. The black flag carried but a faint design. Only one type of vessel sailed under such colors.

Pirates.

My pulse raced. A worse situation I could not imagine. We were defenseless passengers sailing aboard a defenseless ship, and yet I was responsible for the safety of my most cherished family members.

As the ship came closer, the others would also see that pirates were upon us. Before the panicked chaos from that realization erupted, I rushed back to Elizabeth and bent close to her ear.

"Don't act afraid," I whispered. "Pirates are closing on our ship. If they board us, keep Mary by your side and try to not stand out. These men want plunder, not people. If they don't think you can be ransomed, they do not want to kidnap you."

"But no one *would* ransom me," Elizabeth said.

"Just don't make them think otherwise."

From above came the sounds of flapping canvas and creaking pullies. The hull of the ship hummed as the *Maureen Lavelle* increased her speed. The Captain shouted orders echoed by mates around the vessel.

I am no seaman, but the futility of flight was clear even to me. Like a fox after a hare, the larger vessel would overtake us no matter how much canvas we set against the wind. Nothing short of a miracle could save us.

I returned to the port and set my spyglass upon the pirate vessel. Now I could see men rushing about the deck and scaling the rigging. Cutlasses and other weapons hung from their belts. Upon the raised deck at the stern stood a tall, imposing man in a long, black coat. A tangle of dark hair flowed down past his shoulders and a great, braided beard hung to his chest. Intertwined in both were a spate of burning fuses, spitting sparks in all directions.

I lowered my spyglass. Dread swelled in my chest until I thought it might still my heart. From the tales I'd heard, the ship's captain was none other than Blackbeard himself, the most heartless of all pirates.

Those stories told that Blackbeard had started his ignominious career as a privateer in the service of England during Queen Anne's War. Privateers were legal pirates, empowered to act with impunity against enemy shipping. At the conflict's conclusion, Blackbeard loathed to end this lucrative business, and continued to pillage without the consent of King and country. His ruthless reputation was legendary.

A cloud of white smoke erupted from one of the cannons. Seconds later a throaty boom rolled across the wave tops. A whizzing cannonball struck the sea so close to the port bow that the spray of its impact wetted the hull.

Blackbeard had issued his fair warning. The iron ball could have just as easily splintered our decks as splashed into the sea. The target of the next ball's impact was in the hands of our captain.

Orders were shouted across the deck. Canvas fluttered and timbers creaked as the rigging relaxed. The hum of the hull turned to a whisper. Our captain had apparently had enough.

Our plight was now clear to even the simplest of those below decks. Like wildfire, panic spread among them. I retreated to Elizabeth's side. We tucked Mary between us and Elizabeth began to pray the Lord's Prayer for the Almighty's assistance. Hoping God might also listen to one less devout, I added my voice to hers.

The ship passed us so she could come about at our stern and come up alongside. As she did, out a port I could read the name *Queen Anne's Revenge* painted across the stern. The black flag contained the figure of a skeleton pointing an arrow at a red heart. As if I needed any further confirmations, this was indeed Blackbeard's ship.

In no time, the pirate ship was alongside our vessel. Men launched grappling hooks at our deck and then tied the ships fast. Pirates cheered and then came the thuds of dozens of heavy footfalls on the deck above us. There were no sounds of fighting. Our crew was in no mood for martyrdom.

Pirates swarmed down the stairway. Seeing the only cargo here was cowering immigrants, they continued on down into the hold. The last one in the group stopped at our deck. Save for the sword at his waist, he was as ill-clothed and unkempt as the crewmen aboard our ship. The difference was the fire that burned behind his eyes and the malevolent smile upon his lips. He ordered us to bring our belongings and assemble on the deck.

By this point, I'd moved our belongings to the hold, save for my medical bag. Whether this would bode well or ill for us I could not tell. I grabbed my bag and stood between Elizabeth and Mary. The poor little girl was shivering in fear and I could not say that I blamed her. We tried to blend in with the passengers as they tromped up the steps and into the daylight.

Pirates had taken up stations all about the ship. Our crew slumped against the railing along the starboard side of the main deck. Our captain stood before them. The terrified look on his face said that we could expect no heroics on his part.

The pirates lined the passengers up along the port side of the deck. Elizabeth and Mary cowered beside me. I became more cognizant than ever about how much better dressed we were than the rest. Surely that would get us singled out. I moved to stand before them, and nudged them just a step behind me.

A voice boomed from the wheel at the elevated quarterdeck at the stern of the ship. The timbre and intensity of it set my organs aquiver. Never had I heard such a voice. I turned to see Blackbeard standing there. The fuses no longer burned in his beard.

"How lucky all of you are," Blackbeard said, "to be boarded by the one and only Blackbeard. Do as you are told, and you will be even luckier, and live to tell the world about it."

Blackbeard ran two steps and jumped upon the railing at the elevated deck's edge. Then without pausing to balance or judge the distances, he leaped from the railing down to the main deck. I could not believe my eyes as he sailed as high as the yardarm and nearly to the forward mast. I doubted a deer could have made such a leap, let alone a human. He landed to the sound of splintering wood. But he seemed unharmed, hadn't even flexed his knees.

This close to the pirate captain, I could now see his face clearly. I'd already noticed the maniacal look about the sailors he commanded, but Blackbeard's was even more alarming. A ferocity burned behind his eyes. The little of his cheeks exposed above his beard glowed, enflamed with red veins. I'd seen such a condition in men taken to too much drink, but this was something altogether different. The condition in drunkards was a sign of decay, a harbinger of circulatory collapse. This seemed more like a system unable to contain the power coursing through it, one on the verge of exploding.

I reached that conclusion through more than my visual observation. The man absolutely radiated power. Not the aura of authority a school teacher or royalty might display, but more like the sensation one had standing beneath a thundercloud about to burst into storm. The feeling demanded I take flight, while at the same time freezing me with fear.

It was clear that I was not the only one so affected by Blackbeard's presence. Across from me, expressions ranging from trepidation to panic painted the faces of the *Maureen Lavelle* crew, with none more affected than our dear captain. He absolutely shivered in his boots. As Blackbeard stopped before him, a dark stain grew around the Captain's crotch.

Whoops of joy sounded from beneath the decks. Pirates emerged from the hold carrying crates and barrels of the ship's cargo.

"Captain." The title slipped off Blackbeard's tongue with so much disdain it was as if the pirate could barely stomach attributing it to the pathetic example before him. "As with all things in the sea, the strong devour the weak. What was yours is now mine. I'll be taking the pick of your cargo. I'll also be taking the pick of your crew."

The Captain seemed about to object. Blackbeard pulled a dagger from his belt. The Captain cast his eyes down at the deck.

"So," Blackbeard said to the assembled men, "who has the courage to sail aboard the *Queen Anne's Revenge?*"

One young sailor stepped forward. I recognized him as one of the new sailors who had joined the complement when I had boarded. The lad couldn't have been over eighteen years of age, if he was that. A seaman's cap contained a mop of dark hair and a sparse beard sprung from acne-reddened skin.

"What's your name, boy?" Blackbeard said.

"Horace DeWitt," the boy answered.

"You think you're pirate material?" Blackbeard said.

"I went to sea for adventure," Horace said. "None of that happening here until right now."

"Adventure you shall have," Blackbeard said. "And riches to boot. Johnson, take him aboard."

One of the pirates grabbed the boy by the arm, and gave the lad a rough escort over to Blackbeard's vessel.

Two pirates began a physical inspection of the remaining crew, yanking up the men's sleeves and pulling back their shirts. I was taken aback by the number of tattoos the sailors had, as if each carried a visual history of their life and loves upon their skin. In my practice I examined many bodies, but even my indigent patients were above having such skin illustrations.

The pirates gave each of the sailors' tattoos a detailed inspection. One pirate stopped and held aloft a sailor's arm. The pirate pointed at a tattoo of a tall ship on the man's forearm. "Got one here!"

Blackbeard stood before the sailor and peered at the tattoo. "A Royal Navy seaman?"

The stout sailor carried several scars about his face that I guessed had been made by the edge of sharpened blades. Of those cowering in line, he seemed the least intimidated.

"Aboard the *Defiance*." He answered without pride.

"Warship duty," Blackbeard said. "We both served the navy in Queen Anne's War, then."

The sailor spat on the ground. "Privateers ain't Navy."

Blackbeard's eyes narrowed. "No, privateers did what your pitiful navy could not. My ship now has need for good gunners. Join us and you share in our spoils."

"Wouldn't join you thieving cowards for all the King's riches."

Blackbeard leaned closer to the crewman. To the man's credit, he did not flinch.

"Your choice." Blackbeard plunged his dagger into the man's gut and then whipped it straight up to his neck. I caught my breath. As a surgeon, I can tell you that it took unbelievable strength to cut through a ribcage like that with one swipe.

The sailor's face went white. His organs spilled upon the deck like they'd been dumped from a bucket. The familiar scent of coppery blood and bodily waste rolled across the deck. The crew and passengers recoiled in shock. The men beside the victim vomited. Several women screamed.

Before the man could collapse, Blackbeard shoved his hand into the man's chest cavity and grabbed his spine. With an effortless toss, he sent the corpse sailing backward, high over the gunwale, and into the sea.

"Press this worthless crew into unloading the ship," Blackbeard said to the pirate beside him. "Kill the lazy ones."

The pirate shouted orders to our crew and they practically ran down the gangway to the hold, apparently unwilling to be labeled as lazy. Even our pathetic captain joined the queue.

All this time, pirates had been messing about at the passengers' feet, sifting through everyone's belongings. If the men were looking for anything of value to steal, they were certain to come up empty-handed among these people. The growing frustration among the searching pirates proved this true.

One of them finally got to my medical bag and opened it up. He grinned as he plucked out the prize of my new spyglass. Then he pulled out a pair of forceps with one hand, and a clamp in another. With a confused look on his face, he held them up for Blackbeard to see.

Blackbeard's eyebrows arched. He marched over to stare me in the eyes. I confess I felt a bit like wax before a raging fireplace.

"Have we a surgeon here?" Blackbeard's breath felt hot upon my face. The scent of sulfur stung my nose. Terror sent my heart racing.

"Yes," was all I could reply.

"I'm in need of your service. Or my crew is. You will join us."

The idea of being in league with such a monster churned my stomach. My Hippocratic Oath demanded that I treat all who were in need, but to treat criminals in the act of piracy had to be exempt from such a pledge. Indeed, I would be treating them so they could mend and plunder anew. And I certainly could not live in the paralyzing fear of Blackbeard's presence. Full knowing the fate that the deceased Navy veteran had suffered would await me, I still gave the only answer I could.

"No."

Blackbeard looked shocked, then angry. I guessed that after the first killing, he was used to having complete compliance from his victims. "No?"

"I would rather die."

Blackbeard looked over my shoulder to my sister and niece. Then he pushed me aside so hard that I fell to the deck. He grabbed Mary by the neck and placed the tip of his blood-soaked dagger against Elizabeth's breast. "But would you rather *they* died?"

I hoped a lie would save my beloved family's lives. "I don't know those two."

"They happen to be the only two other people on board not dressed in rags, and you don't know them?" He slashed the top button from Elizabeth's dress and exposed her neck. "Perhaps I'll give my men a go at your wife before killing her. I'll let you watch."

Correcting him that Elizabeth was my sister wasn't going to score me any points here. "No! Leave her be. Leave her, and the others here safe, and I will go with you."

Blackbeard released Mary and lowered his dagger. "A learned man can make a smart decision. But you have not driven as hard a bargain as you think. None of these wretches would have been worth me ransoming."

At this point, the crew members looked like a chain of pack animals, carrying cargo from the hold over a gangplank to the pirate ship and returning empty for another load. Jeering pirates on board the vessel belittled the crew on their speed and weakness.

Blackbeard kicked my medical bag across the deck and it slid into my leg. "Get a move on, Doctor."

I picked up my bag and stood. I wanted to say goodbye to Elizabeth and Mary. Mary sobbed as she clenched her mother's skirt and I especially wanted to hold her close and tell her that everything was going to be all right. But I dared not try Blackbeard's patience any further, nor show him just how much these two meant to me. That would inform him of how much leverage he had over me, and he might even force them along as well.

I waited for a gap in the line of laboring crewmen, then fell in behind a thin fellow with a barrel upon one shoulder. He strained under the load as he worked his way up the gangplank between ships.

The bag in my hand was far lighter than the barrel upon his shoulder. But I felt as if the weight I carried overall was far greater. These men would drop their load and be back on the *Maureen Lavelle*. When I stepped upon the pirate ship's deck, I would be facing a daunting task. Treating pirates without all the proper equipment? Practicing medicine without the right medications? Doing this all on the wholly unsanitary conditions aboard a pirate ship? And to top it all off, I had the feeling that any failure on my part could lead to my death at Blackbeard's murderous hand.

I had left London in search of a new life and a bit of adventure. I should have been careful what I wished for, for it seemed that I was about to get both.

CHAPTER THREE

As soon as I stepped off the gangplank connecting the two ships, I sensed a difference, the way one does walking from light into shadow. The ship wore a cloak of darkness and dread about her. I looked about to see what exactly was different, but in general it looked little dissimilar from our vessel, perhaps a bit better maintained, in fact. But I could not escape the sensation that something deeply evil lurked below the decks.

I told myself that of course I'd feel this way. It was a pirate ship flying a skeleton flag commanded by a notorious captain. Only a fool would step aboard and feel anything but fear.

A tall man with long hair and red cap grabbed me by the arm and pulled me away from the line of men delivering the stolen cargo. He tossed me back against a mast.

"What the hell are you doing here?" he said.

I'd scarcely been aboard for seconds, and somehow I'd already run afoul of someone. "Blackbeard ordered me to board," I managed to say.

The man looked at my fine coat with disdain. "Why would he want the likes of you on board?"

"I am a physician."

Now he seemed to notice the bag in my hand. "Ah, that makes sense. There will be work for you here for sure. I'm Mr. Sneed, first mate. All your orders will come directly from me, and they will be followed without hesitation. Understood?"

"Completely."

"Expecting you did not volunteer, eh?"

"No. I was told to join this crew or my family members aboard the *Maureen Lavelle* would be killed."

"And they would have been. Try to desert, or shirk your duties, and they still will be. Blackbeard has spies in most of the ports, that's how he knows where the prime shipments will be. He'll send word to one of them, and that's the end of your family."

It was too early into my servitude to have thought about escape, but Mr. Sneed's warning turned me away from even considering it.

"You'll bunk where the last surgeon did."

"Do I want to know what happened to the last surgeon?"

"He ended up being poor at his job, and no, you don't want to know the consequences for that. Follow me."

I followed Sneed past the ship's wheel, to the stern of the ship where we climbed one of the two sets of steps to the raised quarterdeck. A railing ran along the forward edge of the deck, overlooking the rest of the ship. A U-shape of cabins enclosed the other three sides of the deck. The cabin at the stern appeared to stretch the breadth of the vessel. At its center, a pair of open doors revealed what I assumed was Blackbeard's cabin, though all I could see was a table with two upholstered chairs beside it. A chart lay on the table. Two stones kept the edges from curling up.

Sneed pointed to the open doors. "That's the Captain's quarters. Steer clear unless he orders you in. Even then you might not come out alive."

I had already decided to stay as far away from the pirate captain as possible, so this was a warning I did not need.

To my left, a smaller cabin covered the starboard side of the deck. Smoke slithered out of a crack between the doorframe and the door. It smelled strange and the scent tickled my nose.

Sneed placed himself between me and that door. "You don't never go into this cabin. Ever. For any reason."

Fear tinged Sneed's voice as he issued this order, and I could feel its source. The ominous sensation the rest of the ship exuded seemed twice as strong behind that door. At first blush, one would think Blackbeard's cabin would be the ship's evil center, but that cabin did not give me the chills the way the one behind Sneed did.

He gave me a shove toward the final door on the port side. "Yours is over here."

As I crossed the quarterdeck, I noticed a decoration carved into it, a five-pointed star inscribed within a circle. It seemed ominously familiar, but another prod from Sneed to my spine moved my thoughts back to surviving my present situation.

I opened the cabin door and was hit by a horrific stench. This gut-churning stink was one I'd encountered in only the worst medical conditions. If you can imagine a charnel house with an overlay of gangrene and hints of human waste, you can get halfway to how awful this room smelled. We medical professionals are trained to ignore such things lest they interfere with our focus on a patient's treatment, but it was difficult for me to not gag.

The room was certainly more similar to a closet than a cabin. A rough wall on the aft side marked where the cabin had been truncated and the missing portion re-allocated to Blackbeard's quarters. What remained was about as long as it was wide. A square, closed port let in some meager light. I'd wished someone had left it open to let in some fresher air. To my left, a hammock hung from bulkhead to bulkhead. The only furniture in the room was an unfinished table about six feet long and three feet wide. A single shelf on the forward bulkhead held an oil lamp, along with some rough pewter cups and plates.

I gave the table a closer inspection. Its scarred surface exuded the room's malignant odors. There were great gouges in the wood and dark brown stains in its mottled surface. It was then I realized the table's purpose and went bolt upright.

"This is your operating table?" I said.

"Sorry, your Lordship," Sneed smiled. "Ain't quite the Royal London Hospital now, is it."

"This is abominable. There's no room to work, too little light." I coughed. "There's no air. Working on the deck would be better."

"When there's cannonballs crossing the deck, you'll change your tune about that. You'll be patching up pirates in the heat of battle."

I could not answer. During medical school, Royal Navy physicians had spoken to my class about their combat experiences. The stories were ghastly. Cannonballs snatching away limbs. Huge wooden splinters driven through organs. Men crushed under fallen spars. They did not practice medicine in battle. They were human butchers, chopping off limbs from screaming patients.

"The smell," I mumbled. "I can't sleep in here with that."

"I'd open that window," Sneed said. "You'll get used to it. The last doctor did. Eventually."

On the main deck, boards banged against boards and sails unfurled with the slap of canvas. I opened the window to see that a hundred yards of water already separated the *Queen Anne's Revenge* from the *Maureen Lavelle*. Only my poor swimming skills kept the idea of crawling out the window and swimming for her from being seriously entertained.

Sneed went to the deck and began adding his orders to the cacophony of shouts among the crew. The hull groaned as the sails caught the wind.

In a panic, I searched the faces that lined the railing of the *Maureen Lavelle*. Then I saw them, Elizabeth and Mary standing amidships at the railing. I hung out of the open port and gave them a frantic wave. But Elizabeth's search seemed confined to the deck and she did not even glance in the direction of the cabins astern. Soon the ships were so far apart that the details of her face had melted into the crowd along the railing. My hope of a final farewell exploded and left behind a thick sensation of loss.

I tried to console myself that with Elizabeth and Mary still aboard the *Maureen Lavelle*, they were not prisoners here among the pirates. I dared not contemplate the deprivations that would likely befall them here. I could lament the martyrdom I'd volunteered for, but at the same time I knew I'd made the only decision any gentleman could make.

I wondered if the previous pirate doctor had thought the same thing.

CHAPTER FOUR

After the other ship had become an indiscernible speck upon the horizon, I stepped out of my cramped quarters. I hoped the breeze would cleanse me of some of the offending scents that now clung to me like spilled, rancid whale oil. I hadn't been told I had to stay sequestered. A dose of bright sunlight and fresh air would likely improve my disposition.

As soon as I stepped through the doorway, the first mate appeared and grasped my arm.

"Get your bag and come with me."

I picked up my bag and followed Sneed down to the main deck. Pirates manned the capstan and climbed through the rigging like squirrels in an oak tree. The ship veered to starboard and the sails caught the wind. Crewmen scurried out of his way as Sneed made a beeline for the fo'c'sle. The men closed back in behind him to continue their work, usually bumping into me as if I was invisible.

It was during these inadvertent close encounters that I noticed something all the pirates shared. Upon their necks each one had the same tattoo. It encircled their neck above the collarbone and resembled the crown of thorns worn by Christ, though that was certainly the only Christ-like attribute the pirate crew likely had. At the base of the back of each pirate's neck, the two ends of the tattoo joined at a five-pointed star within a circle. Seeing the same symbol from the quarterdeck again reminded me that it was always associated with the occult. I assumed that Sneed had the same skin illustration as well, but a scarf tied about his neck kept me from confirming it.

We entered the fo'c'sle and a crewman lay upon the deck. The right leg of his trousers had been cut away and exposed a deep slash across his thigh. He held both hands to the cut, pressing the wound closed as if it might decide to knit itself back together with his encouragement. Blood leaked out between his fingers and into a growing puddle on the deck.

The pirate could not have been much past the age of majority, with the patchy facial hair of youth still upon him. His eyes were wide with fear, his face white. Sweat beaded across his forehead. He winced and trembled as he stared at the gash in his leg. Whatever adventure this boy had believed pirating was, it was clear that receiving a severe wound had not been part of it.

I also noticed the faces of the brigands who stood around him, staring. Their countenances were also masked in concern, some in fear. It was hard to believe that these quaking men were the same fearless howling pirates that had boarded my ship less than an hour ago.

I set down my bag and knelt by the injured crewman. "I am Doctor Whitcomb. What's your name, son?"

"Wilkes," he managed to say.

"Okay, Wilkes. Take deep breaths and try to relax. I'm going to look at your wound, all right?"

The pirate nodded a half-dozen times and pulled his hands away. The gash opened up and blood began flowing freely. The wound was deep, through the outer tissue and into the muscle. But not to the bone, thank heaven, nor was any artery severed. But he certainly wasn't walking back to my poor excuse for an operating table.

I hadn't seen any of the crewmen from my ship put up a fight to repel the pirates and wondered how he'd gotten injured. "How did this happen?"

"I tripped," Wilkes said. "Landed on my own sword."

"You're lucky. This will heal, eventually." I applied pressure to the wound to stop the blood flow. "I'm going to sew the wound closed and bandage it. This is going to hurt."

"Not as much as it already does," the pirate said behind clenched teeth.

"You will be unpleasantly surprised." I looked over my shoulder at Sneed. "Where are your medical supplies?"

Sneed pointed at my bag. "Right there."

"You can't be serious."

When Sneed didn't smile, I knew he was indeed quite serious. I was expected to do major surgery with nothing more than the contents of my bag. One might as well be asked to build a house with a handsaw and a hammer. And to add a bit more pressure, this was where I was to prove myself worthy of having Blackbeard keep me alive, unlike the last doctor.

One of the other pirates gave the injured man a bottle of rum. "Here, lad, for courage."

Wilkes took the bottle and guzzled the contents. I was not about to stop him. Passing out drunk might be the best thing to happen to him right now.

I had the ersatz bartender who delivered the rum take my place holding the wound closed. Then I told Sneed I'd need some water, not the fresh water the ship had aboard, but saltwater from the ocean. Sneed sent a pirate to fetch some. Many accomplished doctors would have simply closed the wound, but my experience had validated some of the newer theories that a level of sanitation helped in the healing process. Cleaning the wound with seawater would be as close as I would be able to get to clean, and I'd observed natural healing properties in saltwater.

The pirate soon returned with a bucket of seawater with a coil of rope still attached to the handle. I prepared catgut and a needle for the suturing. By the grace of God, the wounded pirate was a lightweight when it came to alcohol, and was quickly quite inebriated and then passed out. I had two volunteers hold him down anyway.

"Can you disperse this audience so I may work, please?" I asked Sneed.

He sent the pirates off with some curt, profane commands and followed them out onto the deck. The volunteers held the injured pirate down at the ankles and shoulders, and I began treatment. After a splash of rum in the wound elicited no response in him, I went to work stitching him closed. I can tell you I was more nervous here than during my first surgery in medical school, for the stakes in this surgery's success were much higher. My needle slipped from my fingers more than once.

After what seemed like an eternity, I finally finished the last stitch. Owing to a clean wound and my own skills, the result looked as good as I could have done in a hospital. Oh, the man would have a nasty scar, but if he stayed off his leg for a while, he would walk again with only the slightest limp. I washed the wound down in salt water. Someone had come up from the hold with a fine woman's dress and given it to me to use as a bandage. It must have been part of the booty taken from one of Blackbeard's prizes. The crewman must have thought that the quality of the cloth made it a better bandage. I ripped free a sleeve and bound the wound tight.

When I was finished, I had the two crewmen lift the passed-out pirate into a hammock and told them he was not to move from there without assistance until I'd cleared the man to walk. I left the fo'c'sle to meet Sneed standing outside.

"He shall recover given the proper amount of rest. I daresay a week or two before he can even walk about."

Sneed did not look impressed by my accomplishment. I was quite offended given how little I had to work with and how well the surgery had turned out. He grunted and motioned me to follow him back to the stern.

When we got to the cabins, he hustled me past my own and into the Captain's cabin in the middle. My stomach sank and I stopped short of the doorway, remembering Sneed's command to never enter unbidden. Then he pushed me through it anyway.

Stumbling inside, it was as if the pull of gravity increased. The air felt thicker. Movement came slower. As a doctor I knew this had to be some trick of my mind, but that understanding did not allow me to overcome the sensations.

Blackbeard stood behind the chart table. He bit the tip off a dried sausage he held in one hand and chewed it savagely. I recognized the label on the sausage as the same brand I had packed in my baggage as a gift for my Boston brother-in-law. I doubted the pirate knew the sausage was mine, but his action incensed me nevertheless.

But my anger flash froze into ice as I beheld Blackbeard. There are people in the world whose presence makes one happy. They have an undefinable radiance about them, a contagious cheerfulness. Blackbeard was the opposite of that. There was an ominous shroud of darkness about him, and under it there seemed a percolating sensation of rage, ready to boil over. On the deck of the *Maureen Lavelle*, Blackbeard had been scary, but in this confined space, he was terrifying. As Sneed and I entered, the pirate captain looked up, but only at Sneed.

"Did he operate on Wilkes?"

"Yes, sir. Sewed him up good."

I was taken aback being spoken about in my own presence. After all, I was the medical expert.

"Two weeks of rest and he should be back to duty," I chimed in.

Blackbeard continued to only look at Sneed. "Throw him overboard."

Shock jolted through me. I'd done as asked, and done it well if I did say so myself. I didn't warrant being thrown to the sharks.

"Aye, aye," Sneed said.

I dreaded the clamp of Sneed's hand upon my person, but instead he wheeled about and left the cabin. A combination of curiosity and a desire to get out of Blackbeard's malevolent presence bid me to follow him. Sneed went to the railing and shouted an order to the pirates forward to bring out Wilkes.

"Wait," I said, "what are you doing?"

Sneed paid me as much heed as Blackbeard had. Two pirates entered the fo'c'sle and returned dragging Wilkes out, one of them holding the poor man's wrists, the other his ankles. Wilkes was still out cold.

"Surely you aren't going to throw him overboard," I said. "His wound will heal, I promise you."

Sneed ignored me. "Pitch him!" he shouted to the two pirates.

The men shuffled their human cargo over to the railing, swung him back and forth twice, and on the third swing sent him sailing over the side. I ran to that side of the ship and looked over the railing.

Wilkes hit the sea with a splash. The impact and the cold water brought him instantly awake. He surfaced, splashing and gasping among the waves. With the ship's forward motion, he was already nearly astern.

Wilkes cried out for help, called other pirates by name. In my mind's eye, I could see his kicking tearing all his stitches asunder, destroying both my work and any chance he had to stay above water. But as he fell back into the ship's wake, I realized that swimming only put off the inevitable. There was no land to swim to, no other vessel would pluck him safe from the sea. He would stay afloat until exhausted, then drown if sharks did not find him first.

I gripped the railing, equal parts incredulous and furious. As one trained to preserve life, this blatant disregard of it struck me as inexcusable. If my best efforts here were to be wasted, what was the point of my passage?

Sneed grabbed me from behind at the collar and dragged me back into Blackbeard's cabin. The Captain still stood behind the table.

"It's done?" Blackbeard said.

I was so angry that I did not wait for Sneed to answer. "Yes, it's bloody well done. A man is good as dead, a man I treated, a man who would have been back to duty in two weeks."

Blackbeard finally looked me in the eyes. I wished he hadn't. The fury that had fueled my insolence dissolved. His withering, malevolent gaze made me feel like a sheet of paper laid before a blazing hearth, slowly singed and shrinking from the heat.

"Two weeks of him consuming stores and providing nothing," Blackbeard said. "And after that, what do I get? A sailor so clumsy he nearly cuts off his own leg with his own sword. He's of better service feeding the fishes."

"That was barbaric." Only after saying that did it register with me that I was talking to a man who stole and pillaged as a trade.

"Wilkes' death isn't on me, Doctor. It's on you. Your job is to keep the men on this ship fit for combat, not to make them useless convalescents. We are a pirate ship, not a hospital."

"Then why did you have me treat him?"

"A test. Two actually. One of your willingness to work, the other of your skill when doing so. Lucky for you, you passed both tests, or you'd be keeping Wilkes company out in the ocean." Blackbeard turned back to Sneed. "Get him out of here. And then get me an inventory of what we took off his ship."

"Aye, aye."

Sneed did not have to drag me out of the cabin as he'd dragged me in. I turned on my heel and was out the door in an instant. Sneed followed me over to my cabin.

"Now you know how things work here, Your Lordship," he said. "The rule is be useful or swim with the sharks. You need to work hard keeping yourself useful."

I entered my cabin and stuck my head through the port to take away some of the smell. I could not believe it, but this voyage was going to be even worse than I'd expected.

CHAPTER FIVE

As I'd been given no instructions about the basics of my enforced journey with Blackbeard, I wondered how I would get fed. I assumed I would, of course, but knew not when, nor if I would eat with the crew. With the rations aboard my previous ship being quite meager, my interest in these details was soon keen. Knocking on Blackbeard's door and asking was out of the question. I had the feeling that Sneed would reply to any query I put forward with a blow to the jaw, so I wasn't about to ask him. I resolved that I would wait until given instructions.

I did not have to resort to that. As evening approached, a knock sounded upon my cabin door. I opened it to find a short pirate in tattered clothing. He had a horribly crooked nose, likely broken and never reset. In his hands he held a wide pewter plate. An identical plate rested inverted upon the first, acting as a cover. The pirate passed me the plates.

"Dinner, sir."

"Blackbeard ordered you to bring me this?" I really wanted to know if Blackbeard had worried about my hunger, for so far it seemed like I was more of an inconvenience to the pirate captain than an asset.

"Uh, no sir. I serves the officers, and I was serving the last doctor, so I just assumed…"

He motioned to take back the plate. I stepped away out of his reach.

"I wasn't complaining," I said. "And what actually happened to that last surgeon?"

"Well, sir, he fell out of favor with Blackbeard, he did. Not a wise thing to do aboard this ship."

"Blackbeard threw him overboard?"

"Eventually."

I imagined a cat playing with a mouse before killing it, and resolved to ask no more questions about the previous ship's doctor.

"I saw what you done for Wilkes," the pirate said. "He was my mate and you treated him right, you did."

"For all the good it did him in the end."

"Like I said. Don't fall out of favor with Blackbeard." The man pulled a bit of sandstone the size of a fist from his pocket. "You can use this holystone, sir, with a bit of seawater, to get the stain and stink off'n that table there. Make the cabin a bit more livable, that will."

I set my plate on the table and took the stone from him. "Thank you. Your name is?"

"Joshua Barnes, sir." He gave the setting sun a terrified glance. "Best be about my business, sir. Don't pay to be on the quarterdeck after dark."

I was about to ask him why, but he was gone before I could. I closed my door and lit the small oil lamp in the room. Uncovering the plate revealed salted meat, and an assortment of pickled vegetables and fruit. A single piece of hardtack lay across the top. I confess I only recognized the cracker from derisive descriptions I'd read in stories.

With great force, I was able to break the cracker. I despaired over what it would do to my teeth should I try to chew it. I poured some water into a pewter mug and dropped chunks of the cracker into it. I hoped it would soften enough to make it digestible. The process took quite a while.

The rest of the meal proved to be awful, but my growling stomach silenced any objections my tastebuds offered. It was certainly better than starving.

With little else to do, I moved the plates to the floor, and poured the last of my water from the mug onto the edge of the table. I grabbed the holystone with both hands and began to scour the wood.

***

A while later, the monotony of the scrubbing and the growing ache in my shoulders convinced me to give cleaning the table a rest. As far as I could tell by the yellow lamp's light, I'd given about a quarter of the surface a good cleaning. I hoped I'd be lucky enough that no events would arise that would make me stain it again, but I doubted that was possible. I climbed into my hammock.

Even deep into the night, a ship at sea is never silent. Rope and sail and hull are in a constant battle for position, and they creak and moan with every shift in the wind. The ship itself is never still, with the deck tilting to and fro as the bow plows through the waves. The hammock provided some respite, but sleep was still elusive under such conditions.

During the night, I heard the tread of boots upon the deck outside my cabin. I looked out the window to see Blackbeard himself standing on the quarterdeck, illuminated by a lantern sitting at his feet. He held a sextant aloft, took a star sighting, and scratched the result down on a bit of paper. He did this several times. I wondered if he performed this task because none of his crew had the skill, or if it was because he did not want any of them to know their position.

He finished and placed the sextant in the pocket of his long coat.

The door to the cabin across from mine opened. As this was the cabin I'd been forbidden to ever enter, my curiosity piqued.

The lantern glow through the open door backlit a short, stooped figure. The slight build and the long, flowing skirt told me the person was female. She wore some kind of strange, peaked hood, and as she stepped into the light of Blackbeard's lantern, I could see that a cloth across the front of it covered her face below her eyes. Everything the woman wore was black, save a silver medallion on a chain about her neck. The medallion contained the same circle and five-pointed star design I'd seen tattooed on the back of the pirates' necks.

This shadowy figure created the most dreadful sensation in me, like the fear one gets in the face of a towering wave about to crest upon one. There was nothing threatening about the woman, while at the same time everything about her was. I'd never felt this way before.

The woman stopped by Blackbeard and he turned to face her. With both hands, she held out a small gold bowl between her and the Captain. He struck a match that illuminated both their faces, then dropped it in the bowl. The contents caught fire in an instant, but it was the strangest fire I'd ever seen, with flames of bright green and a darker green smoke that seemed to glow as if it too was on fire.

The two bowed their heads over the smoking bowl. The woman lowered the veil from her face. The details were vague, but the features were of an old woman. She recited an incantation in a language I had never heard before. It struck me odd that these were the first words either had spoken since they had met.

Then the rising smoke narrowed and formed what looked like the head of a cobra snake. The woman opened her mouth and the smoke snake passed inside her. A second later, two green tendrils exited from her nostrils and made their way to Blackbeard. Like creeping ivy, they wrapped around his neck, across his shoulders, down his arms, sending more tendrils out with each inch they covered, until a pulsing green glow encompassed the pirate captain's body.

The woman blew into the bowl. It exploded into a cloud of bright blue flashes and then went dark. The glow around the Captain dulled and then vanished. The woman uttered another set of phrases I did not understand. Then she reset the veil to her face, turned about, and returned to her cabin.

Blackbeard took a deep breath, stood erect, and squared his shoulders. A satisfied, wicked grin crossed his lips. It may have been a trick of the lantern light, or a concoction of my own mind, but I could swear that I saw a green fire flash within his eyes.

Blackbeard laughed, a joyous, evil laugh, scooped his lantern from the deck, and returned to his cabin.

My shock upon witnessing this event cannot be overstated. As I said, I am a rational man, a man of science, but what I'd just seen conformed to no science I knew, or even knew of. Clearly something in the supernatural realm was at work on this ship, and on its captain. I struggled for an explanation for what I'd witnessed, but could only come up with one, a reason that in all honesty made as much sense as unicorns, dragons, and specters of the dead.

The woman in the other cabin was a witch.

CHAPTER SIX

I can testify that I endured a poor night's sleep that night. While the events of the past few days had left me physically exhausted, they had also left me mentally hyperactive. Physical dangers and supernatural threats consumed my waking thoughts, and in my brief moments of slumber, rose again in my nightmares. I welcomed the rising sun and the promise of a new day.

Joshua came to my door with breakfast. I uncovered the dish to reveal a morning meal very similar to the previous evening's dinner. I considered myself lucky to be fed, and surmised that pirate cuisine would by nature be minimalist and repetitive.

"Joshua, tell me of the woman in the cabin across the deck."

His eyes widened. "Don't cross paths with that one if you can avoid it, sir. That's Dumitra. She's a witch through and through."

"Blackbeard doesn't seem to fear her."

"Blackbeard's why she's here. I was here when she first came aboard."

This promised to be an interesting story. I waved him into my cabin out of sight of the rest of the crew. He looked left and right, then stepped inside and into the shadows.

"Abouts a year ago," Joshua said, "we stopped in Port Royal to resupply. I'm told that before the big earthquake in '92, the place was pirate heaven. Free reign to do as one pleased. Well, it wasn't no heaven now, but we managed to trade what we had for what we needed.

"While we was in port, I am scrubbing the quarterdeck between the cabins. I stand to take a break to stretch my back. I look to the dock and that's when I seen her for the first time. She comes walking down the dock like she owns it. Hair black as a raven's wings hangs down past her shoulders and she's wearing a dress red as a cardinal's cassock."

That description did not match the old woman in the cabin across from mine. Perhaps Joshua glimpsed her in poor light. I certainly had, so it could just as easily have been my perception that had been off.

"Men laboring on the dock stop working as she passes by. First off, I think it's the usual sailor's reaction to any woman after a long time at sea. But later when she comes upon me, I learn the true reason. She brings a chill down my spine just passing me by, like someone's walking on my grave. Truly I'd never felt such a terrifying thing. You might doubt me, but I swear it's the truth."

I had doubted that Joshua had seen the same woman I'd seen on the deck, but that doubt was now banished. I'd felt that exact same sensation in the witch's presence.

"Dumitra marches up on deck and gets Mr. Sneed's attention where he was working on the bow. Woman or not, no one boards the *Queen* without his permission. He pulls his pistol from his belt and heads straight for her with the same look in his eyes as before he's to administer a flogging.

"Mr. Sneed steps right in front of her to block her way. Maybe he doesn't feel the darkness around her, maybe he is just brave as hell. He asks her who the hell she thinks she is boarding Blackbeard's ship.

"She barely pauses. She puts two fingers on his forehead and says 'Sleep!' Then Mr. Sneed collapses faster than a sail with a parted halyard. He drops his pistol. It hits the deck and goes off.

"That boom is enough to bring a furious Blackbeard out of his cabin. My position on the quarterdeck puts me right between the two, which is the place I least want to be. I back up into the cabin across from yours to get out of Blackbeard's line of sight.

"Blackbeard shouts 'Who fired that gun?' No one answers, likely all balancing between the fear of falling under Blackbeard's wrath and the terror this strange woman inspires. She ain't afraid. She just climbs the gangway to the quarterdeck and stops, facing Blackbeard. At this point, he notices Mr. Sneed collapsed on the deck. He draws a dagger from his belt and bellows, 'You killed my first mate!'

"'He's not dead,' she says. 'And I can do the same thing to you. Or to your enemies. Your choice.'

"Blackbeard lowers his dagger. Blackbeard must not have noticed me slipping into the cabin because he speaks to her as if no one can hear. 'What power is this you have?'

"'The power of magic,' Dumitra says. 'The power to make you invulnerable and your men fearless. You will gather riches beyond your wildest dreams.'

"I could see Blackbeard's eyes light up. If this woman could lay low someone as stout as Sneed, and make it possible for him to become the greatest pirate to ever sail the seas, he was going to hear her out. He leads her back to his cabin, and she's never left the ship since then."

Joshua's story filled in a few blanks. The ritual I'd seen her perform on Blackbeard the previous night might have been that conveyance of invulnerability, or a reinforcement of it. The pirate captain had certainly seemed rejuvenated by it.

"How is it that—"

"Joshua!" shouted Sneed from the quarterdeck.

Joshua went pale. He grabbed my plates from the table and rushed out the door. "Here, sir! Delivering breakfast, sir."

"Except mine, dammit. Get it now."

"Right away, sir."

Joshua scurried away back to the galley. I'd lost my breakfast but gained some insight. A fair trade I thought, considering my position.

At the time, my knowledge of witchcraft was quite minimal, though I have done considerable research since then, trust me. While I'd heard of people accused and convicted of witchcraft, I'd never seen a witch in person, or knew anyone who had. That made the whole idea more akin to myth than fact in my mind. But now I'd seen witchcraft practiced, and heard a first-hand, credible account of some of the extent of its power.

Only Blackbeard seemed comfortable in the witch's presence. Sneed had warned me to give her a wide berth, and I'd observed that he himself stayed far from the witch's cabin door. And the lack of any crewmen on the quarterdeck, which I'd attributed to the fear of Blackbeard, may have been in equal measure due to a fear of the witch, Dumitra.

I shared the crew's trepidation.

CHAPTER SEVEN

I was given no orders to remain in my cramped quarters, and after a while ventured out upon the quarterdeck. Sneed looked up from the main deck, but did not shout for me to return to my cabin. I took this as confirmation that I could walk about the ship. I may have been a conscript among the pirate crew, but oddly had more freedom here than as a paid passenger on my previous vessel. I decided that if I got in no one's way, I could pass around the ship unmolested. Somewhere inside I harbored the hope that the crew, knowing I was a doctor, might understand that should they be wounded or fall ill, I would be the one keeping Death at bay for them. As such, they might look up to me with welcome and respect.

The ship was making good speed with a following breeze and calm seas. I descended the port side steps from the quarterdeck to the main deck. I could make a better assessment of this ship now than in my horrible state when I'd come aboard. Cannons lined both sides of the gunwale, and a look to my left showed several more pointing astern. I estimated the ship bristled with over thirty guns, a match for any merchant vessel on the seas, and even for many ships in His Majesty's Navy. It would take a flotilla to subdue this ship and rescue me, and I held no illusions that anyone would be sending one for that purpose.

Between the gunports were carved a strange symbol, a spiral overlaid with an inverted cross and crowned with a pentagram. The carving went deep into the wood and the inscription appeared charred, as if a fire had burned in it. I wondered if instead of being carved into the wood, the symbol had been affixed with a hot branding iron. I also noticed the same symbol carved into the base of the mast. I did not think that these had been part of the ship's original design, as there was absolutely no other adornment about the vessel. No, these, and the pentagram in the quarterdeck, had to have been added to the ship after the witch's arrival.

As I worked my way to the bow, I also got a better look at this pirate crew as the men went about their business of scrubbing decks, patching sails and adjusting rigging. Indeed, all of them had the same crown of thorns tattoo about their neck, apparently some rite of passage for the crew of Blackbeard.

I came to the conclusion that in the heat of being kidnapped, my imagination must have run away with me. These men were not the robust, bloodthirsty terrors I thought I'd seen board the passenger ship deck. This sallow crew worked their jobs with sunken, glazed eyes. Their bodies showed the effects of the monotonous, preserved diet pirate life had imposed on them. I'd seen the same wasting frames on men in London workhouses, where the combination of poor food and hard work ground down a man as sure as a millstone ground wheat.

If you are not of the medical profession and are reading this, my next statement may sound strange. But even though I was here by force, and the men around me were doing the Devil's work on the high seas, I wanted to treat their plight. I did not know how long the previous doctor had been absent, but it had clearly been long enough that the most common treatments for minor injuries had not happened. It seemed that every one of them had a need, whether it was a slight wound in want of cleaning, a boil that begged to be lanced, or a swollen jaw that betrayed a tooth demanding extraction.

An internal battle ensued between my Hippocratic Oath and my moral outrage over treating the criminal element. The deciding factor was that I had little to treat them with. The *Queen* had a doctor, but had no medicines or supplies aboard. I could no more make his crewmen healthy without medicines than the ship could move without wind.

But there was something I could do to prepare. When I'd treated Wilkes, I'd had no ready bandages. I doubted that future raids would be as bloodless as the surrender of the *Maureen Lavelle*. For that I could be ready. I went to Mr. Sneed on the quarterdeck.

"I should like to prepare some bandages to treat the injured during our next encounter," I said. "One of the men brought me some clothing to tear while treating Wilkes. I should like to gather more so I may have bandages at the ready."

Sneed gave the proposition a few moments of thought. I assumed most of it was determining if his permission might somehow run him afoul of Blackbeard. He pointed downward.

"Plunder's in the hold below the quarterdeck," Sneed said. "Bring your lamp. Confine yourself to personal baggage in the open. Leave be any doors or you'll regret it."

I already had enough regrets about being aboard and certainly needed to add no others. "Thank you."

I returned to my cabin, retrieved my bag and oil lamp, and then took three flights of steps into the hold. This deep in the ship and below the waterline, the hold was quite dark. I lit the lamp and could see for several feet about me in its amber light.

The seawater chilled the hull timbers and condensation glistened on the wood. The air was cooler but much in need of ventilation. To my left were barrels and crates carrying stenciled markings of destinations the contents would never reach. Following Sneed's warning, I did not look closely at them. Stored here in the open, they must have been valuable for trade, but of no value to the crew. Or perhaps the threat of Blackbeard's wrath was enough to keep thieves at bay.

To my right were stacks of trunks and boxes that appeared to be personal items stolen from passengers on captured ships. The luggage was of much finer quality than the bags the passengers on my vessel had in their possession. I wondered if some had been taken during raids of shoreline homes. Partially closed lids and scattered personal items upon the deck told me that these had already been rifled through. That made me no less uneasy at sorting through the personal goods of strangers.

One trunk caught my eye. The lid had been pried open and the sleeve of a man's shirt was pinched between it and the trunk proper, as if the lid had been closed upon it as it tried to crawl out. I surmised that other such clothes would be stored within, and shirts such as that one would make fine bandages. I would be doubly happy not having to paw through multiple trunks, conducting an uncomfortable series of invasions of privacy.

I set the lamp upon a crate and opened the trunk. What I found within exceeded my expectation. There sat a stack of clean shirts made of fine linen. After removing the ruffled sleeves and collars, I would be able to slice them into excellent bandages, and even use the ruffles as padding. There was also a collection of men's cravats which I could put into service as tourniquets. Beneath those I uncovered embroidered silk handkerchiefs, perfect to dampen and place on fevered brows. I noted the name and address on the trunk, and promised myself that upon my return I would look up the gentleman with such fine taste in clothes. I wanted him to know what a beneficial purpose his purloined clothing had served.

As I put these articles in my bag, something in the stern of the ship flashed in the flickering lamp light. I took up the lamp and went to investigate.

What I found was a heavy door with an opening in the top portion covered by a set of iron bars. From between the bars, I glimpsed a trove of treasure in the room beyond, including gold and jewelry. A ruby-ringed hand mirror in the pile must have been what reflected my lamp light and caught my eye.

To my surprise the door had no lock and just a simple bolt kept it secured. Even Blackbeard's fearsome reputation could not have been enough to keep the lowliest pirate from snatching a bit of these spoils for himself. The temptation would be far too great.

I took a step closer to the door. As I did, a symbol appeared in the wood. It resembled a lightning bolt superimposed upon a reversed letter P. The symbol glowed green, and brightened as I got closer.

With that glow came a queasy sensation from within my gut, an acidic bubbling that set my medical mind reeling to a variety of awful diagnoses. Before I could retreat, a discharge of green electricity arced from the symbol and struck me in the chest. The force of it threw me backward across the hold to land flat upon my back. The lamp flew from my hand and extinguished as it hit the deck. In the darkness, the symbol glowed with an intensity I can only describe as malevolent. In the same manner that a lion roars to celebrate a kill, the symbol flared brighter one more time, and then went dark.

The power of the discharge had stopped my heart for a moment and then sent my pulse soaring. Lying on the cold deck in the near-full darkness, I struggled to control my galloping breathing and curb my panic. As I gathered my wits, I sat up and began to feel around for my lamp. I soon found and relit it.

Wary of approaching the door again, I examined it from a distance. I could not see the symbol that had sprung to the treasure's defense. It was not carved or painted upon the wood. Whatever magic spell had been cast had placed it within the door, ready to appear if anyone came too near.

That anyone would not be me again. I crept forward on hands and knees, hoping that such a submissive advance would not stir the spell to anger again. When my bag was within reach, I grabbed it and made a hasty retreat to the steps. I climbed out of the hold and could not have been happier to return to the daylight.

I knew why the unlocked door kept Blackbeard's treasure secure. I also had more first-hand proof than I desired that the witch aboard the vessel had immense supernatural power, and that she was using it in Blackbeard's exclusive service.

I now had another powerful resident of the *Queen's* quarterdeck I did not want to run afoul of. I returned to my cabin and busied myself with turning shirts into bandages.

CHAPTER EIGHT

"Sail ho!" called out a man from the crow's nest.

I stepped from my quarters, alive with the hope that a fleet of British warships had arrived to put my captivity to an end.

Sneed bounded up the stairs to the quarterdeck. Blackbeard burst from his cabin, spyglass in hand, and joined Sneed at the railing. Blackbeard raised the spyglass to one eye and aimed it in the direction the lookout pointed. With my naked eye I could make out the hint of white sails on the horizon.

Blackbeard flashed a malevolent grin. "Beat to quarters, Mr. Sneed. Make for that ship."

My hope of seeing the Royal Navy's arrival deflated. Blackbeard's glee said he'd sighted prey, not a predator.

"Aye, aye, sir." Sneed turned to the main deck. "Joshua, beat to quarters!"

Joshua stood by the main mast. He disappeared into the area under the quarterdeck and reappeared with a drum hanging from his neck. He mounted the quarterdeck steps and when he got to the top he stopped beside Sneed.

The drum boasted some truly horrific details. It was the size of a conventional snare drum, but there was nothing conventional about its construction. The body of the drum was made of human skulls. As a doctor I can attest that these were indeed actual skulls, not some wooden or clay facsimiles. The leathery head of the drum hosted moles and other defects that led me to the conclusion that it had been fashioned from human skin. Given the nature of the drum body, the inference was not unreasonable. On the head of the drum had been painted a pentagram like the one on the quarterdeck.

Joshua held a human thigh bone in one hand and began to beat the drum with the ball end of the bone. The sound the drum made was quite out of proportion to its size. Each strike brought forth a deep, bass boom that sounded more like thunder than a snare drum's snap. The sound rolled across the deck and made the timbers beneath my feet shudder. I was certain even the men down in the hold could sense this summons.

And it seemed the whole crew did. Like a disturbed anthill, suddenly there was activity everywhere. Men came bounding up from below decks and began to load and ready the big guns. Another sailor exited the fo'c'sle with an armful of swords that he handed out among the crew. The men I'd seen approach seamanship lackadaisically earlier seemed full of energy when the object was personal gain.

Our faster ship closed on the fleeing vessel. I could see that she was smaller than the *Queen Anne's Revenge*. She flew the French flag at her stern, and on the deck beneath those colors a pair of cannons pointed in our direction.

The door to the witch's cabin opened. Dumitra stepped out of the darkness and onto the quarterdeck. It may have been my imagination, but I swore the air temperature dropped several degrees. She wore a long, black, hooded cape that went down to her ankles. The oversized hood covered her head and hung far enough forward that her face remained in a dark shadow. She held a ventilated brass globe on a chain in one hand. It resembled the censer a priest used, but I was certain nothing holy would be done with it on this ship. All eyes on the quarterdeck turned to her.

Joshua stopped beating the drum and scurried over to my cabin door. Blackbeard and Sneed stepped to the railing away from the witch.

The witch spoke to no one, did not even acknowledge that anyone was there. She moved straight to the center of the pentagram and faced the bow. Kneeling down, she set the globe on the deck and removed the top. Inside were a collection of leaves and other plant material I could not identify. She struck a match and dropped it into the brass orb.

No fire I'd ever experienced lit as fast and as completely as the one in that orb. And the green flame that flickered in the half-sphere was a color no fire burned. Dumitra reaffixed the top onto the orb and emerald smoke coursed out of the openings in the sides, and in an amount out of proportion to the flames within.

The witch stood and began to chant in a tongue I'd never heard, likely the same language used when she cast the spell for Blackbeard last night. As she spoke, even more smoke now jetted from the orb and spread across the pentagram like a fog. Just as it reached the circle's edge, she clapped her hands together three times.

The pentagram burst to life with a deep green glow. Then all the symbols carved between the cannon and upon the masts began to emit the same green glow.

The witch uttered one more phrase and clapped her hands again.

The crew froze in place, stopped in mid-movement, no matter how awkward the position. Then the circle of thorns tattoos about their necks lit up in the same bright green hue. It would seem that such a hot-looking glow around the neck would deliver great pain, or restrict their airways. Yet none of the men reacted.

The glow subsided and the men were released from their paralysis. Instead of crying in agony as I'd expected, most whooped with joy. Their slack faces became animated and the sparkle of avarice danced in their eyes. The effort put into their tasks doubled. They had transformed back into that maniacal crew who had boarded the *Maureen Lavelle*. The witch had sent an evil wind to fill their sails.

Sneed barked orders to the bow gunners. We were now close enough that I could read *Reine D'or* painted across the other ship's stern. Their captain watched our approach from the quarterdeck. He did not seem as consumed by fear as my last ship's captain had been. I hoped he was not going to put up a fight. He could not know the evil the witch had unleashed in this crew.

The bow gun on our ship fired. A cannonball arced through the sky and landed with a splash along the *Reine's* port side. The warning shot had been made. I prayed their captain would heed it.

My entreaty went unanswered. The two cannons in the French ship's stern replied in unison. Twin balls hurtled through the air and hit the water a hundred yards from our bow. Were we out of range of the French guns, or was their captain's answer just as polite as Blackbeard's warning shot?

The French Captain's intent did not seem to matter to Blackbeard. Anything short of submission enraged him. He drew his dagger from his belt and plunged it straight down into the railing.

"Close on her and board!" he shouted. "No quarter!"

A cheer went up amongst the men. The witch's incantation had them spoiling for a fight, dying to have the blood of the other sailors upon their hands. To see humans so reduced to base animal instincts chilled me to the core.

The bow gunners reloaded and fired in unison. Out of the barrels flew twin cannon balls, with a long chain between them. The balls and chain soared across the water in an almost mesmerizing swirl. This time the projectiles hit their marks. The balls passed through the French ship's rigging, ripping sails and lines. When the chain struck the aft mast, the weight of the balls snapped it free at the base. It toppled over in what looked like slow motion, bringing canvas and yardarms and heavy ropes crashing down upon the Frenchman's deck.

The French vessel's speed dropped. The ship veered to port, and then back to starboard. The downed sails had robbed the craft of power, and buried the helmsman at the wheel. That single volley had delivered a fatal blow.

But I could tell Blackbeard would not be content with a surrender now. Vengeance boiled behind his eyes. A captain and crew had dared refuse to kneel before the skeleton flag. They had to be destroyed.

The *Queen Anne's Revenge* came broadside to the *Reine*. On Sneed's command, all the starboard cannons fired. A deafening report accompanied a bright flash all along the deck. The ship rolled left from the recoil. At this range, I could not imagine the gunners missing their target.

They did not. Iron balls raked the French vessel's gundeck. Cannons and carriages were torn from their locations and sent careening across the deck to take more sailors to early graves.

Two French guns managed to survive the fusillade, and returned fire. Both balls screamed straight for our gundeck. I grabbed the frame of my cabin door and braced for the impact.

But at the last second, the balls made an inexplicable upward change in trajectory. They passed over and beyond the ship, sailing harmlessly between our masts, sails, and rigging, clean as a thread through the eye of a needle. Had I not seen it with my own eyes, I would have professed such an event impossible.

The madmen manning our pirate guns reloaded and fired at will. Cannonballs crashed into the opposing ship, sending boards and splinters flying. Several French crewmembers were struck directly and dismembered.

As the bow of the *Queen* aimed for the French ship, Sneed shouted orders that sent crewmen with grappling hooks to positions along the starboard side. In moments, the *Queen* was alongside the *Reine*. The grappling hook men took aim, let fly their metal claws, and snared the French ship. The boats crashed side to side with a great, wooden crunch.

Then the pirates swarmed over the railing and onto the *Reine*. A tidal wave of screaming, slashing pirates washed over the ship. They overwhelmed the smaller crew.

Following their captain's orders, the pirates gave no quarter. The opposing crew was butchered. Surrendering men were run through. Unarmed men were cut down with their hands still raised. Even men incapacitated by the first pirates had a coup de grace delivered by pirates further back in the pack. In minutes, the sounds of battle ended. The pirates milled about the ship, panting, with no one left to kill.

I slumped against my cabin, stunned at the carnage I had just witnessed. There wasn't an ounce of regret among the pirates, least of all Blackbeard. He surveyed the bloody deck of the French ship with immense satisfaction.

"You have the bridge, Mr. Sneed," he said. "I'm going to board our new prize."

I noticed that Joshua was gone, joined in the fight for the prize ship. The witch, too, had vanished. Her cabin door was closed so I assumed she'd returned there after the effects of her spell had taken hold. Now the glow had left all of the engraved symbols around the ship.

There could be no reason that would justify this slaughter of human beings. And I believed there could be no redemption for one employing witchcraft to do it. As a crewmember, however unwilling, I wondered how much burden of guilt I bore for not trying to stop it.

CHAPTER NINE

As the pirates scrambled over the captured ship, Blackbeard turned and looked me in the eyes. It was the first time he'd acknowledged my presence on the quarterdeck since he'd stepped out of his cabin.

"Find me any wounded still alive," he ordered. "Keep them that way and bring them back here."

I thought this a bizarre request. At his urging, his men had just done their best to leave no one alive aboard the other ship. Now he was dead-set on me saving a survivor, even before ordering me to care for his own crew. But I had heard of his penchant for holding hostages for ransom, and assumed that was the objective.

I nodded my assent, fearing that an "aye, aye, Captain" might sound sarcastic coming from one impressed into service. Blackbeard went to the starboard quarterdeck railing, stood upon it, and then leapt across to the French ship.

I made my way down to the deck and to one of the gangplanks the men had set between the ships. These were anything but stable. The two decks rose to different heights above the sea, and the two ships did not ride the swells in unison. It would be more like walking across a moving teeter-totter than a sturdy beam. But I had no choice.

The pirates moved back and forth between the ships with the agility of monkeys through the trees. I tenderly set one foot and then the other on the end of a less traveled plank. A pirate immediately grunted at me to get the hell going.

I made my way across in an embarrassing shuffle. At the midpoint I made the mistake of looking down between the two hulls. The distance between them varied from three feet to three inches as the ships rocked in the sea. I envisioned me falling and being caught between them like a piece of veal under a chef's tenderizing mallet. In a panic I ran the rest of the way across the plank and jumped off to the French ship.

I landed and nearly fell. Blood had turned the deck to a slippery mess. I grabbed a railing to steady myself and surveyed the scene.

Even with my many experiences with traumatized human bodies, the breadth and the depth of this massacre turned my stomach. Corpses lay scattered across the deck. Some bore the slashed wounds of a pirate's cutlass. Others had been blown to pieces by the cannonade. What none of the bodies did was move. The pirates had followed the no-quarter order with remarkable efficiency. I despaired of returning to Blackbeard emptyhanded.

The men around me were hard at work stripping the ship of items of value. Below I could hear the sound of crates being smashed open and a stream of pirates carried goods from the hold back to their ship. These ranged from handfuls of individual items to unopened barrels marked as gunpowder. I realized that with ports of call unavailable, the pirates took ships as much for resupply as for treasure.

There appeared to be no skimming going on by the pirates. Every bit of booty was stacked in the same spot amidships. Was it honor among thieves that kept the men from taking personal spoils, or fear of retribution by the others if discovered taking more than their share? I resolved that I would never know.

I made my way across the deck, stepping between the corpses as best I could. I came across two French army officers in full uniform. Fatal wounds stained the chests of their tunics. This was clearly not a military vessel. I thought that perhaps the military stores I'd seen the pirates unloading had been destined for a French garrison in the Caribbean under the care of these officers. The decision to stand and fight against a more powerful ship now made sense. Perhaps the *Reine's* captain had been patriotic, or perhaps the officers had ordered it. But someone on board had felt that keeping the stores from falling into the hands of pirates was worth dying for.

Giving up on finding a living soul on deck, I descended into the ship. I discovered more bodies amid the bustle of the pillaging pirates. I was ready to settle for a fatally wounded man at this point. If I could get him back to the ship alive, even if he died soon after, I could spare myself from Blackbeard's wrath.

I came to the ship's galley. The provisions had been cleaned out. The body of a dead sailor lay across something on the deck. I rolled him over to reveal a lumpy burlap sack. Inside I found limes.

I thought that if I didn't come back with a living sailor, my delivery of these to Blackbeard would soften the loss. But I couldn't stop my search for a survivor while I still might find one, and had no desire to risk extra gangplank passages between the ships. I cinched the sack back closed and took it to the corridor outside the cabin. I flagged down a passing pirate.

"Here, this needs to go aboard the *Queen*," I said.

Without hesitation, the pirate clutched the sack, tossed it across his shoulder and carried it off. It seemed my position as ship's surgeon had some authority, or perhaps the pirate had seen my compassionate care of his injured comrade earlier. Either way, it spurred some hope that I could at least pass among the crew without antagonism during the voyage.

As the pirate walked away, a thud came from within a cupboard in the galley behind me.

I whirled about. The noise repeated and one of the larger doors quivered. While every ship harbored rats, no rat was large enough to make a door that size move. Or so I hoped. I looked about for a means of self-defense and spied a two-pronged carving fork. That would have to do. I brandished it as if it was Excalibur, crept over to the cupboard door, and yanked it open.

Inside, folded into the tiny, open space, cowered a young man in simple seaman's clothes. Curly, dark hair hung down to a pair of fearful eyes. He shivered, his face white with terror.

I had hit the jackpot. I'd found Blackbeard a living hostage who wouldn't die on me due to injuries.

"I'm not going to hurt you," I said in French.

The young man seemed relieved someone spoke his mother tongue. "Leave me here, I beg you. Let me die alone on this ship after the pirates abandon it."

I set the carving fork aside. "If I leave you here and someone else finds you, they'll kill you without a second thought. And if no one finds you, well this ship has taken some serious damage. Blackbeard may decide to sink it once he strips it down so he can leave no trace of his crime."

The man pondered this for a moment. I could see he was still clinging to his plan.

"Look," I continued, "Blackbeard will hold you as a hostage for ransom, and free you once he's paid. That means he'll have to keep you alive. I'm the ship's doctor. I'll look after you and make sure that happens."

I wasn't really sure that I could do that, but I thought it would be reasonable that I could.

I waved the young man out of the cupboard and he extricated himself from the miniscule space. "My name is Doctor Baxter Whitcomb. What's yours?"

"Francois Girard."

"Do you have anyone who would pay for your release from these pirates, Francois?"

The young man shook his head.

After Blackbeard's ruthless treatment of the injured sailor, I feared what he'd do to this man if he wasn't worth a ransom. "Then we shall say you are the nephew of William Fielding, a London businessman who will pay for your release. Repeat that name for me."

"William Fielding."

"Excellent."

William Fielding was a London businessman and a friend of mine from the Huntsman's Club. When the time came to make contact, I would write the letter, and then pay William back after all this was over.

I walked the young man out of the galley and onto the deck. He garnered the attention of every crewmember we passed. It was as if the sight of him rekindled the bloodlust that had infected the men after the witch's spell took hold, but the flash of fury seemed to have no staying power within them, and they returned to their thievery.

It felt good knowing that the witch's spell faded after a short time and did not require a second incantation to release the pirates from its bondage. Blackbeard also had his personal spell renewed the night I'd seen the witch with him. Perhaps all her magic worked that way.

I walked Francois back aboard the pirate ship. I adopted a brave face and tried not to display how much the trip across the gangplank between the vessels terrified me. I did not want to break Francois' confidence in my ability to keep him safe by displaying my fear over passing between the ships.

When we returned to the *Queen*, Blackbeard stood at the quarterdeck railing, supervising Sneed as Sneed organized the pillaging. I led the young man up the starboard steps to present him to Blackbeard. The pirate captain gave the Frenchman a visual inspection as he approached.

"Sir," I said, "this is Francois Girard. Alive and uninjured. He says that William Fielding of London would pay to keep him that way."

"What are you talking about?"

"Fielding is a wealthy businessman, more than willing to pay his ransom."

Blackbeard smirked. "Ransom. Yes." He turned to Sneed. "Put the prisoner in irons."

"Aye, aye, sir." Sneed grabbed the captive and practically threw him back down the steps.

I worried Sneed might hurt the poor boy even though I'd slipped in the reminder that Francois was worth more if he remained healthy and sound. Before I could remind Sneed of that, Blackbeard regained my attention.

"And what are these things you made a crewman bring on board?" Blackbeard pointed to the sack of limes which now leaned against the wall of the quarterdeck cabins. "And what made you think you could give orders to my crew?"

I immediately forgot about the future of the Frenchman and worried about my own. "Limes, sir."

"You can't eat them and you can't sell them. What the hell do I need limes for?"

"Your crew needs them, sir. The food they're forced to eat is deficient in vitamins. That plays havoc with their constitutions. Research by a doctor in my hospital has shown that a section of lime will help keep them fit, free of scurvy."

Blackbeard cocked his head at me. It seemed that he would embrace the power of witchcraft but the facts of science were another thing. "How will a rock-hard fruit cure a disease?"

I was going to explain the difference between curative and preventative properties, but this was certainly not the time. "I'll admit the theory sounds odd, but it cannot hurt the crew to put it into practice."

Blackbeard mulled the idea for a moment. "Go forward and treat any of my injured men."

That was an order I was happy to follow. I'd had enough adventure for one day. I backed away into my cabin, grabbed my bag, and hurried to the ship's bow.

CHAPTER TEN

Sneed ordered any injured crewmen to head forward for treatment. I watched them pass glances between them that said they would not be doing so. Blackbeard's tossing the crewman I'd treated overboard seemed to have sent the message that treatment would only highlight the fact that you might not be able to pull your weight. No one on deck approached me.

Just as I began wondering if perhaps none of the magic-enhanced crew had been injured, I felt a tap on my shoulder.

"Sir, if you could?"

I turned to see a pirate of about my age, though the weathering effects of sea life made him look much older. He held out one hand wrapped in a bloody cloth.

"One of the bastards nicked me before I could run him through," he said.

"Let me have a look." I unwound the dressing. The man had undersold the damage. His pinky hung by just the smallest bit of meat and skin. Even in the hospital's operating room, I could not have saved that digit.

"You can sew it back up then?" the pirate said.

I hated to destroy the hope in his voice. "No, but I can keep it from taking the rest of your hand with it."

The pirate gave me a glum nod. I did not want to operate here on the open deck, so I led him back to the table in my cabin.

I plied him with enough rum to make him woozy, and then went to work on his finger. To his credit, he endured well what pain pierced the alcohol's veil. I had done a similar surgery on a dock worker who had crushed his finger under a heavy crate, and I dare say that taking into account the lesser conditions I now toiled under, I did a fair job of the amputation. It helped that a French sword had done most of the work.

I dressed the wound and reinforced to the pirate that he would need to continue to do his duties, or risk being tossed overboard as a useless mouth to feed. He said he'd already ascertained that himself.

Since the rum had loosened the man's tongue, I decided to see what more I could learn about this witch's spell she cast over the crew.

I pointed to the thorns that encircled his neck. "Before the battle, the witch made this tattoo glow. Was it painful?"

Despite having just had a finger cut off, the man smiled and grinned me a display of missing teeth. "Hell, no. Just the opposite. The fighting spell makes you feel twenty-years-old again, fit and ready for anything. All your fear? It melts away like snow in the spring, and all you wants to do is see the bodies of the enemy piled high and bloody."

"The witch controlled you?"

"No. She can control one person at a time, but the whole crew, that's too much by far. It's more like she lets a tiger inside you out to run free."

I pointed to his bandaged hand. "But unlike Blackbeard, you can be hurt, even killed."

"That idea don't even cross your mind. The spell leaves one thought in your head above all others. Kill the enemy and take his ship."

"But the other vessel could still sink your ship out from under you," I said.

"Didn't you see them carvings start a-glowing? Puts an invisible shield around the ship. Been sailing on the *Queen* for years and never seen a cannonball touch her."

That explained what I'd seen during the battle when the French cannonballs sailed harmlessly overhead. The only explanation for that defiance of physics would be a witch's spell.

"All right, then," I said. "Sleep off the rum and then back to duty."

The pirate flashed a goofy smile and gave me a sloppy salute with his bandaged hand. Then he rose and staggered out of my cabin.

As he left, I was surprised to see another pirate waiting in the doorway. I looked out of my cabin and saw several men in line with minor injuries. Apparently having that first patient broke the ice. I ushered the next man in and went back to work.

***

As I treated the crew, the noise of moving naval stores and cursing pirates provided a chorus of background noise outside my cabin. From the captured vessel came the sound of sharp blades chopping against timber. I surmised that the pirate crew was hacking out anything valuable that could not simply be stolen.

It turned out that I'd been right to not let the French survivor remain secreted within his vessel. Blackbeard deemed the ship too damaged to take as a prize, and had his gunners sink it after everything of value, even down to the cleats, had been ransacked.

If you have never seen a seafaring vessel sink, it is a sight to behold. One moment the *Reine D'or* floated strong and tall above the waves. A pair of cannons blasted the waterline. In moments, it slipped beneath the sea, leaving no trace that it had ever been there. As a doctor I'd witnessed something similar when a patient died, but in those instances the corpse remained behind as a reminder of a man's existence. A mighty ship left nothing.

The *Queen* sailed on. With my medical duties completed, I observed the pirates as they stored all the stolen goods below. Blackbeard personally locked away the captured gold and other valuables in the supernaturally-protected storeroom. Crewmen averted their eyes as he performed the task, as if unwilling to be seen displaying any interest in the pirate captain's cache. Once he'd finished, he ordered the bounty of the pillaged French food stores to be prepared for a celebratory feast that night. After sunset, the celebration commenced.

Most of the sails were furled, leaving just two fore and aft to make some headway. With the midships open, blazing torches were lit and set along the gunwales. They cast the middle of the deck in an eerie, yellow glow.

Joshua still brought my meal to my cabin. The fare was much improved. Some of the food was fresh, and the items that weren't had been preserved with the French flair for flavor, rather than the English desire for tasteless practicality.

The rest of the crew ate al fresco on the main deck instead of the galley below. Captured rum flowed among the rambunctious men. Soon arm wrestling and displays of knife-throwing skills began, neither of which were improved by the alcohol. Blackbeard looked on from the quarterdeck alongside Sneed. Neither joined in, but clearly approved of the bacchanal. As the revelry reached a crescendo, Sneed rang the ship's bell four times.

Winches creaked and what at first looked like a very knotted rope began to rise at the main mast. The other end had been tied to the forward railing of the quarterdeck. When the rope ran parallel to the deck about ten feet up, the winching stopped. Now I could see what the knots were.

Every foot or so along the rope hung a human head. The rope had been run through one ear and out the other. Blood soaked the matted hair and mouths hung agape as if in shock at their circumstance. It explained the chopping noise I'd heard aboard the other vessel. The pirates had been collecting heads.

This revolting display of inhumanity roiled my stomach, but the men on deck only amplified their revelry at the display. Under the rule of Blackbeard, and with the power of the witch behind them, the crew had plumbed humanity's depths.

Sneed rang the bell six times. The crew fell silent and all heads turned to the quarterdeck. Blackbeard stepped up to the railing.

"We have had another great victory." Blackbeard pointed to the string of heads. "And another crew learned that I mean business when I say 'surrender or die.'"

I reasoned that Blackbeard may have wanted a living survivor for more than just a ransom. Someone had to tell the tale of the ship's destruction to encourage others to surrender.

"And having proved their mettle in battle," he continued, "now we initiate the new recruits into the pirate brotherhood!"

The drunken men cheered. Two of them grabbed Horace DeWitt under the arms and hoisted him to his feet. This was the first I'd seen of the lad since we'd left the *Maureen Lavelle.* He seemed quite inebriated and overly happy. He'd certainly taken to pirating and decapitation faster than I'd expected.

The pirates brought Horace up to the quarterdeck. Blackbeard and Sneed stepped aside as the men bent Horace face-first against the railing that faced the main deck. Before he was quite aware what was happening, his hands and arms were lashed to the railing. The smile slipped from his face.

I feared that his initiation would be some sort of corporal punishment. I'd heard such things were common in London street gangs and such.

Then the witch Dumitra stepped out of her cabin and I feared what was about to happen to Horace was going to be worse than what any street gang would dole out.

CHAPTER ELEVEN

Dumitra wore the same hooded robe as before. The shadow over her face was so dark it was as if the hood concealed an abyss.

The crowd went silent. At the far end of the deck, Joshua appeared with the skull-lined drum. He began a four-count beat, three pounds on the skin and a pause. The men began a low chant in sync with the drum.

"All as one. All as one."

The pirates who had carried Horace to the railing leaned their body weight against his arms and shoulders. It seemed that adrenalin had burned away the alcohol's haze as Horace screamed out for them to let him go.

Dumitra stepped up right behind Horace. The witch carried what looked like a stone mortar and pestle in one hand. In the other was one of the needles the sailors used to stitch repairs into the sails. She cast a spell in the strange language she used and a puff of green smoke rose from the stone cup.

She dipped the needle into the mortar. When she pulled it out, a viscous, black liquid dripped from the tip. She bent down and set the point against the base of Horace's neck.

"All as one," the crowd chanted. "All as one."

What transpired next I could scarcely believe. The witch's hand moved in a blur, as a hummingbird's wings do in flight, so quickly that my mind could not see it in any one location. Horace cried out in pain and an image began to glow on the back of his neck.

The beat of the drum came faster. The voices of the pirates grew louder. The flames in the torches that ringed the deck brightened.

Seconds later, Dumitra stepped away. Horace stopped screaming and went still. Upon his back glowed the green pentagram the rest of the crew displayed. Of its own accord, the necklace of thorns grew out of the pentagram from both sides, and like lengthening strands of poison ivy, stretched out and encircled Horace's neck. The poor boy shrieked, and then passed out. The skin illustration went dark. The two pirates untied his arms.

The witch set forth another incantation. The tattoo glowed green again. She hopped and Horace's body jumped unsteadily to its feet, though his head hung at an odd angle and his eyes stayed closed. She raised both her arms and Horace's arms jerked upwards like a marionette with a poor puppeteer.

Here the crew on deck roared with laughter. It seemed this was a rite of passage ritual all new crewmembers endured. As the injured sailor had told me earlier, the witch could control one pirate at a time. I could see why only Blackbeard did not carry the necklace of thorns tattoo.

The witch clapped her hands together. Horace collapsed across the railing and then slid to the deck. His eyes fluttered open. He grabbed the railing and pulled himself back up. His face was white, his legs wobbled. The witch's spell had drained him, and I had to assume that letting an alien consciousness inside him had to have changed him for life, and not for the better.

The drum beat began again. The renewed crew's chant returned. "All as one. All as one."

A heavy hand clamped down upon my shoulder. I spun about to see Blackbeard behind me.

"Next new crewmember up!" he said.

My gut sank. I never wanted to be part of this crew. I sure as hell did not want a witch mucking about in my mind. Above all, I did not want to lose control of myself.

"Sir, not me," I pleaded.

"All as one," the Captain said.

I scrambled for an excuse. "Captain, you've seen my skills. I've put all your injured men back on duty today. The witch does not have those skills, does not know how to treat patients. If she were inside me, she would slow my hands, make them falter. I couldn't fulfill the only reason you have me here."

Blackbeard laughed and pushed me forward. The two pirates who'd dragged Horace up to the quarterdeck caught me, one on each arm, and pulled me to the railing.

"I'll fail," I cried over my shoulder, "like the last doctor."

The pirates slammed me down chest-first on the cold wood. The position gave me a direct view of the men on the deck below. They chanted in beat with the drum, faces alight with torchlight and animated by some kind of mass hypnosis. Several still bore the bandages and other signs of my treatments, but there would be no rescue from the crowd for me.

Rough ropes bit into my wrists as the pirates bound me in place. Heavy hands pressed my shoulders down into the railing. I could not struggle, nay I could barely breathe.

A chill went up my spine and I felt the dark presence of the witch behind me, like a weight pressing against my soul. She chanted the same spell she'd uttered before dooming Horace to being a slave to witchcraft. A wisp of green smoke curled around the side of my face. I closed my eyes and awaited the painful prick of the poisoned needle.

"Belay that!" Blackbeard ordered.

The drum beat stopped. The crew's chant petered out to nothing. Disbelief and fear crossed their faces.

Behind me, Dumitra hissed in frustration. "You dare stop the ritual?"

Heavy boots thudded against the deck and Blackbeard walked to the witch's side. He spoke low enough that only the three of us could hear. "I'm the captain here. I give the orders, witch."

"All on board must be under my control," she said.

"Like the last doctor?" Blackbeard said. "This one is under *my* control. That will be more than enough."

Then Blackbeard shouted so the rest of the crew could hear. "Mr. Sneed. These men look thirsty. More rum!"

A cheer rose from the crew and animated conversation returned between them. The ropes on my wrists loosened and the two pirates pulled me to my feet. I turned around to thank the Captain.

Instead, I faced the witch. The torchlight from below lit a bit of the area under her cowl. Her face looked unbelievably old, lined and worn worse than any poor soul I'd seen even at the indigent clinic. I blamed the poor light, the shadows it cast, and my imagination. What I was certain of was the anger that burned in the witch's eyes. She turned and marched back to her cabin. The door slammed shut without her touching it.

Blackbeard stepped up to me. Before I could extend my thanks, he grabbed my shirt at the collar with one meaty hand. He twisted the fabric until I choked, then lifted me so I balanced on the tips of my toes.

"Fail me," he said, "and your death will take days."

He dropped me and I collapsed against the railing to regain my breath. Blackbeard, Sneed and the two pirates left me alone on the quarterdeck. I staggered back to my cabin.

The Captain had saved me from the witch's spell, only to expose me to her fury. I did not know which one would prove worse.

***

Even after the carousing pirates vacated or passed out on the main deck, I did not sleep easy that night. I'd seen a display of witchcraft that no one would believe and came within a hair's breadth of becoming a victim of it. I realized that the point I balanced upon to stay alive on this ship had only become more precarious. Each time I drifted off to sleep in my hammock, a sense of dread forced me back awake.

Then something far worse awakened me, a hand pressed against my mouth.

I attempted to cry out, to roll away from this assailant. But I was frozen in place. A cloth pouch pressed against my lips. I caught the smell and taste of some unidentifiable, earthy herbs. They numbed my lips and the rest of my body as well. My heart raced with panic.

The witch's gravelly voice came out of the darkness. "A risk to Blackbeard is a risk to me. That cannot stand."

I was certain that she was about to kill me. I broke out into a cold sweat.

An ice-cold hand pulled open my shirt. Nails so long they felt like claws dragged across my skin.

Then came the stab of a needle upon the center of my chest, just at the base of my sternum. The piercing felt like fire had been injected into my skin. Then the process repeated faster than a woodpecker drilling into a rotten tree. The needle inscribed a searing circle into my skin. Though the poultice at my lips immobilized me, I could see a greenish glow emanate from my chest. That glow lit the inside of the witch's hood as she bent over me. The sight of her ghastly, wasted face amplified my terror. Her vengeful, maniacal look compounded it so much that I thought I'd go insane.

The needle completed the circle. The pain and the glow began to subside. My pulse slowed, but more from emotional and physical exhaustion than from any lessening of my fear. Dumitra pulled away and the night swallowed her again.

"This mark will bind you to Blackbeard," she said. "Should you stray too far from his side, you will die in agony. And should he ever die, life will drain from your body as well. So pray my protective spell over him never fails. Tell anyone of this spell, and I will cast one upon you that will be even worse. Blackbeard be damned. No one aboard can be beyond my reach."

She took the strange poultice from my mouth. The door to my cabin opened and closed. I felt like all the life had been drained out of me.

As my sensations began to return, I rolled out of my hammock. I felt my way to the table, and lit the lamp upon it. I pulled open my shirt to examine my chest. There, where my last set of ribs met, was inked a black circle with a strange symbol in the center, almost like the Egyptian ankh, but with a misshapen head. Before I could commit the symbol to memory, it faded away, leaving only bloody pinpricks where the needle had violated my skin. I wiped at them, and the skin beneath was unblemished.

The witch had played her cards with skill. She left no proof of the spell cast. Indeed, if I had not been wide awake at the time, I would have written the incident off as a nightmare. She also did not violate Blackbeard's order that I not be under her power. Finally, if somehow the spell was exposed, she could say that it had all been to Blackbeard's benefit.

The moment on the quarterdeck when I'd been saved from the witch's spell of coercion, relief had consumed me. Now depression fully took its place. In some sort of power struggle between Dumitra and Blackbeard, I was square in the middle. And the spell she'd cast upon me banished the faint hope I had of someday escaping the ship. I would have to sail with Blackbeard forever.

CHAPTER TWELVE

The men I'd treated for battle injuries had spread the word that I was there to heal them. Rumors that the crew was about to eat daily servings of limes for their health had been met with skepticism, but at least my championing of the regimen had shown I had their best interests at heart. Up until the tattooing ceremony, I'd sensed a growing acceptance of my presence onboard.

Morning came and my status among the crew aboard the *Queen Anne's Revenge* had definitely changed. Joshua kicked my cabin door once. By the time I opened the door, he was gone and had left my uncovered plate at the threshold. Later when I walked the deck, the crew pointedly ignored me, looked through me as if I wasn't there, or not so roughly bumped me as they passed. It seemed that my failure to become "all as one" meant I was now officially on the outside. Whether their reaction was because they were insulted or incensed, I did not know. I wondered if they would even let me treat future injuries, or would they stubbornly die before addressing me.

Sneed was worse, becoming downright antagonistic. While the other crewmembers ignored me, he appeared to boil with anger at the sight of me. Blackbeard remained largely in his cabin, studying maps and referencing books. Whatever his next point of plunder was, he was not sharing it with the crew, and certainly not with me. Save the two times he came out to give the helmsman course adjustments, he remained sequestered.

I ended up doing much the same. The discomfort of enduring the crew's disdain was difficult to bear. This may seem odd to you, that I would wish to garner the fellowship of a band of cutthroat brigands, but that is my nature. I joined the medical profession to help and heal others. Rich or poor, smart or simple, good or evil, I made no distinctions. Now I feared that my unfortunate sojourn on this vessel would be one of social isolation, on top of a constant fear of death at the hands of the witch or Blackbeard.

This terrible turn of events engendered an awful insomnia in me that night. I lay in my hammock, still wide awake well after midnight and wondered if I would ever rest well again. With the deck clear save the minimal night watch, I decided to venture out and seek consolation in the stars.

Compared to the previous evening's chaos, this night was quite silent. The subdued crew on duty seemed to keep to themselves, and the ship continued on course with a slight following sea. I stood in the shadows at the port railing and let the breeze caress my face.

From below came the muffled voice of Blackbeard and the thud of his heavy boots. Light appeared near the base of the starboard steps.

"Hurry him up, damn you!" Blackbeard's voice was now close and crystal clear.

I tucked myself back into the corner. The last thing I wanted to do was gain Blackbeard's attention.

He appeared on the main deck, hatless and with his long curly hair unrestrained. His usual captain's jacket must have remained in his cabin, for all he wore was his shirt and trousers. It was as if he'd been summoned from sleep, but without an emergency on board, I doubted any crewmember would have dared do so.

A pirate walked up beside Blackbeard, dragging Francois along with him. The Frenchman had his hands bound behind him, a gag in his mouth, and a heavy blindfold tied over his eyes.

Guilt swelled within me. Overwhelmed by the initiation ceremony and the witch's attack upon me in my cabin, I had neglected to even inquire about the prisoner I'd brought aboard the ship. My heart hurt for the man if he'd been enduring his captivity in such a state as this. My promise to watch over him had been broken.

"Step lively," Blackbeard said.

Blackbeard marched up the starboard steps. The pirate followed, pushing Francois before him with violent shoves. At the bottom of the stairs, Francois bumbled into the railing and lost his balance. The pirate caught him by the shirt and reset him upright. Then he pushed him into the steps.

"Climb, you bastard," the pirate said.

I could not see how any of this mistreatment was necessary. It certainly would not reflect well on Blackbeard when Francois was ransomed and told the world about his ordeal.

I assumed that they were taking the man to Blackbeard's cabin for some kind of interrogation. But Blackbeard mounted the quarterdeck and stopped before the witch's cabin. He banged on the door and a light went on inside.

Francois got to the quarterdeck. He paused and then the pirate gave him another forward shove. He staggered two more steps closer to Blackbeard. The pirate paused atop the last step. He glanced nervously about the deck, and especially at the door to the witch's cabin.

"What the hell is your problem?" Blackbeard said to the man. "I'm sending the Frenchman in there, not you."

I gripped the railing. There was a large difference between being a hostage in the hold and some kind of victim in the witch's cabin. I was furious that I had been party to putting Francois into this situation.

The pirate stepped up and grabbed Francois from behind at the shoulders. Blackbeard banged on the door again. This time it opened, though the witch was not there when it did. The lamp light within lit up a large, wooden chair in the center of the room. It looked very heavy, with much of the wood to construct it being unfinished branches with the bark intact. The pirate shoved Francois through the doorway. The door slammed shut by itself.

The pirate wasted no time departing the quarterdeck. He nearly tripped over his own feet scrambling down the steps. I expected Blackbeard to again berate him for cowardice, but the Captain retreated to his own quarters with almost as much haste. Blackbeard closed the door behind him and left the quarterdeck deserted.

I freely admit that nothing in life had ever sent terror coursing through my veins the way Blackbeard's witch had. The idea of approaching her cabin was as appealing as walking to the edge of a rain-slickened cliff. But I'd convinced poor Francois to surrender himself, promised him that he'd come to no harm. I had to know his fate. My weak hope was that Dumitra was going to interrogate him, and nothing more.

I slinked across the deck, fearful one of the crewmen below might spot me. But none of them sent up an alarm, in fact they were making it part of their duty to look away from the quarterdeck. It was as if even the hardened, thieving men aboard the ship did not want to acknowledge what was about to transpire in the witch's cabin.

As I stepped closer, the thick, dark sensation of evil returned. It oozed from the cabin stronger than ever, so heavy it seemed to slow my movements, though that may have been a result of my own trepidation. As I reached the cabin wall, I stopped and listened.

Inside, Dumitra chanted one of her strange incantations. Francois cried out, muffled by the gag in his mouth.

I worked my way around the forward wall to a spot where light escaped through a split between two boards. I dropped to my knees and set one eye to the gap.

I had a side view of the strange chair. Francois sat in it, immobilized by what at first looked like rope lashed about his limbs and chest. But closer inspection revealed that these were vines with the same color and texture of the wood in the chair. It was as if they'd grown from the chair to restrain Francois, though I knew harvested wood could do no such thing.

Two lanterns lit the scene, one on each side of the chair. These at first appeared to hang from the ceiling, but nothing suspended them. They floated in the air, still and independent of the motion of the ship around them. I gasped at the sight.

At the foot of the chair stood Dumitra, facing Francois. She wore the dark robe and from this side view, her oversized hood obscured her face. I thought that perhaps the blindfold was a gift to Francois now, saving him from having to stare at the witch's ravaged visage.

The witch produced a slender, silver tube about four inches long. One end was pointed, the other wider and ending in a shape like the petals of a lily. As the witch spoke her spell, an indiscernible inscription along the side glowed green.

She completed her spell with one, louder, more emphatic incantation. Then she drove the silver shaft into Francois's trachea.

I winced. Such a wound would draw a copious amount of blood, and likely block Francois' windpipe. Instead, it did neither. Francois went still. His chest still rose and fell, but his struggle against the chair's restraints stopped. No blood came from the wound, no raspy breath echoed from the tube.

Instead, a bright, white light began to glow in the silver shaft. Then smoke with the same brilliant glow drifted out from the silver petals. As a trained physician, I know all the fluids and humors within the human body, and what came from Francois's body was unknown to me.

The witch inhaled, and the silvery smoke disappeared into her hood. Three long draughts seemed to drain whatever this was coming from Francois' body. She leaned away and pulled the silver device from his chest like taking a cork from a bottle.

Francois' head lolled to one side. His chest hitched once, then twice. Then his body went still. As the color drained from his face, I did not need to check his pulse to know that Dumitra's actions had killed him.

Then I saw that she had done much worse. His lightening pallor went from the familiar corpse gray to a bleached white. Holes opened in his skin, as if he'd been transformed into pumice. Then his whole body vanished in a puff of white dust. Francois' clothing held its shape for a moment, then it collapsed into the boy's grainy remains. The restraining vines retracted back into the chair, and the whiter sections of the wood shifted back to dull brown to match the bark.

This ritual had left me shocked beyond words, immobilized by the horror. Then I remembered how exposed I was on the quarterdeck. If I was found out, perhaps the witch would treat me to the same deadly ritual she'd just performed on Francois. I certainly did not want to risk that. I scurried back to my cabin and closed the door. I hopped into my hammock and feigned sleep.

I was certain that true sleep would not come. My mind reeled under the weight of all I'd witnessed. Dumitra had killed poor Francois, and by some method beyond what the latest science understood. She had drawn something from the man I'd never seen, and without it, he did not just die, he disintegrated. One puff of wind and any remains of him would be forever scattered.

Worse, the witch did not just draw that light of life, that soul, if you will from Francois. She appeared to ingest it herself. I'd seen no evidence of food being delivered to her cabin, as it had been to myself and the Captain. Could it be that she survived on a more cannibalistic and unnamed sustenance?

From the reaction of the pirate who'd delivered Francois to his death, the crew was aware that something bad happened inside the witch's cabin, and that some who entered never came out. And Blackbeard was party to whatever it was. His capture of live prisoners to feed this wicked woman must have been what he bartered for her spells.

So far, I'd been kept unaware of all of this, and it seemed Blackbeard wanted me to remain so. I vowed to continue to act as if I was still ignorant of how twisted the evil was that powered this vessel. Otherwise, I was certain I'd be the next one to sit in the witch's chair.

CHAPTER THIRTEEN

I spent the next day near my quarters. I felt uneasy around the crew, afraid around Blackbeard and Sneed, and terrified that I might encounter the witch. Perhaps paranoia was getting the best of me, but I was certain that as soon as Dumitra spied me, she would detect that I'd seen her horrible act with Francois, and she would decide I needed to be her next victim. Sneed and the crew would certainly hand me over.

By midday, the lookout in the crow's nest called out that he'd spotted land. Soon I could see it off to starboard, a small island that barely peeked up out of the sea, populated by scrubby bushes and a stand of lonely, stunted palm trees. Such a place with no harbor and no water was of no value to most mariners. But as we rounded the northern side, I saw the value to Blackbeard.

This island was a fixed rendezvous point. On the western side anchored three ships. All were smaller than the *Queen Anne's Revenge*, but they were all armed, and they all flew Blackbeard's skeleton flag.

The realization that this pirate commanded a fleet made my heart sink. Any hope of rescue, even inadvertent, drained away. It would take an armada of ships to defeat this fleet, and even then, Blackbeard's protected ship would come out of it unscathed.

A worse outcome came to mind. What if each ship had a witch aboard? The four vessels would be invincible and I'd spend my life serving evil and observing bloodshed.

Blackbeard ordered a set of signaling flags raised. They made no more sense to me than the witch's incantations, but the other ships responded with their own. As we passed the three, sails unfurled and anchor chains rose. The *Queen* continued westbound, now at the head of a murderous, pillaging convoy.

After my meager evening meal, I sat beside the portal in my room and watched the ship to port sail in formation with us beyond our ship's wake. I wondered what prayers I would need to utter to have God exchange her for a British man-of-war. I wondered if God could even hear the prayers of one who so rarely addressed Him, spoken from a place so shrouded in evil.

Sneed burst into my cabin looking worried and anxious. "Blackbeard wants you. Now."

Before I could respond, he grabbed my arm and hauled me out of the cabin. I'd spent the day in my tiny corner of the ship, so there was no way I could have made any transgression to earn the Captain's ire. I feared there was no way this encounter would end well for me.

We crossed the quarterdeck and did not head for Blackbeard's cabin. Instead, we went straight for the witch's. Sweat broke out upon my brow.

"You-you said Blackbeard wanted me?" I said.

"He does."

The suffocating, oppressive sensation of the witch's cabin began to weigh me down. I tried to dig in my heels but Sneed just pulled me across the deck. Surely the witch had told Blackbeard I'd seen her ritual, and now the two of them were going to exact some gruesome revenge.

At the cabin, Sneed threw open the door. Using my arm, he swung me inside like a coachman cracking a whip. I skidded to a stop just short of the killing chair where Francois spent his last, painful moments. I leaned over it, then righted myself to keep from touching the wood. The door slammed shut behind me.

"Over here!" Blackbeard stood to the right beside a bed with a simple mattress and a gray wool blanket. Beyond the soul-sucking chair and against the far wall stood a small table and chair, with a medium-sized chest on the deck beside them.

The witch's robe hung on a wall hook by the foot of the bed. The open port let a shaft of light fall on the deck just short of the bed, leaving most of it in shadow. But there was a small human form beneath the blanket. From the way the evil in the cabin oozed from that side of the room, I knew the witch had to be under that cover.

"Goddam it, get over here," Blackbeard said.

I went to the side of the bed. The corner of the room smelled of a dozen different herbs and an unnerving amount of sulfur. Dumitra lay beneath the covers. The blanket was pulled up to just below her exposed neck and shoulders. Her head lay on a stained pillow. Her appearance shocked me.

A fan of frazzled, gray hair reached down to her shoulders. Lines creased her gaunt face so horribly that she looked more like a bleached, dried fig than a human. Her nose seemed elongated and unnaturally pointed, but that deformity was nothing compared to her ears, which had shriveled in the center and become pointed at both the top and bottom. Her eyes were closed within sunken sockets, but I could see them dart back and forth under their paper-thin lids. I could not even guess at her age.

"Dear God," was all I could muster.

"She hasn't left her bed," Blackbeard said. "What's wrong with her?"

"What isn't? I've never had a patient look this ill."

"She always looks like that, well, mostly. But something else is wrong."

"I don't even know where to begin."

Blackbeard struck me on the back so hard that I nearly fell across the bed.

"You'd damn well better figure that out. I need her alive."

I could perform a basic examination, but did not want to do so under Blackbeard's watchful eye. "I will need to examine her. I trust she would prefer I did it alone."

Blackbeard looked like he was about to object, then thought better of it. "Be quick about it."

The pirate captain left the cabin. Before the door closed behind him, my medical bag sailed in and skidded across the floor to near my feet. Seemed that Sneed didn't want to set foot in this room any more than I.

Everything about being this close to Dumitra made my body shiver. I closed my eyes, took a deep breath, and tried to convince myself that this creature before me was just a patient, one mandated treatment by my Hippocratic Oath. Witch or not, she was human, or had started out that way.

I began as I would with any patient and checked her pulse. Touching her skin engendered a feeling of repulsion, like touching a snake, but I did not recoil. Her pulse was quite difficult to find, very weak and quite slow. Between that and the eye movement, at least I could confirm she was alive. Most doctors attributed the eye movements to a sleeper's dreaming state, so while she was physically immobile, she was likely still mentally active.

I needed to check the witch for any signs of injury. Her bare neck and shoulders hinted that she was naked beneath the blanket. I rolled it down and indeed that was true.

There seemed to be little left of this woman. In medical school we'd examined Egyptian mummies, and she could have almost passed as one. The aging process had not stopped at her face. Shriveled skin clung to bone. Her breasts and buttocks looked desiccated and deflated. So scant was the fat and muscle upon her that I could see her weakened heart beat within her chest. There was no way this was the same woman Joshua thought he saw board the ship years ago.

What I did not see was any sign of trauma, any lesions, any bruising or discoloration. Whatever was ailing this witch was doing it from within. I reached to push her hair away for a better examination of her head.

Her hand shot up and grabbed mine. Thin, claw-like fingers gripped my wrist like an animal's leg trap. Her eyelids snapped open to reveal orbs that were solid black and staring straight at me. A green glow formed around them.

I gasped and tried to pull away, but the frail witch seemed to have the strength of several men.

"Touch me again and you'll die in great pain." She almost hissed the words.

"I'm here to help you."

"You are far too late, and too incompetent even if you weren't."

I brushed off her insult. "Where do you hurt?"

"Everywhere. The bill is coming due." She pulled the blanket back over her withered body. "Get out of my cabin."

"Blackbeard has ordered me to treat you. Which of the two of you do you think I'm going to listen to?"

"I'm more powerful than he could imagine."

"Yet you cannot heal yourself." I doubted she could cast much of a spell in this state, so I decided to take a risk to get some answers. "You didn't seem ill after you killed Francois."

Her eyes narrowed. "That was you I sensed outside the wall. I was so deep in the consummation I could not be sure."

"What happened to you after that?"

"It's what didn't happen during it. You would not understand." Dumitra began to cough, the kind of deep, choking cough only those with diseased lungs delivered. "You don't even understand healing *people*, though you think you do."

I again ignored her verbal barbs. If this witch had a lung disease, it would account for her loss of weight and energy. I'd seen coal miners so afflicted. How she could contract such a disease in this open sea air I could not guess, but treatment was the important part, the part that would keep Blackbeard from feeding me to the sharks.

I was not going to get any more information from the witch, and I was certain she'd claw me if I tried to touch her again. I picked up my bag and left the cabin. To my surprise, Blackbeard stood right outside the door.

"You have treated her?" he said.

"I have nothing to treat her with," I said. "She appears to have a respiratory problem. There are plasters I can mix that will relieve the symptoms, draw out the ill humors from her chest. But the ingredients are not onboard. Do the other ships have medical supplies?"

"No."

"I can't treat her with good intentions. We need medicines."

Even with the medicines, I wasn't sure I could help someone who seemed as close to death as the witch was. But the excuse would keep Blackbeard from killing me. I hoped.

Blackbeard stormed away to his cabin. From within I heard the rustling of charts. A minute later, he returned to the quarterdeck. He ordered Sneed to change course to a more northwesterly heading and to signal the other ships to follow. Then he stepped over to me.

"We're going to get your medicine," he said. "The good citizens of Charleston will hand over what you need."

I knew he meant they would do so encouraged by the barrels of his cannons. "If they don't have what we ask for?"

"Then people will start to die until they do, with the last victim being you if the witch dies."

CHAPTER FOURTEEN

The next sighting of land was the coast of the Carolina colony. I greeted the coastline with mixed emotions. While my goal had been to get to the New World, this was neither the location nor the type of arrival I'd envisioned.

Thus far, my life had been spent in and around the environs of London. In the city, save for small parks, there stood scarcely a tree. Outside the city, what we considered the country was far from untrammeled forest. Those lands had been tilled and transformed for over a thousand years into neat squares of meadow, agriculture, and manor estates. To my shock, this shoreline of the New World appeared to be nothing but wilderness as far as I could see. The safety net of civilization I had taken for granted wasn't in place here. The immensity and the danger of this untamed land now hit me full force.

Daunting as the prospect of joining the colonists was, I would have preferred it to staying bound by witchcraft into Blackbeard's service. But I doubted I would leave this ship now, or ever. To have my longed-for freedom beckon so close was excruciating.

We sailed north and began to encounter smaller fishing vessels. All fled at the sight of our skeleton flags. Blackbeard's ships entered Charleston Harbor and dropped anchor between Sullivan's and James Islands so that any vessels transiting the harbor entrance would pass under our guns. Wharves and buildings rose on the western shore and it felt good to see elements of the world outside the pirate realm, even if I could not return to being part of it.

The three other pirate captains came aboard the *Queen* to meet with Blackbeard. They retired to his cabin. I found that if I pressed an ear against the aft wall of my cabin, I could make out most of what the group discussed. Blackbeard made no mention of Dumitra's illness, but instead said all the vessels were in need of medical supplies, and that they were here in Charleston to take them.

One of Blackbeard's land-based spies had reported to one of the other captains about the condition of Charleston, and his news was not good. The city had recently girded itself against the growing pirate threat. A battery of cannons covered the south end of the city and batteries were being built on the two islands bracketing the approach channel. A militia regiment had been mustered and was stationed just to the west. In addition, a gunboat anchored in wait just upriver. Blackbeard cursed as his plan for a quick shore raid disintegrated.

The strategy shifted to a blockade. The pirate ships would close the harbor until the city fathers delivered the demanded medicines. At the request of the other pirate captains, a healthy amount of gold and silver were added to the ransom.

But Blackbeard sanctioned only half the amount the other pirates first wanted. I got the feeling that Blackbeard did not want the medicines delayed while the people gathered up precious metals scattered across the county. The captains returned to their vessels.

The harbor had been quiet since we'd arrived, the townspeople likely trying to ascertain the pirate armada's intentions, but not curious enough to sail out and risk striking a hornet's nest with a stick. Finally, a local cargo sloop left the docks and set a course for the harbor exit.

Blackbeard ordered Sneed to load one of the bow guns and fire at the sloop. Sneed relayed the order and several pirates made the forward guns ready. Sneed watched the approaching boat through a spyglass. When it came within cannon range, he barked the order to fire. The cannon boomed and a puff of smoke rolled out over the water.

Sitting at anchor, against a slow-moving boat, the expert pirate gunners could not miss. Turning the usual warning shot across the bow into something a bit more intimidating, the cannon ball punctured the ship's mainsail dead center. Blackbeard's men sent up a raucous cheer. The cargo vessel swung hard about, reset the sails, and headed back for Charleston.

No sooner had the boat passed back out of range than a new set of sails appeared upriver from the town. The city's little gunboat sailed into the harbor. It seemed its captain had been waiting for Blackbeard to signal his intentions. Since they were hostile, I imagined he thought it his duty to sail out and bring us to heel.

I am no naval warfare expert, but even if the gunboat captain could not tell how well armed the *Queen* and her sister ships were, the fact that there were four of us and one of him should have been enough to keep him within range of the harbor batteries' cover fire. But either due to underestimating the pirates' skill, or overestimating his own crew's, he came out to do battle.

At this, Blackbeard's eyes lit up with excitement. He pounded the railing with one fist and ordered anchors weighed and sails unfurled. As some men cannot contain themselves at the offering of strong spirits, so it seemed Blackbeard had an addiction to combat. He ordered Sneed to beat the men to quarters.

Sneed complied. Joshua came on deck with the skull-and-skin drum. He took up his usual position, and began to pound out the special beat.

But the witch did not participate, the sigils around the ship did not catch fire, and the crew did not swell with a warrior spirit. The men instead stared at each other in confusion. They reminded me of actors who had taken their marks to begin a stage show, but the houselights were still lit, the costumes were still in the dressing rooms, and the orchestra had not arrived. Something special was supposed to be happening, and nothing was. They'd become dependent upon the witch casting her combat spell before each encounter, and for the first time in years they were on their own.

The *Queen Anne's Revenge* set sail and the other ships followed right behind her. Blackbeard's forty guns would be more than enough to subdue the smaller vessel, but like schoolyard bullies, the other captains seemed to want a piece of some easy action.

As the distance between the ships closed, I could make out the solid blue flag at the gunboat's stern with the Union Jack in the upper corner, and a longing to be back in England came over me. The ship's proud captain watched our vessel through a spyglass from the stern of his ship. His resplendent blue tunic looked like it had been cleaned and pressed for this occasion. Though it might mean my own demise, I did root for David against Goliath in this impending battle.

The *Queen* sailed an intercept course and as soon as the boat was in range, Sneed asked for permission to fire. Blackbeard refused, once, twice, three times. Bloodlust made itself manifest in his twisted smile. It seemed he wanted this defiant little vessel blasted out of the water at so close a range that he could witness every detail of its destruction.

The gunboat captain felt no need to grant Blackbeard the opening salvo. Cannons spit smoke and fire and his boat sent its tiny broadside flying at the *Queen*.

The Carolina gunners had been practicing. Cannonballs pounded the side of the *Queen*. One gun was blown from its carriage, skidded across the deck, and smashed two guns on the other side of the ship. Wood splintered and rigging snapped. Another cannonball sailed over the gunwale and decapitated the helmsman. His lifeless body dropped to the deck. The ship's wheel spun like a child's top and the *Queen* fell away from the approaching gunboat.

Chaos reigned on the *Queen's* main deck. These pirates had fought under the shield of the witch's spell for so long that they acted stunned by the results of unprotected combat. I ducked down to use the quarterdeck cabins as shelter from the gunboat's next salvo.

A bolt of pain lanced my left forearm. I didn't think anything had struck me, and indeed my coat had no tear in the sleeve. I pushed my coat and shirt sleeves up to my elbow. That revealed a gash in my forearm, appearing from nowhere as if by some awful magic.

I remembered the witch's binding spell she had cast upon me. A circular area below my sternum began to itch. I searched the deck for Blackbeard.

Across the quarterdeck, Blackbeard leaned against the cabin wall. The furious glee that had animated him moments ago had disappeared. With an ashen face, his glazed eyes stared down at a thick, wooden splinter that stuck from his left forearm. Blood ran down from the cuff of his jacket and dripped off the end of his fingers. Not only was his ship now exposed, he also had proof that his personal invulnerability had fizzled out. He'd gone from immortal to mortal and the shock seemed profound.

In a flash I realized what that meant to me. The witch had bound my life to Blackbeard's, and my mystery wound proved that unlike Blackbeard's immortality spell, my spell did not require reinforcement to stay active.

I grabbed my bag and crossed the deck. The potential personal risk to me from cannon fire paled in comparison to the actual personal risk of Blackbeard bleeding to death. The pirate captain did not acknowledge me when I arrived by his side.

"Captain?" I said. "Let me see that arm."

He held it out for me. I could see inches of exposed splinter, but could not tell how much more had penetrated within. I took a scalpel from my kit and slit Blackbeard's coat and shirt from the bicep down, and then exposed his lower arm. I sighed with relief when I saw that the splinter did not protrude out the other side.

Cannons boomed again, this time from the rest of the pirate fleet. As the out-of-control *Queen* had sheared away, the others had held course. Cannon balls found their mark. Smoke and shattered timbers exploded from the Carolinian vessel.

Sneed shouted orders to the *Queen's* crew and they pitched in across the deck to get the ship back under control. Men slipped on bloody decks while others kicked corpses aside to get to the guns.

The splinter that stuck from Blackbeard's arm had to come out, and had to do so in one piece. Should it leave lesser bits behind in the wound, I did not envision Blackbeard calmly letting me probe about in his flesh looking for them. I had just the tool for this, a small pair of forceps I'd acquired from one of the more forward-thinking colleagues in London. I took them from my bag and gripped the splinter. Warning Blackbeard of what I was going to do seemed condescending, and given his state of distraction, useless.

I pulled. My forearm felt every bit of the pain Blackbeard did at the splinter's removal. I stifled a scream.

Blackbeard did not react. The splinter came out as easily as a sword from a greased scabbard. It seemed to be in one piece. A quick check of the wound did not reveal anything left behind, but the oozing blood made the diagnosis difficult. One of the innovative treatments I'd brought in my bag was sphagnum moss, which could stanch bleeding. I took a sample from my bag and packed it into the wound. I bound it with a few turns of the shredded linen shirts. When blood did not penetrate the make-shift bandage, I became quite proud of my work.

I checked my own forearm. The bleeding had stopped and the wound had closed up. I'd treated myself, even if it was indirectly.

Blackbeard yanked his arm away. Perhaps it was the end to his bleeding, or the fact that the cannonade from the pirate fleet quieted, but he'd regained his composure and a measure of his piratical bearing. He stepped over to Sneed without even acknowledging my contribution to his continued existence.

"The gunboat's dismasted," Sneed said. "She's dead in the water."

Indeed, the overmatched defender of Charleston's honor now listed unmoving in the water. Her mainmast had been snapped halfway up. The broken section and the tangle of ropes and canvas it contained leaned half across the deck and half dipped in the sea. The dead littered the deck, red as fallen autumn leaves. The ship's defeated captain stood by the helm with blood splattered across his once-fine blue tunic.

"Come alongside and board the ship," Blackbeard ordered. "Bring me the Captain."

The other pirate ships backed off to a safe but still intimidating distance. The *Queen Anne's Revenge* came alongside the gunboat and the pirates lashed the ships together. This time there was no reckless, whooping charge across gangplanks to subdue the captured ship. Blackbeard gritted his teeth as his men guardedly commandeered the gunboat. The stunned pirates made cautious work of the boarding, with the survivors of the defeated crew held at bay by sword points, not dispatched by them. The witch's spell had been the driving force behind their bloodlust and bravado.

Blackbeard turned to me and pointed to the chart table in his cabin. "Make me a list of what you need to cure the witch."

I wanted to tell him I could give him a list of what *might* cure the witch, because the vagaries of the human body had still not been mastered, even with our leaps in scientific progress. Instead, I repaired to the chart table, found a bit of paper, and made a list of medicines which, if they arrived in time, might save two lives: the witch's and my own.

CHAPTER FIFTEEN

An hour later, Blackbeard sent the chastened gunboat captain back to Charleston in a skiff. The Captain carried my list which included mercury, opium, cinchona bark, and camphor. I'd listed some basic herbals and plasters as well. With my life hanging in the balance along with Dumitra's, it was better to have too many options than too few.

I resolved to do all I could between now and the medicine's arrival to keep the witch alive. A standard practice for the release of the bad humors wracking her body would be bloodletting. I decided to give that a try.

I reentered the witch's cabin. The foul miasma that pervaded it oppressed me in an instant. While the pervasive evil still filled the air, now had been added the sensation of decay, the feeling that Death was coming upon his pale horse.

It was a sensation I'd felt most acutely in plague clinics, where the mass of dying bodies exuded a near tangible form of the despair they felt. That same scent was in the air here, and just as strong, though it came from only one victim. Perhaps all the evil power she possessed in life would make her passage into death that much more difficult.

I retrieved the knives from my bag to begin the bloodletting process. I admit that it took me several tries before I could even touch her arm, so great was my fear that her malevolence would slither from her and coat me like I'd touched tar. When I did set fingers upon her, her dry skin felt more like parchment than any patient's skin I'd ever encountered.

I took a deep breath, and then went to work to pierce a vein. The near transparency of her skin made that task simple, and the blade pierced the witch's skin with no pressure. I opened the vein, but the blood within barely flowed. Its thickness and low flow rate caused immediate clotting. I concluded that the witch's low heartrate might have made this treatment impossible.

A sense of desperation descended upon me. I had no idea when, or even if, the medicines I required from Charleston would arrive, and I needed Dumitra to survive until they did. I recalled that some physicians had reported success with sweating out the bad humors if bloodletting had been unsuccessful or impractical.

I left the cabin, swallowed my intimidation, and approached Sneed to ask him for a metal container and a supply of firewood to heat the witch's quarters. He did not question my request, which might have been a telltale that he also knew how important the witch's survival was.

In no time I had what I'd asked for delivered. Joshua set down a battered cooking pot a healthy distance from the witch's cabin and beat a hasty retreat. He soon returned to lay an armload of splintered firewood beside it. I knew that asking him to bring it into the cabin would have been futile for several reasons. I undertook the task myself and set everything up between the witch's bed and the soul-leaching chair. I considered making the horrible chair part of the pyre, but was certain that it would fight back against the process.

The fire caught in moments and soon a small blaze lit the room in an orange glow. The temperature quickly rose, accompanied by a healthy smoke I was certain would invigorate her lungs. As I waited to gauge her reaction to the treatment, I glanced about the room.

Carvings dominated all four cabin walls. They did not match the ones carved around the ship. These looked like a crescent moon with a jagged line running between the two crescents' tips. If the symbols on the ship delivered protection when charged by the witch's spell, I wondered what power these diagrams held.

Then I noticed a large, leather-bound volume atop the small table. It had the heft and thickness of some of the finer family Bibles I'd seen, though I knew there was no possibility this could be a copy of that holy book. I stepped over to give it a closer look.

The book's handstitched leather cover boasted a brown pentagram symbol burned into the face. It reminded me of the results of using a branding iron, and then to my horror I realized why. This was no ordinary leather. Like Joshua's drumhead, this cover had been made from tanned human skin. Whether the pentagram brand had been added pre- or post-mortem I could not tell, but certainly hoped for the latter.

Whatever was within this witch's book, I did not want to know it. Mentally and spiritually, I recoiled at the thought of reading whatever filthy spells or disgusting sentiment waited within. Physically, the book was even more repellent than the room itself, and not just due to the human skin cover.

The witch coughed. I'd considered her sleep quite deep and the sudden noise startled me. I whirled about to see her pointing a bony finger at the book.

"That book can answer all your desires," she said in a weak and raspy voice.

Seeing her so frail, my fear of her powers abated. "I can assure you I have no interest in your repellent book."

"You want to heal people, but all you can use are the foolish rituals you learned in schools run by the ignorant. Inside that book is real power, magic that can heal in an instant."

"The way you healed Francois?"

A weak smile crossed Dumitra's lips. "All kinds of magic are within those covers. You can use the spells you choose. They don't have to be the same ones I've used."

The idea intrigued me. Clearly there was some kind of power the witch tapped into. What if it was used for good instead of evil? British warships could be protected from pirates, instead of the other way around. But more alluring was to have magic cure the ills our science as yet could not, like the undiagnosed blackened lungs and enlarged hearts discovered only in autopsies. Perhaps I could heal the shattered bones that now I had to amputate.

Just then the aura about the book changed. No longer repellent and dangerous, it now felt welcoming and benign. The pages practically whispered to me that it could make me the greatest physician the world has ever know, and the richest. Doctors the world over would come to me to learn the secrets the book promised to share. I would join the ranks of Hippocrates. I reached out to touch the cover.

With my finger a fraction of an inch away, I froze. The book had promised fame and riches. I had never sought out either. All I wanted to do was help people get well.

"Go ahead," the witch said. "Afraid of success, are you?"

"The book betrays its true character," I said. "It promises what it supposes I would want, not my true desires."

The witch's hand returned to her side. She wheezed out a long exhalation. "You couldn't have withstood the power. But it would have been fun to watch."

In an instant, the book reassumed its vile, repugnant character. A wave of evil pushed me away. I turned to brag to the witch of my triumph over its tricks. But Dumitra had returned to her deathlike slumber.

I took her return to consciousness as proof of the efficacy of the smoke and heat treatment. I knelt by the pot and tossed a bit more wood into the blaze. The thought occurred that perhaps I could cure her illness before the medicines arrived at all.

At this point in the voyage, I still had the luxury of indulging in wishful thinking.

CHAPTER SIXTEEN

Two days later, I entertained no such illusion. After her one resurrection to taunt me, the witch did not respond again. Given her weakened state, I feared she'd spent the last of her waning strength trying to trick me into practicing witchcraft. During those days, I kept a vigil in her cabin until the malevolence it exuded threatened my own health. Then I would retreat to my cabin until cleaner air revived me.

That morning of the third day, I left my cabin to see Blackbeard pacing the quarterdeck. He'd been wearing out that section of decking near continuously since he'd dispatched the defeated gunboat captain to Charleston carrying the pirate's ultimatum. There had been no word back from the city, but neither had any ships tried to venture out of the harbor. That mixed message did not sit well with a pirate whose ultimatums were usually answered within the minute.

Ships within the harbor knew not to try to leave, but there was no way to warn arriving ships not to enter. With the sun still low on the horizon, the lookout called out that he sighted sails approaching the channel.

This time, the opportunity for combat did not set Blackbeard's face alight. He did not call his men to make ready for battle. Instead, he ordered signal flags raised to send one of his other ships, the *Avarice*, out to intercept the incoming vessel. Sneed was flabbergasted when Blackbeard gave the order, and as the men saw their sister ship depart while they remained at anchor, they were stunned.

The *Avarice* met the incoming vessel well east of the harbor's mouth. It only took one salvo for the merchantman to come about and head for a different port. A half-hearted cheer came across the sea when the merchant vessel beat a retreat. It seemed the crew would have been happier with an outcome that left them in control of a new stash of booty. But Blackbeard needed the retreating vessel to spread the word that the port of Charleston was officially closed by the fleet that sailed under the skeleton flag.

With Charleston's blockade secured, I began the day as I had the last two. I entered the witch's cabin to tend to her and rekindle the fire for the sweating process. It struck me that the oppressive, malicious air of the place was considerably diminished. Strange as this may sound, instead of relief, the sensation filled me with fear. In addition, there was a new sound. A new, wheezing rattle of the witch's breath echoed off the walls.

I rushed to her side. By a lamp's light I inspected her. Dumitra's skin now clung to bone so tight it was if she was a painted skeleton. Nearly all the color was gone from her, and even her eyeballs seemed to have shrunken and receded deeper into their sockets. I could not believe that someone could be so manifested with death and still be alive. But I knew she would not be so for long.

I rekindled the fire to get the room warmer. After soaking a cloth in water, I wrung it out across her parched, flaky lips. I'd seen her consume a soul for sustenance, but did not know if in addition she ate or drank. She had done neither since falling ill. At worst, the water could do no harm.

"Ship approaching from Charleston!" called the lookout from the crow's nest.

My heart leapt. Perhaps this was the answer to my prayers, and life-saving medicine was to arrive in the nick of time.

I left the cabin and ran to the railing facing the city. A small sloop was making a beeline for the *Queen*. It flew a white flag.

The vessel came alongside. There were several crates on the deck, rigged to be hoisted up to the pirate ship. The Captain of the sunken gunboat stood between the crates wearing a new, or at the least laundered, uniform. The pirates unrolled a rope ladder down the side to the sloop. Two crewmen held the sloop fast under the ladder.

The Charleston officer grabbed a leather valise and scaled the side of our ship. A few laughing pirates tossed down a rope that the sailors on the sloop tied to one crate. The pirates began to haul up the first crate of the ransom payment.

The Charleston Captain reached the *Queen's* deck. Blackbeard already stood facing him.

"Your ransom is in those crates," the Captain said. "Silver and gold and jewelry in one crate. All volunteered by the finest Charleston families. Foodstuffs in the second crate."

Neither of these boxes of tribute interested me. Blackbeard seemed to share my sentiment.

"The medicines?" he said.

The Captain handed his leather valise to Blackbeard. "Almost everything you asked for. We scoured the city and these were all we could find."

Blackbeard snatched the valise from the man. He turned around to shout for me, but I was already halfway down the stairs from the quarterdeck. I went straight for the two men and grabbed the case. Without a word to either, I sprinted up the steps and back to the witch's cabin.

Outside the door, I stopped to take an inventory in the brighter light. Opening the case revealed a plethora of lifesaving medicines including mercury, laudanum, and potassium nitrate. There were even bottles of some of Britain's newest patent medicines. I finally had some ammunition in my fight to save Dumitra's life and my own.

I reentered the room and instantly coughed from the smoky air. After setting the case down on the soul-sucking chair, I went to the port and opened its hatch to admit a fresh sea breeze and some brighter daylight. Out with the old treatments, in with the new. I went to Dumitra's side.

The sunlight revealed an awful sight. All the witch's facial muscles were slack, her skin so bloodlessly transparent I could make out the specifics of her skull. I hurriedly placed a mirror before her lips. It did not fog.

The medicines had come too late. The witch was dead.

An avalanche of awful repercussions was about to cascade upon me. With no reason to delay the inevitable, I decided to pull the keystone loose myself. I left the cabin to tell Blackbeard this awful news.

CHAPTER SEVENTEEN

I stepped out of the witch's cabin to find Blackbeard already waiting there. "The witch?" he said.

Many times in the past I've had to break bad news to family members. I always worried about how much pain my report might cause them. This time I worried about how much pain my report would cause me.

"The medicines arrived too late," I said. "She is dead."

Blackbeard roared with disapproval. He grabbed me by the front of my jacket and lifted me off the ground. Then he threw me back against the cabin wall. My head hit the hardwood with a loud crack. Then I dropped to the deck.

Blackbeard pointed to the Charleston officer. He had foolishly remained onboard as the last of the crates from the sloop were transferred. It hung just a few feet over the deck.

"This is your fault!" Blackbeard shouted. "Three days we waited!"

The Captain paled. "It wasn't my fault! The-the city fathers dithered. Gathering valuables takes time. We-we paid as fast as we could."

No excuse could quell Blackbeard's rage. I doubt he even heard the man through his own anger. He growled and drew his sword. Then the pirate captain vaulted over the quarterdeck railing and landed on the main deck with a crash. Crewmen scattered out of his way. Blackbeard charged the unarmed Charleston officer.

The officer turned and retreated to the ladder over the side. He did not make it. In two bounds, Blackbeard was upon him. The pirate sent his sword through the man's back with a quick, violent thrust. The tip exited the man's chest in a fountain of blood.

With his sword into the man up to the hilt, Blackbeard drove the jerking, dying Captain to the gunwale of the ship. He slammed the man against the railing, set a boot against the base of the man's spine, and extracted the sword. The wounded Captain uttered a garbled last word, and then collapsed bent over the railing. Blackbeard drove his sword into the deck, grabbed the corpse's legs, and flipped it over the side. It dropped down onto the deck of the sloop with a splat.

The men on the sloop cried out in shock and pushed away from the pirate ship. The wind caught its sail, and the ship peeled away back toward Charleston.

"Bring guns to bear on that sloop!" Blackbeard shouted. "Sneed, get us underway. We're going to level that city."

Powerful as Blackbeard's fleet was, the pirate captains had already agreed in their meeting it would be no match for the longer-range shore guns along the Charleston waterfront. Blackbeard's fury had overwhelmed his reasoning. The fearful look on Sneed's face said that his view had remained more rational.

Sneed spoke to Blackbeard in a whisper. "Sir, we have the ransom."

Blackbeard grabbed Sneed at the throat. "But I don't have the witch, do I?"

"An attack is suicide," Sneed rasped. "And even if it isn't, no one will ever pay again after we double-cross Charleston. And the ship we turned away three days ago might have sent warships back to bottle us up in here."

The anger in Blackbeard's eyes faded. He set Sneed free. The first mate rubbed his neck and coughed. Blackbeard looked across the deck and realized his crew had gone silent, and all were staring at him. He turned back to Sneed.

"Set sail and raise the anchor. Signal the other ships we head to sea."

Sneed nodded and Blackbeard mounted the steps to the quarterdeck. He marched past where I still sat on the deck without looking at me.

"Dispose of the remains," he said. I had to assume he was speaking to me, no others being nearby, though he still did not look in my direction. He entered his cabin and slammed the door shut behind him.

The crew still hadn't moved. Sneed climbed to the quarterdeck and stood at the railing overlooking the main deck.

"Set mains and topsails!" he ordered. "Prepare to weigh anchor. Secure that ransom below."

The orders awakened the crew from their trance and they set about their tasks. Sneed gave the signalman orders to signal the other ships to follow.

I rose to my feet. I now had one more duty to perform for the witch. I assumed there was some ceremony for burial at sea. Blackbeard would likely not wish me to toss her over the side like trash, though I was sure more out of fear of some sort of ghostly retribution by her than out of common decency. I resolved to shroud her body in her bedsheet in preparation.

I reentered the cabin. The witch's death had diminished the sensation of evil inside, but the amount that remained was more than enough to be unnerving. I went to the bed and found that the body was gone. My first instinct was that somehow my diagnosis of death had been incorrect and she'd gotten up.

But a quick look about the cabin proved that wasn't the case. I reexamined the bed. Gray ash lay upon the mattress in a rough outline of the witch's body. There was no disease that could make that happen. I would have no way to explain this to Blackbeard.

I took one edge of the mattress, with the intent to shake the ash free onto the floor. But as I moved it, the ash transitioned into the mattress as easily as flour through a sifter.

I placed the mattress back into position and looked under the bed, but the ash had not made its way through. Whether it be moss or straw or some other bits of vegetation that gave the mattress its cushion, the ash had apparently clung to it. I was relieved that I did not have to deal with the corpse, though still confounded as to what had happened here.

I returned to the quarterdeck as the ship exited the harbor. The rest of the little fleet followed us. From within the Captain's cabin came a string of curses and the sound of rustling charts. With no desire to return to the witch's cabin, I went back to my own. Before I could enter, Blackbeard returned to the quarterdeck. The anger and fear he'd displayed earlier was gone, replaced with the resolve that was more familiar.

I hoped that we would be heading further out to sea and away from any armed vessels patrolling the harbors of the New World. Blackbeard's new vulnerability was as much a threat to me as to himself. The further we all stayed from flying cannonballs and the sharp edges of swords, the more content I would be.

Of course, Blackbeard did not ask for my opinion. He ordered Sneed to set a course up the coast.

**

By dusk the next day we were off the northern coast of the Carolina colony. Sandy islands of the outer banks blocked a direct view of the lagoons and land beyond. I had heard that there were many small settlements along the coast, and that these outer banks were treacherous waters.

Blackbeard stood beside Sneed and scanned the shoreline with a spyglass. He stopped and examined a spot up ahead, then collapsed the spyglass.

"Sneed, we go in through the next pass. Big Pine Point will be south along the coast. That's our destination. Drop anchor short of the docks."

We still flew the skeleton flag, Blackbeard's calling card to all who saw the *Queen Anne's Revenge*. I imagined the panic it would sow among the townspeople. At least we were not sailing in with cannons blazing.

We went through the narrow pass Blackbeard had mentioned. On one side was a tall lookout tower made of rough-hewn logs. As Blackbeard watched the tower, the lookout within checked over our ship with a spyglass and then gave us a wave. The lookout could not have missed seeing our skeleton flag. Blackbeard's influence did indeed extend inland from the sea.

By dusk we had dropped anchor just off Big Pine Point, a small town with two docks. Then despite Blackbeard's rush to get here, we did nothing.

After nightfall, Sneed entered my cabin. "Get up. Raiding party's going ashore. Blackbeard says you're in it."

"Me?" I said. "I'm no pirate. What good would I be?"

"Ask Blackbeard." Sneed slammed my door.

I dressed filled with dread. I could not bring myself to carry a weapon, could not engage with innocent people as part of a pirate raid. I was a doctor for the love of God. I could not fathom the purpose taking me ashore would serve. Even worse, I could not even use the raid as an opportunity to escape. Separation from Blackbeard would kill me as easily as a cannonball. The occasional itch of my sub-dermal tattoo reminded me of that. Then I wondered if I could even survive if Blackbeard was onboard and I was on the shore. Would that be too far apart?

I went on deck to where men were climbing down rope ladders to a small skiff. Blackbeard arrived behind me. I had to try and get out of this unwelcome assignment.

"Sir, what am I doing on a raid?"

"This raid's *for* you, Doctor. We're not going to be caught short of medicines again. We're going in to steal them, and you're going to tell me what we need among what we discover."

The pirate captain was leading the raid. My concern about being separated from Blackbeard was allayed. My concern about participating was not.

He handed me a sack and then looked me straight in the eye with a malicious grin. "No more excuses for someone dying on my ship."

Having access to every medicine known to mankind could not guarantee that. Blackbeard had just made it clear that the next patient I lost aboard the *Queen* would be my last patient ever.

CHAPTER EIGHTEEN

From the appearance of the Big Pine Point docks and the boats around them, fishing seemed to be the town's lifeblood. I wasn't sure how well-stocked an apothecary such a place would have. A larger city would have a better chance for success, but also more likely to put up a strong defense. I was in no position to second-guess Blackbeard, and if the smaller town made it less likely anyone would get hurt, then I was all for it.

I embarked on the same skiff as Blackbeard and a half-dozen other pirates. A similar skiff loaded with men already floated a few yards away, though whether they came from our ship or one of the others, I could not say. Blackbeard sat in the stern and I sat just forward of him.

Blackbeard leaned close to my ear. "Try to desert my ship while we are ashore, and I won't kill you on the spot. I'll bring you back aboard so I have time to do it slowly. Understood?"

Blackbeard had no idea the witch's binding spell made his threat completely unnecessary. "I understand."

As we approached the docks, the town appeared deserted. The few lights burning in some windows were all that indicated the place wasn't abandoned. The buildings were all simple, single-story affairs, some even constructed of rough-hewn logs. I began to worry that such a place had no apothecary at all.

The pirates rowed with near-silent oars through the darkness. It chilled me to think of how many surreptitious attacks they'd executed in the past, and how many hapless victims they'd left behind each time.

The other skiff reached the dock. It touched a piling with just the slightest bump. Men mounted the dock soundless and stealthy as cats. They crept down to where stacks of fish traps lined the shore and then they disappeared into the shadows.

Our skiff reached the dock. Blackbeard and most of the men disembarked. Being unarmed and worried about a locals' attempt to repel the pirates by force, I kept myself in the middle of the group. As we made our way down the dock, I prayed that the townspeople would remain nestled in bed until we departed.

When we reached the end of the dock, one of the men lit a lantern and handed it to Blackbeard. He then took the lead. A number of pirates stayed back to guard our escape route and Blackbeard marched down one street and up the next. He seemed to know exactly where he was going. He stopped in front of one building and raised the lantern to the sign by the door. It read:

Samuel Wainwright
Provisions and Apothecary

Blackbeard waved one of the pirates forward. The man arrived with a blacksmith's hammer in one hand. With one quick swing, he punched the door knob and lock into the shop with a minimum amount of noise. Blackbeard pushed the door open, then he shoved me inside.

We passed by several well-stocked shelves and went to a rear corner of the small store. Blackbeard held the lantern high and lit up a shelf of medical supplies, including bandages and multiple corked and labeled bottles of medicines.

"Take what we need," he said.

A new dilemma presented itself. I realized whatever I took would leave the town short in an emergency, but if I left something behind and I required it later, that might cost me the life of the patient, as well as my own.

Blackbeard began to give orders to the others about what provisions to steal and was not paying attention to me. As I reached into shelves, I pushed some bottles into the shadows in the back as I pulled a few bottles forward and into my bag. If Blackbeard did not look closely, it would appear that I'd taken all the shop had, which I assumed was the pirate way. I soon had a full sack.

"That's it," I said.

Blackbeard glanced at the apparently empty shelves, nodded, and ordered everyone out of the shop. We gathered on the street. The pirates had been much more efficient than I at their thievery, and the men were laden with provisions. Either no one in the town had noticed our arrival yet, or no one was brave enough to contest it.

"Iverson," Blackbeard said to one pirate, "take all of this and the doctor back to the dock." He pointed to two other pirates. "You two come with me."

The tattoo on my chest itched and reminded me how closely my life was tied to Blackbeard's. I had no intention of testing if the distance between the dock and wherever Blackbeard was off to was more than the witch's spell would let me tolerate.

"Sir, I should stay with you," I said. "In case you need me."

I hoped the implication that his invulnerability was gone would be subtle enough to remind him without bringing it to the attention of the rest of the raiding party.

"Fine," he said. "Iverson, take the doctor's bag."

Most of the group headed back to the skiff, save Blackbeard, two crewmen, and myself. Blackbeard led us through town and onto the porch of a small, simple house. It was in need of paint and the porch roof sagged. If that was what I could discern at night, I was certain daylight would reveal it to be near-unlivable.

Blackbeard did not wait to make a stealthy entrance this time. He reared back and gave the door a mighty kick. The lock exploded the doorjamb and the door swung open so hard that one of the hinges broke. Blackbeard entered with the two crewmen right behind him.

The lantern light revealed a sparse main room with a simple table and three chairs. The walls held no decorations and what passed for drapes on the single front window were faded and frayed. A cornhusk doll lay by the table on the bare wood floor. A strange scent filled the air, not quite the wood of a fireplace, not quite cooked food, but still familiar.

A young woman stepped into the room. She wore a long nightgown and squinted against the lantern's glare. A tangle of black hair cascaded past her shoulders. She looked at Blackbeard and her jaw dropped.

"Blackbeard," she whispered.

Apparently his personal appearance was as recognizable as his skeleton flag.

"Get dressed," he said. "You're coming with us."

Now my jaw dropped. I'd already disgraced myself by becoming a thief tonight. I had no interest in being party to a kidnapping.

The woman's eyes widened. "No, no you can't. Promises were made."

"And now they're being broken."

"I-I won't go," the woman said. "My husband will call the town to arms to defend me."

Blackbeard laughed. "There's no husband here, and no courage in these empty streets to save a woman like you."

A sleepy little girl wandered in and stood by the woman. The resemblance was uncanny. "Mommy? What's happening?"

"Nothing, Abigail. Go back into bed." She pushed the girl back into the other room.

Blackbeard drew a dagger from his belt. "You can come with us peaceable and I leave the little girl alive here. Or I kill her and my men take you anyway."

I could only think of one reason a pirate crew would want a pretty young woman on board, and the scenario repulsed me. Blackbeard's use of family for leverage had worked on me, and I could see in the young woman's eyes that it was working on her as well. I hoped she would grab her child and escape out some back door and be swallowed by the night.

"I'll go once I see my daughter is safe," she said.

I wanted to scream at her to stop, that it would be better if both she and her daughter died than she subjected herself to a shipload of brigand scum.

"Dress and pack what you need," Blackbeard said. "You have three minutes."

She stepped back through the doorway. One of the pirates moved to follow her. She raised a hand. "I don't need an audience."

"I think you do," Blackbeard said. "To keep you from doing something rash. Johnson, you stay here." Blackbeard pointed at me. "You watch her. Allow no tricks."

"He's no better!" the woman said.

"Of course he is. He's the ship's doctor. A proper gentleman and all that." Blackbeard ran a finger along the side of the dagger's blade. "Or we can do this the other way."

The woman gritted her teeth, then disappeared into the other room. Blackbeard pointed the dagger at me, and motioned that I should follow her. I reluctantly obeyed.

The woman lit a candle. The room had two beds, one much smaller than the other. The little girl sat on the smaller bed. The woman pulled a sack from beneath her bed and began to fill it with clothing from a dresser between the beds.

"Mommy, what's happening?"

The woman did not stop packing. "I need to leave for a little while. You'll stay with your grandfather while I'm gone."

"No!" Abigail wailed. "Father left and didn't come back. Now you're going to leave and not come back!"

The panic in Abigail's voice broke my heart. The woman knelt down before her daughter and held her at the shoulders.

"That's not going to happen," she said. "We'll be back together. In fact, we'll never really be apart."

The woman pulled a medallion up from under her nightshirt. It hung from a chain around her neck. She placed it against the edge of the bed and struck it with the palm of her hand. It bent. She flipped it over and struck it again. This time it broke. The lower third fell to the floor with a clink. She picked it up and handed it to her daughter.

"Every night you'll hold that," she said. "And every night I'll hold this piece. And no matter the distance, we'll be together. You'll feel me. We'll do that until I come home."

Abigail gripped the broken medallion like a drowning sailor would a raft. "Promise?"

"I promise." The woman threw a few more items from the dresser into the sack, then laid a long dress on the bed. She gave me a hateful stare. "Turn away."

I made a half turn to the right so she was out of my field of view. "Madame, I assure you, I am a doctor."

"If you sail with pirates, you're filth, no matter what you call yourself."

The truth in her words cut me to the core. Whether involuntarily or not, I was an accomplice in theft and kidnapping and the unimaginable trauma being inflicted upon this poor little girl.

"I didn't know you were going to be kidnapped," I explained. "I came ashore to..."

To do what? I thought. *To steal medicines? That wouldn't make me sound better.*

"Let's go," she said.

I turned back to see her fully dressed with the sack in her arms. I backed out of the doorway. The front door was open and Blackbeard and the pirates waited on the porch. The woman led her daughter out the front door and onto the street. I followed behind her. Blackbeard watched with his dagger at the ready in case of a double-cross.

The woman knelt and kissed her daughter on the forehead. She held out her medallion. Abigail held out her piece and joined them together at the jagged break.

"Every night," the woman said.

"Every night," Abigail repeated.

"I'll be back soon. Now, run across the street to your grandfather's house and tell them what happened and to not come after me."

Tears welled in the girl's eyes. She nodded, whirled about, and ran off to one of the houses down the street.

"Good instructions," Blackbeard said.

The woman did not answer. She threw her bag up upon her shoulder and started to walk toward the docks. She did not give her daughter one last look, did not give her home a departing glance. She seemed resigned to this pirate fate. There had to be much more to this story than I knew.

As we walked back to the dock, I vowed to do two things. First, find out about this strong, alluring woman. Second, do everything I could to get her back to her daughter.

CHAPTER NINETEEN

All the way back to the docks, the crewmen kept their distance from this mysterious woman. When we got back to the skiffs, Iverson handed me my sack of medical supplies and led several other pirates who'd come ashore in our boat over to the other. The four left behind looked like they wished they hadn't been.

Blackbeard sat in the stern again. The woman and I sat side by side in the seat in front of him. The rest of the men sat as far forward as possible. We pushed off from the dock and headed back to the *Queen Anne's Revenge*. As they rowed, the pirates manning the oars looked about in every possible direction except at the woman beside me.

Blackbeard had kept his lantern burning on the trip back. It sat on the deck between the seats and cast a flickering yellow glow upon the woman's face. The track of a tear ran down her cheek and her lips trembled as if she held back anguished sobbing. I wanted to give her some words of comfort, but from her initial reaction to me, I dared not try.

We came alongside the ship and stopped with the stern beneath the rope ladder. Blackbeard climbed up. When he'd cleared the boat, I stood and grabbed the ladder with one hand. I extended the other to help the woman to her feet. She looked up at me like I was offering her poison. She went to the ladder without my assistance and scaled the side of the ship with her bag in hand.

"Idiot," one of the pirates said. "Certain death it is to touch a witch."

A witch? Her? I could not fathom where the man got that idea. This was a young mother from a common house, with a beautiful little daughter to boot.

I ascended the ladder. My sack of medicines ensured that I did it with no grace. At the top of the gunwale, I rolled it over onto the deck with great relief. I set foot beside it, close to where Blackbeard and Sneed stood beside the kidnapped woman. Sneed looked wary.

"This is Justinia Florescu," Blackbeard said.

I was surprised that somehow Blackbeard knew the name of a woman he'd barely spoken to. I was more surprised when Sneed nodded, as if somehow her presence aboard the ship now made sense.

"Take her to quarters." Blackbeard turned to me. "You start taking care of her as of now. I don't want any more dead witches on my ship."

I was a bit stunned. This woman was indeed a witch. She didn't object to the appellation, which I thought would be the first thing a non-witch would do in such a situation.

Sneed led Justinia up to the quarterdeck. I followed the two of them and he directed her to the witch's cabin. After she entered, Sneed looked at me like I was a simpleton.

"Well, you heard the Captain," he said. "Make sure she ain't sick."

Between Justinia's icy attitude toward me and the general sensation of evil that still pervaded the cabin, I had no interest in being in there alone with her. Unfortunately, I had no choice. I sighed and entered the room. Sneed closed the door behind me. I struck a match to light the lantern hanging on the wall.

Justinia whirled around. She saw me and balled her fists. "What are you doing in here?"

"You heard the Captain. I'm supposed to make sure you're healthy."

"If you think I'm consenting to a leering examination from some incompetent pirate doctor, you're sadly mistaken. Get out of here."

I would have been happy to comply if I was certain that Sneed or Blackbeard wasn't waiting on the quarterdeck for the report of my examination. But I also did not want to miss this opportunity to make our relationship less adversarial. After all, we were the only two involuntary crew members. I lit the lantern before the match burned my fingers.

"Please, Justinia. Let us start all this over. I'm Dr. Baxter Whitcomb. I was kidnapped off a ship heading for the colonies. Blackbeard gave me the same choice he gave you. I could join his crew, or he would kill my sister and niece."

The tension in Justinia's face lessened. "Truthfully?"

"Do I look like pirate material?"

"No, I suppose not."

"I have to say, neither do you look like witch material."

"And what would you know about witches?" She practically spat the words at me.

"Just what I learned from treating the one who'd occupied this cabin before you."

Justinia grabbed my arm. "Dumitra? Where is she?"

"I'm afraid she died. Did you know her?"

Justinia released me and slumped down on the bed. "She was my sister."

I was taken aback by the impossible age difference between them if Dumitra was her sister, but I let it go by. "That's how Blackbeard knows who you are?"

"Of course. Now I understand it all. He didn't want to pillage without the power of witchcraft behind him, so he came to get another witch." She shook her head. "This will be a long story."

"I'm supposed to be giving you a thorough exam, so we have the time."

"My family is Romani, Gypsy most people call us. We have no real homeland to call our own in Europe. Our practices and beliefs made us outcasts centuries ago."

"Practices of witchcraft?"

"That's what you people call it. With that justification, you hunt us down and then turn us out. My parents moved us here when the colony was new, so we too could be new, and start again."

Many had fled Europe to gain religious freedom in the New World, whether Pilgrims or Catholics or Quakers. But I was certain none of them were planning on this place being a haven for practitioners of witchcraft.

"I can tell what you are thinking. Witches have no place among good people. Burn them. Stone them."

I was embarrassed that my face had betrayed me. "No, I…really…"

"It's fine. You're ignorant of much, like the rest. Every culture thinks they're superior to all others, and dismiss anything unlike their own. The magic we practice can be white or black, depending on how it's used. But others treat it all as evil. Your people are no different."

"I think we're quite different."

"If you British are so different, why are these colonies filled with people trying to escape you?"

She made a good point that I promised myself to mull over later.

"When we arrived," she continued, "it was as my parents had hoped. It was live and let live in the colony. Life was too harsh for anything else, really. We were able to fish and farm and feed ourselves in peace. I married a local fisherman and had Abigail. But that life was not enough for Dumitra.

"My older sister had been exposed to more magic in the Old World than I had. She'd seen the white magic my parents practiced, but she'd also seen the bad, the black magic others had conjured. As she endured the hardships this new place forced on us, she began to look at black magic as a way out of all this."

"I witnessed some of the spells she cast," I said. "The power seems limitless."

"And so is its price. Every spell cast takes something from the witch. The darker the magic, the more draining it is. That's why she had that horrible rendering chair behind you."

"I viewed her using it. The man in the chair did not survive."

"That is how the dark magic works. Addictive, like opium. The witch who practices it becomes enmeshed in the power, changed by the force of the magic itself. She will use more and it will take more from her, until the only way she can live is to draw the life force, the soul if you will, from others. Draw too much from the victim, and the witch kills him."

"Back at your home," I said, "you mentioned a promise Blackbeard had made."

"It was part of the deal my sister made with him. Blackbeard would protect the rest of the family, my sister, my parents, my daughter. That included protection from pirates, including himself."

"Pirate honor is an oxymoron. He had you protected in Big Pine Point?"

"The mayor and town council were easily and cheaply bribed. Why do you think all of you could walk the town unmolested?"

The ease of our raid now made perfect sense.

"Knowing all that," I said, "what will you do when Blackbeard demands you serve him?"

"You're in the same situation, doctor to a crew of murderous pirates. What do you do?"

"As little as possible."

"And that's what I'm going to do."

"Once we're out to sea, and your daughter is safe with your family, why don't you use some magic spell to help you escape?"

"You don't understand Blackbeard's reach. He has spies everywhere, especially in the Carolina colony. He would pay to hunt Abigail down, and someone would be willing to take his money. What about you? You were just ashore kidnapping me. Your sister and niece are far away and Blackbeard probably doesn't even know who they are. Why didn't you escape?"

I stepped closer to her and pulled aside the collar to my shirt to expose the location where Dumitra had left the disappearing tattoo.

"Dumitra tattooed an image here, and it bound my life to Blackbeard's."

Justinia placed her hand a scant inch from my chest. She whispered an incantation in the strange Gypsy tongue. My chest began to itch, and like a surfacing whale, the tattoo rose to the top of my skin.

Justinia winced at the sight of the tattoo. She traced it with her index finger. Her gentle touch gave me goosebumps and made me quiver. Then the mark dissolved away again.

"A binding spell. By its nature, tough to break. This one is more intricate than any I've ever seen. My sister had grown very powerful, much stronger than I am. A counter-spell would be difficult."

"Difficult differs from impossible," I said.

"I'll have to search the grimoire and see which one a counter-spell would be."

A soft shoot of hope emerged from the soil of my despair. If I asked any more questions, I feared a negative answer might wither it. "I had better go. This is supposed to be an examination, not a conversation. Since I'm here, do you have any maladies that require treatment?"

"I assure you I am completely healthy, except for a broken heart over my daughter."

I nodded and left the cabin. Blackbeard waited on the quarterdeck.

"Well?" he said.

"She is quite healthy. I'm certain she'll serve you well."

"I don't need a doctor who can't cure the sick. You need to make sure she serves for a very long time."

As Blackbeard went back to his cabin, I realized that was one order I would certainly follow. I would make certain she was healthy, though not to serve, but to survive. For the day would come, when the opportunity for her to escape would present itself, and I wanted her to be able to take it. I might never reunite with my family, but I could make certain that she would reunite with hers.

CHAPTER TWENTY

That night I had a terrible dream.

I stood alone on the *Queen's* main deck. No sails were set, yet the ship plowed forward. The mast and bare yardarms hung unnaturally bowed, more like clawed hands reaching down to pluck me from the deck and toss me into the ocean. But the sea around the ship wasn't water, but lava, with great waves of it rolling past the hull. I could feel its heat, smell the sulfur and tar scents it exuded. How the ship did not burn was beyond me.

Justinia appeared on the bow, facing me from atop the fo'c'sle. The wind blew her long, black hair toward me. As it whipped about it obscured most of her face. She wore the same long dress she'd put on when we'd brought her onboard.

From the quarterdeck came Blackbeard's furious roar. The pirate stood at the railing, cutlass in one hand and his dagger in the other. Blood dripped from both blades. Behind him flapped a skeleton flag so large that it covered the ship's stern. Fuses blazed in his beard and hair, but not as brightly as the red fire that burned in his eyes. And those eyes were fixed on Justinia.

On the bow, Justinia reached out both hands to me. She mouthed the words "Help me."

Blackbeard crouched and then sprang from the quarterdeck. He sailed through the air and landed with a crash several feet from me. Deck planks splintered from the impact. His glowing eyes felt like they were burning a hole in me. He growled like a tiger and raised his cutlass.

I tried to retreat to Justinia's side, but I could not move my feet. The deck had sprouted vines just like the ones from the rendering chair. They wrapped all the way to my knees and it felt like I was encased in stone. I pulled and twisted to no avail. I would not be saving Justinia. I would not even be able to save myself.

Blackbeard charged me. With one great swing of the sword, he sliced my head from my body. I felt no pain. My head fell to the deck and I remained completely conscious. I could see my body, still upright for some reason with my arms flailing about. I also had a full view of the deck.

Blackbeard did not pause over my demise. He barely broke stride as he made a beeline across the deck to Justinia. I watched in horror, beheaded and helpless.

As he neared the fo'c'sle, a dark oily ooze bubbled up from the fo'c'sle deck. It contracted around Justinia, the opposite of a spill spreading across the deck. The liquid disappeared beneath the hem of her dress.

As it did, Blackbeard leaped for her. He rose high in the air, over a sagging yardarm, and toward the bow, aimed for a landing at Justinia's feet. He held both blades overhead, ready for a double strike when he did. He bared his teeth like a rabid dog.

Justinia's dress transformed. The hem spread wide, the collar closed and rose. From the rear, a hood bloomed and swept forward to cover her head.

As it did, Justinia's face burst into the same green glow that had accompanied all Dumitra's witchcraft. The protective symbols along the bow and forward mast burst into green flames. Justinia's pleading outstretched hands rotated and her fingers pointed at Blackbeard like ten tiny weapons.

Blackbeard's eyes turned the brightest of red in the split-second before landing. Green lightning flew from Justinia's fingertips. The space between the two of them exploded into blinding shafts of green and red light. In that flash I saw not the lovely face of Justinia under the cloak's hood, but the shriveled visage of Dumitra.

A shockwave rolled across the deck. The ship lurched to starboard. My head rolled toward the railing and my world turned into a spinning alternation of wooden deck and black sky. Then I rolled through the gap below the railing.

The heat of the lava sea hit like the breath of a furnace. My head stopped spinning with my face to this vision of Hell. As I plummeted to a fiery demise, I felt my skin shrivel and catch fire. I shrieked and disappeared into the molten waves.

I awakened with such a start that I rolled out of my hammock and landed hard upon the deck. The pain of the impact was a relief compared to the soft landing in the fiery sea my mind had conjured. I jumped up and patted my body all over, confirming that I was in one piece, unsinged, and back on the real-world pirate ship.

The horror of the dream left me wide awake. Out my portal the eastern sky offered no hint of dawn, and so recently terrified by fire, I could not bring myself to light a match and check the time on my pocket watch. Instead I returned to my hammock, stared at the inky darkness of the ceiling and pondered my dream as I waited for the sun's arrival.

As dawn broke, the sun's rays offered comfort. Once reminded that darkness and the horrors it harbored were never eternal, I was able to drop into a light sleep. A racket upon the deck soon re-awakened me. I left my cabin to find the crew had the ship rigged and anchor weighed. The *Queen* and her escorts were riding the receding tide back out to sea.

When Joshua delivered my breakfast, I looked across to the witch's cabin, which I promised myself to now think of as Justinia's cabin. I saw no meal set there for her. Indeed, the previous witch may not have eaten, surviving on the souls she drained from others instead. I considered mentioning this oversight to Sneed, but he was quite busy moving about the deck and piloting the ship out of the harbor. I decided that for now I'd share my repast with Justinia.

It would also be a good excuse to check on her physical and mental state. The level of guilt I felt about my participation in her kidnapping had only increased after my nightmare. So had my fascination with her.

I carried my meal across the quarterdeck and knocked upon her door. She bid me enter.

I'd hoped that with the witch Dumitra gone and Justinia in her place, the cabin's sensation of evil would depart as well. It had not. The room still exhaled a repellent charge. I wondered if the wood itself had absorbed too much evil, the way a table in a tavern continued to smell like the alcohol spilled upon it long ago.

Justinia leaned against the bulkhead, looking out the port at the sea. The morning light allowed me to see her well for the first time, and I could not deny her ravishing beauty. Her skin was flawless as fine porcelain. Sunlight glistened on her luxuriant, dark hair. High cheekbones gave her a regal air that would have been at home at any meal in Buckingham Palace.

She turned to me and looked at the covered plate in my hands. "You have double duties as a serving boy?"

"In this instance, I guess I do. The crew grudgingly feeds me twice a day. I never saw them feed the wi-" I stopped myself, remembering that the one I thought of as a witch was this woman's sister. "Dumitra. In case they were not ordered to serve you anything, I came to share mine."

"That was thoughtful of you."

"You may change your mind when you eat it."

She came to me and uncovered the plate to reveal the standard, unappetizing pirate fare. One difference was the addition of a handful of fresh cherries, no doubt part of the ransom paid by the residents of Charleston. She plucked them up and left the less appetizing items for me.

"I trust you were able to sleep?" I said.

"A little." She munched on a cherry. "These are good."

"The fare is quite poor on average. The cherries are an exception. I'm glad to see you're eating them."

"Unlike my sister," she said, "I don't eat using the rendering chair. I'm not that kind of witch."

"Blackbeard will expect you to become that kind of witch."

"He's going to be disappointed."

"If you don't practice black magic, how will you know what spells to cast anyway?"

Justinia walked over to the corner table and opened the massive, old book. "This is where my sister got her spells. This is a grimoire. Think of it as a magic recipe book. These are passed down through generations in Romani families, with the next generation recording new spells on later pages."

"Then this is your family's book?"

"Oh, no. We never strayed from white magic. I don't know where Dumitra got this book. But she took to using it very quickly."

"How long was she sailing with Blackbeard?"

"She left home two summers ago. Blackbeard had been granted clemency, but took up pirating again. Now I wonder if he recruited my sister to help him, or if she brought black magic to him and volunteered."

Given the witch's advanced age, this timeline made no sense to me. "Your sister was very old to still be at home, very old to even be your sister."

"My sister was thirteen months older than I."

"That can't be. I examined her, treated her. She was geriatric."

"That's the toll black magic takes, even if you are consuming souls. Empty and refill a wineskin many times, and it will quickly crack and leak. The same for a human body going through the stress of performing black magic. Why do you think all the fairy tales tell of old and ugly witches? Because the bad ones are."

"She was emaciated."

"Practicing black magic is always fatal, eventually. The temptation, the addiction to the power becomes too great for anyone to resist."

The revelation horrified me. But I'd seen men do something similar. Alcoholics addicted to drink would indulge their vice to the exclusion of all else, eschewing food and common hygiene in pursuit of the next bottle. The addiction to dark power must have been much worse.

"If she was that damaged," she continued, "and harvesting souls wasn't keeping her alive anymore, nothing you could have done would have saved her."

That made me feel better. My medical training gave me a sense of responsibility for any life placed in my hands, even pirates and witches.

"If you start practicing the magic in that book," I said, "won't the same thing happen to you?"

"Eventually. So I'll have to practice it sparingly."

"Your sister wasn't. Just in what I saw her do, she cast a spell of protection on Blackbeard, had another similar spell for the ship, and cast another one before combat to turn the pirates into fearless, reckless killers."

Justinia looked down at the floor. "That's a lot of magic. I'll need to have a good plan to keep from having to do all that many times."

I'd seen just how ruthless Blackbeard could be when his orders were not followed or the results he wanted not delivered. I feared that Justinia underestimated Blackbeard's intolerance for half-measures.

CHAPTER TWENTY-ONE

Later that day, I observed Justinia leave her cabin and enter Blackbeard's. I surmised she was going to put in motion her plan to survive under the pirate's imprisonment. I certainly wanted to be privy to that proposal. I returned to my cabin, pressed my ear against the thin wall to Blackbeard's cabin, and listened.

"What are you doing here?" Blackbeard said. "I told you Sneed would take care of having meals sent to your cabin."

If nothing else, this conversation allayed my fear of living on half-rations to keep Justinia from starving to death.

"This is about something else," Justinia said, "about making a deal."

Blackbeard scoffed. "You're in no position to bargain."

"What is it you want, Blackbeard?"

"To be rich," he said without hesitation.

"Seems like what you really want is to practice piracy. I mean, you gave it up once for amnesty. And yet, here you are now."

There was a pause. I doubted anyone had ever asked Blackbeard anything so introspective before. I doubted anyone else would have gotten away with it.

"Life on land didn't pay worth a damn," he said. "And I did miss the freedom of the open sea."

"What if I helped you get enough riches that you could not possibly spend it all. You could buy your amnesty and protection from Spain, and then be free to sail between all the Spanish crown's possessions, no longer hunted by the authorities."

"Then I'd say you were doing what you were ordered to do when I took you onboard."

"Hardly," Justinia said. "You expected me to do what my sister did for you. But she just kept you sailing from one small ransom to the next, from one plundered cargo to the next. Why didn't she ever deliver a huge treasure to you? Because she needed you to feed her victims so she could stay alive. She was so addicted to evil that she kept you at it until it killed her."

"And now you're taking her place."

"And if I start using black magic the way she did, I'll suffer her same fate. Addiction to power is inevitable. But since I'm casting these spells under duress, my decline will likely happen sooner, and without warning."

I did not know if that was a bluff on Justinia's part or the truth. But if it was the truth, it made her casting spells of black magic even more worrisome for me.

"You risk that at a crucial moment," she said, "say in the middle of a battle, my magic fails you completely. And with me gone, the last practicing witch in my family, where will you find another?"

Silence followed. In my mind I imagined Blackbeard lost in thought as he processed Justinia's inescapable logic. "What is your point, woman?" he finally said.

"That I'll direct you to a ship with cargo so valuable, you'll be wealthy beyond your wildest dreams. After you're victorious, you quit the pirate business, and let me go."

Again there was a pause. "We have a deal. You can trust me."

"No, I can't. But the important thing for you to know is that right now, *you* can't trust *me* either. Dumitra was here voluntarily, I'm not. I can cast an imperfect spell that is supposed to help you, or secretly cast a perfect one to do you harm. You'll never know until you see the effects, and even then, you'll never know if what befell you is just bad luck, or the result of me making my own luck."

"I can have your daughter killed, or worse, with one message."

"Which you can't send if you're dead."

Justinia's steely resolve as she figuratively stood toe-to-toe with Blackbeard impressed me no end. I'd already demonstrated that I could never do such a thing.

"My crew will kill you in return." Blackbeard's response sounded more like a wish than a prediction.

"And my daughter will still be safe. After they kill me, they wouldn't bother with her. They'll be too busy killing each other for control of the ship. For control of *your* ship."

There was another long pause. I could hear Blackbeard's heavy boots pacing the deck.

"You have a bargain," he said. "Find me that treasure ship."

Justinia's bold move had truly astounded me. Blackbeard's acceptance of it was even more astonishing. If indeed riches were his motivation, the deal would make sense to him. But what if he was lying about that, and was already planning to double-cross Justinia after she delivered the great prize?

The last thing she should do is take Blackbeard at his word. That I was certain of.

CHAPTER TWENTY-TWO

I was thrilled to think about the consequences for myself from the deal Justinia had struck. Blackbeard's retirement should give her the chance to cast the counter-spell that would ensure my freedom as well as hers. That was all the more reason to hope for her plan to succeed.

Later that afternoon, I heard Justinia casting a spell within her cabin. Sneed walked the main deck, supervising crewmen at work mending deck planks. He took no notice of me as I crossed the quarterdeck and took a spot at the railing on the forward side of Justinia's cabin. My plan was to try and hear what she was saying within, without too blatantly eavesdropping.

Alas, the spell was in the same tongue the witch Dumitra had used earlier. But from this new vantage point I could smell the sweet-scented smoke drifting out from around the cabin door. I wondered what she was conjuring, and if the spell she cast to do it was white or black magic.

It did not take long for that question to be answered. The previously reduced sensation of darkness that had radiated from the cabin now amplified. Justinia had once again brought dark magic upon the world, and its residue was impossible to miss.

Moments later, Justinia left the cabin and went straight for the Captain's quarters. She entered without knocking and through the open door I could both hear and see their interaction. I would guess that Blackbeard would have torn the head off any crewman who dared disturb him in such a manner, but for Justinia, he just looked up from the book on his chart table.

"What have you found?" he said.

"A ship laden with treasure. Bars of gold with such weight that the ship is slowed to a crawl even under full sail." She pointed to the chart on the table. "The ship is here and sailing south-southwest."

Blackbeard pounded the desk with his fist. "Excellent. We'll be on the poor bastards in a few hours. I need my invulnerability spell renewed."

"Of course."

Justinia left Blackbeard's cabin. I ducked back out of sight. I heard the door to her cabin open and close, then open and close again. I peered around the wall just in time to see her enter Blackbeard's cabin with the grimoire in one hand and the silver spell bowl in the other. This time she closed the door behind her.

Soon the crack at the base of the door glowed with a pulsing green light. I'd seen Dumitra cast this spell, and though Justinia had hidden its delivery from the rest of the crew, my memory painted a picture of what was transpiring beyond the door. My imagination replaced Dumitra's withered face with Justinia's lovely countenance as it replayed the spell of smoke and evil spirits. My heart broke for Justinia.

At a flash of blue, I knew the spell had been completed. If it wasn't a success, I knew an awful fate would befall Justinia.

Blackbeard burst from his cabin and stepped to the center of the quarterdeck pentagram. He took a deep breath and roared with laughter. He flexed his arms and then stretched up on his toes. Apparently, he could feel the effects of this spell before any calamity tested it. No wonder he knew to be more careful when its power had dissipated.

Justinia seemed quite the opposite as she left the cabin with the grimoire tucked beneath one arm. Casting the spell had taken its toll. Unsteady on her feet, she carried the silver spell bowl in one hand so weakly I was certain she would drop it. My first instinct was to rush over and help her, driven only partly by my physician's responsibility.

But I did not want the Captain or crew to see me hurrying to assist her, both because it would highlight her weakness and because it would betray my interest in her. I did not want Sneed or Blackbeard entertaining any paranoid thoughts about Justinia and I working together against them. I preferred to save that revelation for a last-minute surprise.

As she staggered away from his cabin, Blackbeard brushed past her without any acknowledgement of her distress, or even her presence. He slammed the door shut behind him and I heard the rustle of charts. Justinia entered her cabin and closed her door. Then came the creak of her bed, followed by soft sobbing.

Sneed climbed the steps from the main deck and took up a position at the forward railing. A moment later, Blackbeard emerged from his cabin and marched straight to Sneed. "Reset course to 165 degrees and spare no sail."

Sneed acknowledged the order and began to bark commands to all points of the ship. Blackbeard returned to his cabin. With both of them preoccupied, I saw my chance to talk with Justinia. I slipped around to her cabin door and knocked.

"It's Baxter," I said.

"Come in."

I entered to see her slumped on the bed, head in her hands. She looked up with bloodshot eyes.

"Are you okay?" I asked.

"A little drained. That was a lot more magic than I usually do in such a short time period."

"And black magic, to boot."

Fear crossed her face. "How did you know?"

"I can feel it, the darkness, the aftermath."

"I didn't know non-Romani could sense that."

"Now you know there will be no lying to me about anything you do. Just what is it you've done now?"

"I used a spell to search the sea around us and found a ripe target for Blackbeard. Then he asked for his invulnerability spell, and I hadn't planned on casting that. I'll need a bit of time to recover."

"You don't have much. Once we sight that ship, Blackbeard will be expecting the ship's protection spell to be cast and for you to cast another spell as the crew beats to quarters. Even Dumitra seemed exhausted by casting those spells."

"I'll have to do what I must," she said. "This will all be over soon."

I hated to bring my next set of reservations up, but I felt I had to. "But before it's all over, these pirates will attack and much innocent blood will be shed. I can't say my freedom is worth another man's life. Can you?"

"I have a plan for that."

"Which is?"

"You'll see when the time comes. For now, leave me so I can prepare. I have to gather the necessary elements, study the incantation."

"Can I help you?"

"All I've eaten today are a few cherries. If you could fix that, I'll be recharged much faster."

"Your wish is granted."

I left her and went to Sneed. As soon as I said I had a request, he gave me the surliest look I've ever seen. His demeanor changed when I explained that I was asking for food for Justinia, and not something for myself. He called Joshua over and ordered him to make Justinia's comfort his primary job. Joshua left, and Sneed went back to managing the crew and ignoring me. I returned to my cabin.

A black demon of dread settled into my soul. We sailed into a battle where if Justinia's spells proved strong enough to save us, they might be so strong as to kill her. The part of me that worried about that outcome increased the more time I spent with her.

CHAPTER TWENTY-THREE

Just as Blackbeard forecast, a few hours later the lookout spotted a sail on the horizon. Blackbeard was out of his cabin before the echo of the pirate's cry died out. I stepped out onto the deck as well, anxious about all I feared was about to transpire.

The *Queen Anne's Revenge* adjusted course for an intercept and the rest of the little pirate fleet followed. The distance to the victim vessel closed quickly. Justinia had been right about this ship's reduced speed. I hoped that meant she was right about its cargo as well.

"Beat to quarters, Mr. Sneed," Blackbeard ordered.

Sneed gave the order and Joshua rushed up to the quarterdeck carrying the skull-head drum. Justinia just stood on the deck, watching the other ship. I wondered if she knew what was expected of her now.

Blackbeard fumed and went to her side. He grabbed her arm. "Cast your spell, witch!"

She responded without a trace of fear. "Your crew won't need it."

"Then the ship's protection spell must be cast."

"You won't need that either."

Blackbeard looked at Justinia, then at the shrinking distance between the vessels. Worry wrinkled his face. It seemed that an unwilling witch was something he was not used to. And while she'd made her position immovable, the ships were not. The other vessel would be in cannon range soon.

Blackbeard released Justinia. "Damnit, Sneed. Beat to quarters!"

Sneed relayed the order to Joshua. Joshua began the patterned beat that called the brigands to man their guns. The crew responded slowly, shooting glances at the quarterdeck as they did. They'd gone into the last battle without a witch's power behind them and been smashed. With a new witch aboard, they'd clearly expected that to change, and it hadn't. The looks on their faces said they were afraid the outcome of this fight wouldn't change either.

Justinia reentered her cabin, then returned with a handful of bottles and the silver bowl the witch had used during her spell casting. She set everything down in the center of the pentagram on the quarterdeck and sat before the bowl. She cut a section from a coiled leather belt and placed it in the bottom of the bowl. Then Justinia sprinkled the contents of several different vials over the belt. The last container held rum which she splashed around the inside of the bowl.

Now I could make out the details of the other vessel. The three-masted ship looked to carry just a third of the Queen's armament. Rents split one of the forward sails. Alone she would be no match for our ship, let alone the entire pirate fleet.

Sun glinted off the ship's quarterdeck and someone with a spyglass pointed it in our direction. There was no way that crewmember could miss the big skeleton flag flying from our mast. The only question now was whether knowing Blackbeard was approaching would make them fight it out or surrender.

A flag ran up the other ship's mizzen mast. The wind unfurled it. The flag sported a red diamond on a black background. Blackbeard's skeleton flag was known throughout the world. This ship's flag was as well. It was flown by the Spanish pirate Rodrigo de Conception.

Perhaps de Conception hoped that one pirate would not plunder a fellow brigand, invoking some code of conduct among this brotherhood of murderous thieves. Perhaps he was flying it as a warning to Blackbeard that he'd put up a fight, certainly a losing one, but pirate-on-pirate combat promised to be bloody. The flash of the spyglass returned as the man on the other ship watched for our response.

"Give them a taste of iron as soon as we are in range, Mr. Sneed," Blackbeard said.

Apparently the glimmer of gold blinded Blackbeard to any professional courtesy between pirates.

Justinia chanted an incantation, then lit a match and dropped it into the pewter bowl. The rum caught fire in an instant, but burned with a strange flame that shifted in color from red to purple. Justinia said a new incantation and the flame rose in a tight, green swirl. The tip at the top bent and pointed at de Conception's ship. Justinia cast the final portion of her spell. The flame leapt out of the bowl and extinguished.

At first the spell seemed a failure. Then the thundering sound of flapping canvas came from de Conception's ship. To my amazement, it stood perfectly still, all forward momentum gone. The sails hung down from the yardarms, useless as bedsheets on a clothesline. Somehow, Justinia had stopped the pirate ship in its tracks.

Blackbeard checked the ship through his spyglass. "Hold your fire, Mr. Sneed. Prepare to board her."

We closed on the other vessel. The name *Random Chance* graced her stern. Our quarterdeck was taller than the smaller ship and I surveyed her deck from bow to stern. Not a soul moved upon it. As we got closer, I could see why. The entire crew lay dead upon the deck, as if a plague had felled them all.

My shock was quite profound. Justinia claimed to despise black magic, yet the spell she cast to help Blackbeard slaughtered dozens of men in an instant. Pirate or not, these had been human lives snuffed out. Even her evil sister had not practiced such barbarity.

As the *Queen* came alongside the other vessel, the pirates pulled her close with grappling hooks. The supernatural stilling of the other ship had changed the crew's apprehension into excitement. The first wave of the boarding party tensed for action. But at the sight of the dead crew, they froze on the gunwale of our ship. If the scene on the other ship's deck reminded me of a plague, I assumed the same thought went through the men's minds.

"What are you waiting for?" Blackbeard thundered. "The witch has killed them all!"

Justinia stood up. "Not killed, they're in a deep sleep, and will be for an hour."

"Then we'll kill them where they lay," Sneed said.

"Leave them be," Justinia said, "and when they awaken, they'll remember nothing at all about seeing your vessel. They won't know they'd been boarded. All they *will* know is they woke up and their treasure was gone. They'll have no clue about who to hunt down to get the treasure back. But kill even one of them, and that spirit will see what you've done. It will return to inform the others or haunt your ship itself. There are no spells I can cast to keep the vengeful spirits at bay."

The men did not move and all eyes turned to Blackbeard for his next command. The pirate captain cast a suspicious look at Justinia. He squinted at the prone figures on the *Random Chance*, then turned to me.

"Go check."

"Me?"

"You're the doctor. You should be able to tell asleep from dead from faking fainting. Make sure she's telling the truth."

I didn't like this plan at all. Everything from walking the teetering plank between the ships to standing unarmed among a hostile crew wasn't the least bit appealing. What if Justinia had given the entire crew an invulnerability spell, and they were all waiting to ambush the first person to board the ship?

I looked to Justinia for some sign of reassurance that I would indeed find a sleeping crew aboard the other vessel. She did not look me in the eye. Now I was truly worried.

Blackbeard pulled his dagger from his belt, pointed it at me, then pointed it at the *Random Chance*. I swallowed hard and went to the ship's railing.

The gangplank laid between the vessels angled down quite steeply. My fashionable imported leather shoes weren't meant for navigating such a passage. I executed a half-shuffling, half-sliding crossing with my arms out for balance. The view beneath me of the two vessel hulls bumping reminded me of a miller's wheels at work. I did not want to be a grain of wheat between them. I made it to the other side and hopped onto the deck.

The nearest prone pirate was just two feet away. He lay upon his back, face up to the sun. I resolved to check this man first, the one closest to my only avenue of retreat. I knelt beside him.

The first thing I did was check for breathing. Indeed, his chest seemed to rise and fall, but the rhythm was slow, the movement shallow. The slow rocking of the ship might be tricking me. I would need to check for a pulse. In my mind I saw me touching a finger to his carotid artery and then having his eyes pop open and his hands grab my wrist.

I held my breath and reached for his neck. I lightly pressed two fingers against his skin. A pulse beat beneath them. It was very slow, but regular.

I turned back to the *Queen*. Blackbeard stood at the other end of the gangplank with an impatient look on his face.

"He's asleep," I said.

"Try and wake him," Blackbeard said.

"What?"

"Kick him. See if the sleep is as deep as the witch says. I can't have them all awakening when we're half-way through robbing them blind."

It offended my sensibilities to kick a sleeping man, even if he was a pirate. Instead, I shook him at the shoulders. He did not react. I raised one of his eyelids with my thumb. His iris did not contract, his eye did not move. He was in a state much deeper than any normal sleep.

"Sound asleep," I reported.

"Check a few more."

I did as ordered, but with far less fear than when I'd boarded. Justinia had done what she said she'd do. A quick check of several other pirates confirmed shallow breathing, a slow, weak pulse, and no reaction to external stimuli.

"All asleep," I called back.

Blackbeard turned to Sneed and the crew. "Board the damn ship! Clean out the holds. Disturb no one. Be quick about it or forfeit your share."

The men who surged across the last captured ship like wild-eyed maniacs now dropped one by one onto the *Random Chance's* deck. Seemingly unwilling to take my word for it, the men picked their ways around the bodies as Blackbeard ordered, but I could not help but think the fear of the spell the other crew was under played a part in their trepidation.

Standing in the midst of this supernatural event was quite unnerving. Once the boarding party embarked and the gangplank was clear, I re-crossed the gangplank and returned to the quarterdeck of the *Queen*.

The pirates made their way into the other ship's hold and soon began to return carrying crates and chests. Sneed went to the main deck to supervise the loading. Blackbeard watched from the quarterdeck and grinned with avarice.

Justinia staggered back to her cabin. I followed her inside. She collapsed on the edge of her bed.

"That was a lot of magic," I said. "Are you all right?"

She nodded. "I'm very tired, down to the marrow of my bones, it seems. I've never cast such a powerful spell. Never cast any black magic at all, until today."

As a physician, examining patients happens automatically for me. But it did not take a physician's eye to see that the conjuring effort had affected Justinia. Dark, puffy semicircles hung beneath her eyes. Tiny wrinkles sprouted across her forehead. Were these manifestations temporary? Had they always been there and her overall beauty blinded me to them? I hoped that either explanation was true, but my memory of Dumitra's ghastly demise was not encouraging.

"I was afraid that you'd killed that whole crew," I said. "I'm glad you didn't resort to that."

"I'd sacrifice myself before doing that. And I was able to find a pirate vessel to plunder. Stealing from thieves might be considered more like delivering a punishment than committing a crime."

"Now that Blackbeard has seen you can provide bloodless treasure, he'll renege on his deal and demand you do it forever."

"I couldn't repeat the spell if I wanted to. That sword belt was owned by the pirate de Conception. Blackbeard bragged that he'd won it from the pirate in a card game at Port Royal. Using that personal effect, I could locate his ship, even see through his eyes about what he had aboard. Then I could send the sleeping spell to him across the water, and make it so strong that it would affect those around him."

"Blackbeard won't be happy that you can't repeat this spell."

"There's so much gold on that ship," Justinia said, "he won't care."

"Now we have to hope he keeps his end of the bargain."

"Yes, we do."

CHAPTER TWENTY-FOUR

As soon as the crew had cleaned out the *Random Chance*, Sneed had them set the pillaged ship free. Despite the breeze that filled our sails, the other vessel remained becalmed. By the time an hour had passed according to my pocket watch, the tips of the other ship's masts had disappeared over the horizon. Justinia's spell had delivered as promised.

Justinia slept in her bed as the ship sailed west. I would have prescribed she do so had she not made the decision on her own. The magic had exhausted her the way a day digging coal exhausted a miner. I returned to her cabin on the hour to check on her comfort. The miasma of the spent dark magic hung in the air like stale smoke, but knowing Justinia had been the source made me more tolerant of it. Neither Blackbeard nor Sneed questioned my visits. I assumed they knew proper medical care for their witch was in their own best interests.

My third visit found her awake and sitting in the strange rendering chair, reading the grimoire. She showed more bravery than I possessed. Though apparently inert without a triggering spell, I would not trust that chair enough to sit upon it. I'd seen what it could do.

"You feel rested?" I asked.

Justinia looked up at me. "Yes, much better."

"It must have been awful casting those spells."

"I was afraid it would be, but I'm ashamed to admit that it wasn't."

I was shocked to hear her say that. "What?"

"In my heart I knew that using the black magic spells was wrong, that touching that side of the mystic world was forbidden to all good Romani. But while I was doing it, the rush of power it gave me was unlike anything white magic delivered. I felt invincible."

"And how do you feel about it now?"

"Both ashamed to have used it, and ashamed over the temptation to use it again."

"The good news is," I said, "that you won't have to. You've fulfilled your part of the bargain."

"With Blackbeard off the high seas, we'll both be free."

A terrible realization struck me. I touched where the witch had inscribed the invisible tattoo upon my chest. "Maybe I won't be. That spell still binds my life to Blackbeard's, wherever he is and whatever profession he pursues."

Justinia tapped the book. "If the spell that created the bond is in this book, I can create a counter-spell to dissolve it. I've already started searching for it."

The door to the cabin opened and Sneed pointedly remained outside the threshold. It seemed the residue of the dark magic spells was more than he wanted to experience. "Blackbeard wants to see you."

"Me?" I said.

Sneed pointed at Justinia. "Her."

Justinia stood and placed the grimoire on the chair. We left her cabin. She went to Blackbeard's and I went to mine. I took up my favorite listening post at our shared wall. I wanted to hear the good news of her (and my) release first hand.

"Everything occurred as you foretold," Blackbeard said. "De Conception's ship was laden with gold."

"More than you imagined, I'm sure. Now you can uphold your part of the bargain. Abandon piracy and set me free."

"There's one more thing you will do first."

"No there isn't." There was fire in Justinia's voice. "That wasn't our deal."

"I am adjusting the terms of our agreement. Count yourself lucky I'm not completely tearing them up."

I'd feared that Justinia's faith in Blackbeard was misplaced, and now the pirate was proving me correct. With the gold in Blackbeard's hold, her leverage had diminished. She could use a black magic spell against him, but now that she'd experienced the toll such magic took on her, I believed that she'd be quite hesitant to do so.

"What do you want?" Resignation tinged Justinia's voice.

"I can't bring this gold ashore in Carolina. Once someone found out about it, I'd be fending off thieves for the rest of my life."

It seemed the irony of that particular situation was completely lost on the pirate. The crinkle of parchment sounded in the Captain's cabin, followed by two thumps.

"This is a map to get to an island," Blackbeard said. "It's off the trade routes and uninhabited. I would not have found it myself if a storm hadn't pushed my ship so far off-course. We'll sail to this island first and hide the gold there. I can come back and get it as I need it."

"That has nothing to do with me. Hide it wherever you want. Set me free first."

"But that's where you're still needed. I need a spell to keep others from finding the gold while I am gone."

"You said it's an unchartered island."

"If I found it by accident," Blackbeard said, "so might someone else."

"No witchcraft is strong enough to make an island invisible."

"But you can make it impenetrable. You can cast a spell to have the island defend itself against intruders. Dumitra cast such a spell once. Once, she hexed a cobra snake to defend a chest full of items she used to create her magic."

"That may be true, but defending a box and an island are two different things."

"Lucky for you, you'll have two days to rest and restore your powers to maximum. I'll let you know when we're approaching the island. Go back to your cabin."

I heard the sound of a door closing and got to my doorway in time to see Justinia returning to her cabin. Her head hung low.

In my heart, I'd hoped Blackbeard would keep his word, but in my head, I knew a result like this was more likely. I was certain we'd experience further treachery when we arrived at Blackbeard's island.

CHAPTER TWENTY-FIVE

As soon as Justinia left Blackbeard's cabin, Blackbeard appeared on the quarterdeck. Without explanation, he gave Sneed the orders to set a new course, and Sneed had the crew execute them without asking for details. The crew responded with vigor. It seemed that the successful subjugation of de Conception's ship, the enormous gold haul, and the return of a witch and her magic spells to the *Queen* had sent the message that all was once again right in the pirate world.

That evening when the decks were relatively clear and I felt I could proceed unobserved, I went to Justinia's cabin. She bid me enter.

I did not want to admit my eavesdropping on her conversation with Blackbeard, so began a more circumspect conversation. "Blackbeard had us change course this morning from northwest to southwest."

"We're not going home, at least not right away." She handed me a parchment scroll. "We're going here first to hide the treasure."

I unrolled the scroll. It was a hand-drawn map, done in the style of a navigation chart. It contained the outline of a C-shaped island with a good-sized lagoon. A set of arrows and numbers surrounded the island. I assumed these were some kind of navigation notations. The lower right-hand corner contained a picture of a skeleton pointing an arrow at a heart, just like on Blackbeard's flag.

"He wants a spell to protect the island," Justinia said. "A whole island! He thinks this map will help me create the spell. It's laughable how little he knows about magic even though he sailed with my sister for so long."

"Is protecting an island something magic can do?"

"The lost city of Atlantis was protected by magic. Forests in the Transylvania homeland have spells to help keep werewolves contained. Magic's power is unlimited if the witch is willing to pay the price. I will have to find the right spells in the grimoire."

"I'm sure there's a spell for it in there." I traced the symbol carved in the wall beside me with my finger. "Dumitra carved these into the ship and they served in its protection."

"Lest you remain as ignorant as Blackbeard, I'll correct you here. The symbols in this cabin are warding, a screen if you will against other witches sensing the witchcraft being conjured within. Dumitra knew white magic witches might band together to stop her black magic practices. It had happened before. Within these walls, she would be invisible to all."

"Another reason she rarely left her cabin."

"Correct. And the spell over the ship was a passive, defensive spell, a shield if you want to call it that. To protect the island will require an active, not a passive spell. Visitors must be repelled."

"Like one cannot win a sword fight with only a parry," I said. "He must also thrust."

"Exactly." Justinia patted the grimoire. "Somewhere in this book is that thrust."

"Thrusts often kill."

She sighed. "Black magic knows no boundaries. Its spells are relentless in their execution. Once I cast it, it's out of my control."

My heart went out to her. I imagined how I'd feel if I was forced to do unnecessary amputations as acts of torture. The idea of turning a skill I loved into an instrument of evil would make me hate myself to the core. I tried to cheer her up.

"But in the same way that stealing gold from thieves is hardly a sin, anyone coming to steal a pirate's treasure is probably quite nefarious themselves."

Justinia managed a small smile. "I'll try to keep that in mind."

"The point is, once the gold is hidden, Blackbeard will set you free to return to your daughter. The island on that map looks fairly large. We need to make certain that neither of us knows exactly where the cache is buried. If we're ignorant of where it's buried, and even where the island is, he has nothing to fear from letting us go."

"You would think so." She turned away from me and went to the portal. Through her dress, she gripped the broken medallion that hung around her neck. "But bad dreams have plagued me since I was taken aboard the ship."

"Nightmares are a normal result of a stressful situation. I see that in patients all the time. I can't think of a more stressful situation than this."

Justinia waved her hand dismissively. "Dreams are different for the Romani. The rest of you dream. We have visions. We touch a different world, one where spirits speak to us and the future is glimpsed."

I tried not to look amused. Every patient who'd ever told me of their dreams swore the same thing, that they were some type of supernatural manifestation. Whether Justinia practiced witchcraft or not, dreams having any connection to reality was naught but superstition.

"My visions foretell a horrible future," she continued. "Blood and death, fear and fury. I can't see all the details yet, but each vision is clearer, and each more frightening than the last."

The light through the window lit her face in a near-angelic glow and I saw within her the opposite of the dark magic she'd been forced to practice. I could imagine the horrible culpability she felt for the effects of that magic. Now the guilt of casting those spells was reaching into her sleep to torture her there as well. I went to her side and placed one hand lightly upon her shoulder.

"Those nightmares will not come true," I said. "You will go home again and be with your daughter."

She reached one hand up and touched mine. Her skin felt soft as silk. Her touch spread warmth all the way up my arm.

"Thank you," she said. "It's so rare for a non-Romani to treat me as something other than a fearsome witch."

"The last thing I am is afraid of you."

I longed to take her in my arms, to hold her close, to make all of her fears and worries go away.

She stepped away and my hand fell from her shoulder. Suddenly I felt like a ship cast adrift.

"I found the spell my sister cast to bind you to Blackbeard." She went back to the grimoire and paged through it. She stopped at a page with a picture of the symbol that Dumitra had inked into my chest at the top. "It's right here, with the counter-spell beneath it."

Excitement built within me at the thought of my freedom. "Do you have the elements you need to cast it?"

"Yes, but I dare not do it now. The spells I will have to cast upon the island will tax me to my limits. If I don't have the strength to complete them, I don't know what will happen."

"What would happen is that Blackbeard would kill you."

"That wouldn't be the worst outcome," she said. "A poorly completed spell could be a disaster. It would still be a spell, but it would have unpredictable results. It may do nothing, it may do something unintended, or it may kill us all. These are all chances we shouldn't take."

"I agree and understand. And I don't need my bond to Blackbeard broken until we get you home anyway. It's not as if there is any way for me to escape the ship between now and then."

"As soon as the island spell is cast, I'll burn that tattoo from you and you'll be free."

Actually, we would both be free. In an instant, a wonderful scenario flashed through my mind. This moment we had shared just now could turn into a lifetime of such moments. With both of us free in the New World, there would be no restrictions on where we could go. As I was told over and over after I booked my passage, any town in the colonies would be thrilled to have me hang my doctor's shingle there.

My imagination raced ahead. We wouldn't be restricted to these colonies. Any British possession in the Caribbean would be open to us, or even across the globe.

I wondered if somehow I'd been being prepared for this moment. Over the past year I'd been thrilled to spend time with my niece Mary. Perhaps that was practice for helping raise Justinia's daughter.

Reality poked holes in my expanding fantasy. I realized that I did not know her daughter's age. I did not even know how old Justinia was, or her legal marital status. Other than being a witch, I knew almost nothing of this woman.

I begged off that I should let her rest and read her grimoire, and she agreed. I backed out of the cabin and closed the door behind me. A blast of salty air hit my face and I realized how oppressive the air had been in the warded cabin. I returned to my cabin half-dazed.

Something like this had never happened to me before. While my medical studies and subsequent practice had consumed much of my life, that did not mean that I hadn't been romantically involved many times, and several times quite seriously. But in each event, one or the other of us broke off the affair. Sometimes she would, due to a lack of my attention, but more frequently I would, feeling my lack of commitment. In each case my initial attraction to the woman had been mild, and the relationship tepid. I had never entertained the thought of sharing my life forever with any woman I'd met.

Until now.

And do not misunderstand me. I was completely dumbfounded by the way Justinia had enchanted me from the start, how she'd stirred within me a passion I'd watched displayed in plays and found to be laughably unrealistic. Whatever armor I thought I wore against this version of Cupid's arrow had stopped working. Perhaps it never had, and I'd simply never met anyone like Justinia before.

I was still pondering my situation when a knock sounded at my door. It was Joshua, holding my evening meal. It seemed I'd fallen back into the crew's good graces, or at least his.

"Your dinner, sir. Didn't want to leave it on the deck. Might slide all the way across in this sea."

The sea was as calm as I'd ever seen it, but if Joshua wanted to use that excuse, I would give him the latitude to do so. I took the plate from him. "I appreciate that."

"Still leaving it at the door of the cabin across the way, though. The previous witch didn't eat nothing, but this one, she eats enough for two."

"Who can turn down the fine cuisine the ship has to offer?"

The sarcasm was lost on Joshua. "You don't want to get too close to one of them witches. They have spells that make you do as they wish, make you lovesick as can be."

"Really?"

"Oh, yes, sir. Seen it at home myself. Witch arrived in my home town, of course, mind you we didn't know she was a witch back then. Well, my mate since my early years meets her and his whole disposition changes. All he can do is dote on her. Wait on her like she was the Queen herself."

"Sounds like a love story."

"Not when they caught him stealing it wasn't. Burgled a commissioner's house he did, and was caught red-handed. He told how the woman had bewitched him. Cast a spell to make him steal for her. The town rose up to put her on trial, but she'd vanished, didn't leave no trace."

Joshua shot a quick glance over his shoulder to Justinia's cabin. "Nothing like that's going to befall me, rest assured."

Joshua hurried away and left me to my own interpretation of his story, one where a man decides to take a shortcut to wealth, and when caught, blames his misfortune on a woman who'd supposedly bewitched him, a woman who had the foresight to flee before she had to defend herself from the indefensible.

But the story did set me thinking of my situation, of the unnatural response I had to Justinia. From my first sight of her I felt something stir within me, something that now verged on being all-consuming. Justinia herself had said I did not know how much I did not know about the art of witchcraft.

Now I was quite confused. While I could discount Joshua's second-hand story, suddenly my own emotions had come into question. Was I besotted or bewitched? Could I know the difference?

Whatever the cause, I could not deny its effect. My feelings for Justinia were getting stronger.

CHAPTER TWENTY-SIX

The next morning the sun rose and painted a blood-red sky. I remembered the bit of doggerel that claimed this meant foul weather lay ahead. I hoped that did not turn out to be true. Having the ship wrecked at sea when I could see the light at the end of my kidnap tunnel would be more than I could bear.

In this instance, the old maxim turned out to be true. Great counterclockwise arcs of clouds soon raced across the sky. The wind picked up and the ship moaned under the added pressure of rushing water against the hull and wind in the canvas. A hope that the storm would pass us by, and instead favor us with its outer winds grew in my mind.

The hope died soon after. The white clouds grew increasingly dark. The wind rose high enough that Sneed had the men reef the sails. The bow soon crashed through rising waves.

Prior to my departure, all my veteran-traveler friends assured me that while travel by sea might be uncomfortable, it was generally safe. The only exception being sailing through bad weather. I was about to experience that exception.

Sneed and the crew seemed to share my concern. The first mate's orders became sharper and more profane. The crew's responses to them quickened. Everyone cast their eyes to the sky much more often. Blackbeard even took a more regular position on the quarterdeck, watching over the *Queen* and the three trailing pirate ships.

A lifetime of enduring tempests upon land is absolutely no preparation for experiencing a storm at sea. On land, the shelter of a stout building is unquestioned, for the wildest winds will not topple stone walls or shred slate roofs. But at sea, there is no such safety. The weather assaults the wooden vessel that is supposed to provide refuge. Indeed, where a solid home is respite from the storm, a ship is another probable victim of it, and in turn becoming another potential instrument of my demise.

As the winds increased, the pitch and roll of the deck followed suit. At first, I tried to ride out the storm in my hammock in the mistaken belief that I would hang there while the ship moved about me. But the hammock seemed to amplify every motion of the vessel, and the swinging action made me dizzy and nauseous. Violent crashes of the bow into waves often catapulted me up from the hammock and by God's grace its canvas caught me on the way down. I abandoned the hammock and stood on the cabin deck, holding the surgical table with both hands to stay upright.

I'd closed the cover on the port to cut down on the amount of wind and rain rushing through the cabin. But as the ship pitched to and fro, the air began to feel oppressively thick, further amplifying the seasick sensation that threatened to send me to my knees. I shuffled over to the port and swung the cover up. Gray sunlight lit the cabin.

Then a blast of spray-laden air hit me in the face. Wind-driven drops stung like needles against my skin. My hammock slapped against the ceiling like a landed fish on the planks of a dock. I squinted against the weather just in time to see a wall of green water approaching the ship. The rogue waves I'd heard fearful sailors tell of were no myth after all.

The wave slammed the ship and sent a tremor through the hull that seemed to travel all the way down to the keel. Gallons of seawater blasted through the open port and sent me tumbling across the deck and against the wall. The ship heeled so far to starboard that I thought I'd roll up the bulkhead.

But the weight of the extra gold in the lower hold did the vessel a favor. She came back upright and I landed on the cabin deck on my back. Seawater sloshed past me and more spray splattered on my face. I crawled across the deck and pulled myself up the outer bulkhead high enough to slam the port cover closed.

The ship rolled again and my feet slipped on the soaked deck. I grabbed the table. The boat lurched up and crashed down so hard my teeth clacked together. My nausea was about to be beyond my control. I didn't want to add the stink of my own sick to the mélange of awful smells inside my cabin.

I skated across the deck to the cabin door and threw it open. Wind and rain lashed the quarterdeck so heavily that Justinia's cabin was almost invisible. Holding the doorsill, I hung my head out into the storm. I wretched so hard that it brought me to my knees.

The rain obliterated my sick and saved me having to keep it company. The regurgitation had sapped the strength from my body. My head spun like a child's top. I'd never felt so ill.

Men shouted above me and I looked over my shoulder to see several up in the rigging, working to secure a sail that the storm had torn loose. The man on the far end was having the worst of it. Then the ship heeled to starboard and pointed the yardarm he clung to down at the sea. He lost his grip and with an anguished cry he tumbled overboard and into a wave. He did not resurface.

Across the quarterdeck, the cover to a port on Justinia's cabin opened. I could just make out the outline of her face against the gloom. My manhood demanded I not act as ill as I no doubt appeared. I raised a hand to wave at her.

Just then, a wall of seawater crested over the gunwale. It struck me and I lost what little grip I had on the doorway. Icy seawater washed me across the deck and against the wall of Blackbeard's cabin. I flailed about for something to hold onto, and found nothing.

The bow dove down into another trough. I cartwheeled down the quarterdeck and into the railing that overlooked the main deck. My head slammed into the balusters and I saw an explosion of stars.

I struggled to stay conscious. I reached for the railing's supports, but while I could touch them, my mind could not make my numbed fingers grip them. The ship rolled to starboard and I slid across the deck with my hands slapping uselessly against the balusters.

I skidded toward the starboard railing. Beyond it, the angry sea that had just taken one crewman pounded at the ship's hull, begging for the next sacrifice. A wave washed over the deck and propelled me faster still.

I hit one of the balusters with both feet. But relief that it would save me was short lived. The impact shattered the wood and I continued over the side.

As I cleared the deck, I was yanked to a stop. My back slammed into the side of the ship with wave tips slapping at my feet and my arms raised shoulder-high. The roiling sea stretched out before me, seething as if frustrated its sacrificial offering had been delayed. I squinted up through the storm to see that my coat had caught on the broken baluster end. The skill of my Saville Row tailor was all that was keeping me from a horrible death.

I tried to reach for the railing, but I could barely move my exhausted arms. Even if I could, the deck was out of reach.

The stitching in my right sleeve burst. That side of my body sagged. Even the finest cloth could not bear this abuse. I knew that any second now, I'd be drowned and forever lost.

Suddenly, what felt like the hand of God grabbed the collar of my jacket and shirt and with unrestrained violence yanked me up and through the opening in the starboard railing. It released me and sent me skidding across the deck.

I looked up to see it wasn't the hand of God at all, but the hand of one of the larger pirates on the ship. Wind and rain pummeled him, but he stood strong against the storm. The gloom only amplified the glow of the ring of thorns around his neck.

He stomped across the quarterdeck and clamped a hand on my upper arm. Before I could respond, he dragged me across the careening deck to my cabin. When we arrived, he threw me through the open doorway. I slid across the deck and landed against a bulkhead. He slammed the door behind me.

I curled into a ball on the floor. Soaking wet and freezing cold, I hadn't the strength to do anything else. As the ship pitched and rolled, the motion sent me rocking on the floor. Thoroughly miserable as I was, I gave thanks to the Lord that I was still alive.

But the Lord had not been the one to save me, one of the pirate crew had. But he hadn't done it out of any sense of altruism, and he had not done it alone. The glowing tattoo upon his neck was proof of that. Justinia had compelled him using the puppet-master spell, and that spell was clearly from the book of black magic.

That meant that to save my life, she'd sacrificed a part of her own.

CHAPTER TWENTY-SEVEN

By noon the storm had passed us by. The wind returned to being just a stiff breeze and calmer seas quelled the ship's excessive rolling. I hung my head from my cabin port that faced the quarterdeck. I watched the crew return to the main deck like bees exiting a hive and then immediately become just as busy. Under Sneed's bellowing direction, sails were unfurled and repairs began for the minor damage the storm had inflicted.

I was much slower to recover. My hellish seasickness left me physically weak and my brush with death going over the ship's side had mentally exhausted me. I returned to my hammock and dozed off for a while. I awakened with a bit more strength and opened the seaward port. The flood of sunshine was a welcome relief, but also made clear how wet my tiny cabin had become and how the storm had left everything in disarray. I opened the door to the quarterdeck in the hope of the breeze drying it out. As my body sorted itself out, I reorganized the meager items in my cabin.

When I felt recovered enough, I went on deck. I scanned the sea and saw only one of the three ships in Blackbeard's fleet still sailed in our wake. I wondered if the other two had foundered, but later overheard that the standard procedure if separated was to meet back up at a rendezvous point along the Carolina coast. Blackbeard swore draconian punishments for the ship captains who'd lost contact with the *Queen*. Given the severity of the storm, I thought it unbelievable that even one of the ships had kept within sight of ours.

As the time came for dinner, I'd still not seen Justinia on deck, and her door and port had remained closed all day. I feared this might be a sign that the after effects of the storm, or more likely the black magic she'd conjured to save me from it, had been too much for her. When Joshua arrived with my meal, I took it and offered to deliver Justinia's for him. He seemed quite relieved to avoid knocking on the door of the witch's cabin, and almost dropped both meals in his haste to hand them to me.

Having emptied my stomach most thoroughly during the storm, it took great willpower to not immediately wolf down my meal. I crossed the deck, balancing the two covered plates, and knocked on Justinia's door with the toe of my shoe.

The door opened and she looked surprised to see me. "I thought you weren't going to be the cabin boy permanently."

"The job seems to be growing on me." I entered and she closed the door behind me. She took one plate and sat on the rendering chair. I took the seat from the desk and slid it over. Despite her assurances and my recent benign experiences with the chair, I still feared if I sat close enough, it would reach out and entangle me.

I looked about Justinia's cabin. It had weathered the storm far better than mine. Perhaps she'd been smart enough to keep her door and ports closed during the blow.

I tried to maintain some decorum by not scarfing down my food.

"I'm relieved the ship made it through the storm," she said.

"Two of the ships may not have. We are reduced to a fleet of two. Should I lament the possible loss of pirate lives? The physician in me says yes, but the kidnap victim in me disagrees. Thank you for saving my life during the storm."

"Me? I never left my cabin."

"But you compelled someone else to. Don't deny it. I saw his thorn tattoo glowing."

Justinia sighed. "I saw you struggling on the deck. I sent that pirate to take you back to your quarters. Just as he arrived, you went sliding off into the sea."

"I dare say I was literally hanging by a thread." I weighed whether to say what I next thought and decided I had to do it. "You put that man's life at risk for mine."

"First, he's a pirate. Second, I didn't know you'd be hanging over the side of the ship by the time he got here."

"Those rationalizations aside, that spell had to require black magic, did it not?"

"Your gratitude at being alive seems to be disappearing," she said.

"I can be grateful and still concerned about you. I saw the toll black magic took on your sister."

"I seem to have a stronger constitution. Besides, it was a small spell. There were no after effects."

I gauged her with a physician's eye. Several streaks of gray ran through her hair. She was either lying or unaware of what damage her spell had wrought. I did not see the need to probe further and find out which one was the truth.

Her attitude about using black magic had shifted. Earlier, she had been defensive, almost embarrassed to admit she'd used it. Now, when confronted, she freely confirmed casting the dark spell. I'd seen teetotalers travel this same path on their way to becoming drunkards. They'd be embarrassed at having taken a first drink, and soon comfortable in a tavern. The problem was their next stop was frequently the gutter.

"The pull of dark magic isn't too great?" I asked.

She laughed. "Certainly not. I think my people oversold its addictive properties to keep witches from dabbling in it. My sister was right about that, it seems."

"You wouldn't speak so cavalierly of the magic's effects if you'd seen your sister at the end."

Justinia stood up and dropped her plate on the chair. She looked at me with disdain. "Who are you to lecture me on the use of magic? A few days ago, you thought it all myth and superstition. I have been immersed in it all my life."

I thought her defensiveness misplaced. "There is no denying that using it killed your sister."

"No, there's no denying my sister is dead. You say magic killed her. Would that be a shield you raised to deflect a charge that your pathetic skills couldn't cure her of a common human ailment?"

My pulse quickened and I felt my cheeks flush red. This attack seemed to come out of the blue. My diagnosis of her sister's condition had been rock-solid, my treatment of her the best I could provide given the medicines and tools available. But I bit my tongue rather than respond in kind.

I stood up. "It has been a very trying day. I think it best I retire to my cabin."

"There's one thing you're right about."

I left her cabin and closed the door behind me. Her accusation had made me angry, but not as much as her entire demeanor distressed me. I'd had feelings for Justinia that I'd hoped she'd reciprocate, at least a little. Instead, she seemed enraged by my presence.

I began to worry that the practice of dark magic might have more effects than just physical aging.

CHAPTER TWENTY-EIGHT

Late the next morning, the lookout sang out that he'd sighted land. Given Blackbeard's description of how isolated the island was, I had no doubt that it would be the one we sought. I went up on deck and dodged my way around the working pirates until I got to the tip of the bow. I wanted the first views of this pirate hideout and wished I still had my stolen spyglass.

At first, I doubted the lookout's word. As far as I could tell, the horizon remained empty. But soon what he'd seen from the vantage point of the mast's crow's nest I could see from the bow. A black bump sat where the sea met the sky. The helmsman adjusted course and we headed for it.

As we closed on the island, more details became clear. I estimated that the island stretched a few miles long. A barren peak soared over a thousand feet tall near the center. It bore an uncomfortable resemblance to paintings I'd seen of volcanoes. Waves lapped at a white beach that fringed the island. Beyond that, palm trees, ferns, and other tropical plants covered the ground. A few seabirds circled the island, but there were no signs of people.

That last development suited me fine. If we could hide this treasure without shedding more innocent blood, I'd be thrilled.

The ship tacked north of the island and then made a hook to follow the shoreline south. The shore became a spit of sand and the entrance to the cove appeared, just as the map had depicted. The *Queen Anne's Revenge* entered a circular lagoon. Within it, the waters calmed considerably. On the east side of the cove, the water touched the mountain's dark brown base. It was indeed a volcano, or at least had been. No smoke issued from it and the surface appeared well-weathered. The final proof was that a wide waterfall ran down the extinct volcano's face and created a wall of mist over that part of the lagoon. The shore to both sides of the mountain had curving white sand beaches backed up by a palm forest.

Pirates stepped up onto the bow to drop anchor and I took that as my cue to get out of the way. I headed back to the quarterdeck as our anchors splashed into the water. The ship that had accompanied us dropped anchor nearby. I could make out the name *Avarice* on the bow. Blackbeard rechristened his captured ships appropriately.

Blackbeard stood at the railing looking over at the waterfall. Where I'd looked at it in wonder for its beauty, his face was filled with gleeful greed. He was going to make this island his personal strong box, and use Justinia's powers to lock it up. I could practically see his gluttonous plans being imagined behind his eyes.

He ordered Sneed to make ready longboats to go ashore. Justinia stepped out of her cabin. I steeled myself for an icy reception at best. She looked past me to the island. Her face turned grim and she shook her head. She went to Blackbeard.

"If you're going ashore," she said, "I'm coming. I can't design a spell without knowing what I'm casting the spell on."

"Very well," Blackbeard said.

"I should go as well," I piped in. "Your physician should accompany you in case anything happens."

In reality I was much more afraid that in wandering across the island, Blackbeard would get outside the range our binding spell permitted.

Blackbeard laughed. "My invulnerability spell will protect me better than you could."

Thinking fast, I pointed to Justinia. "But it won't protect her. She is the key to your plan."

The pirate captain thought a moment. "Fine. Get in the boat."

Blackbeard went to the side of the ship where several pirates had fixed a longboat to davits and had just finished swinging it over the gunwale.

"Can't expect a woman to climb down the side of the ship to get in the longboat," Blackbeard said. "Board here before we lower it."

He turned to me. "You too." Disgust dripped from his tone.

Accepting his insult meant I was less likely to be crushed between the two hulls, and would have the moments alone to talk with Justinia. So I nodded and climbed into the longboat. I sat beside Justinia. The men began to lower the boat.

"That was quick thinking," Justinia whispered to me. "I would have hated to see Blackbeard go to the far side of the island and have you die on board before I could break your bond."

Her concern surprised me, given the tenor of our last conversation. My face must have betrayed that.

"I'm sorry about what I said last night," she said. "I really don't know what came over me. You're a doctor, so I know you're looking out for my well-being."

I wanted to tell her with her it was more than that, but as we were about to board a longboat full of pirates, it was certainly not the time for that conversation. "We're all under a lot of stress. You became defensive when I talked about the effects the black magic was having on you. Do you think your reaction might have been one of those effects?"

She sighed. "I…I don't know. After casting the first spell, something very--"

The longboat splashed into the water. We both had to hold onto the side to keep our balance. Blackbeard barked orders and four pirates climbed down to the longboat so rapidly I could have mistaken their descent for falling. The pirates acted as oarsmen amidships and Blackbeard took a seat in the stern, manning the tiller himself.

My concern for Justinia had deepened during our interrupted conversation, but sitting before the pirate crew was no place to delve deeper into the subject. I contented myself with looking out across the bay and being thankful I'd not also been tasked as an oarsman for the trip.

Off to one side, I observed twin bumps surface above the water. My first thought was a bobbing log of some sort, but the bumps did not bob and were far too uniform in appearance. Another pair surfaced, then another. In short order there was quite a collection between us and the shore.

Then a pair of the bumps blinked and displayed a set of wicked-looking yellow eyes.

I gasped and involuntarily grabbed Justinia's hand. "There's something in the water."

"Alligators," she said in a dismissive tone. She slid her hand from under mine. "They are all over the swamps in the colonies."

"These are caimans," the pirate rowing next to us said. "Meaner than alligators."

The boat passed close to one of the creatures. It floated just beneath the surface. Its green skin looked tough as armor, with a long wide snout. Twin ridges ran the length of its elongated body and all the way down a powerful-looking tail. It floated motionless on the water, unafraid of the boat full of men pulling past it.

"They do not look friendly," I said.

"If one is larger than you," Justinia said, "it might consider you a meal."

"How large do they grow?"

"I've seen them at almost twenty feet."

That was considerably larger than I was. "Will they attack the boat?"

"No. They'll wait until you're on the beach. They look slow, but they can run fast enough to catch a deer by the water."

Somehow in my head I'd assumed a deserted island was deserted of everything, not just people. London and its environs had civilized all the wildlife in the area long ago, and encountering anything more fearsome than a rat had never happened to me. The New World was going to be decidedly different.

CHAPTER TWENTY-NINE

The longboat's bow ran up on the sandy beach. The oarsmen had put their backs into the last few strokes, trying to get as far up on land as possible before having to jump into the water. It appeared I wasn't the only one harboring concerns about tempting the caimans.

Since the bow was well-beached, I opted to waste no time getting out. I stood and turned to help Justinia up. To my surprise, she was already out of the boat and two steps up the beach. I was used to the London women being far less independent. I thought that maybe the rigors of the New World required more self-reliance. I have to say that it only endeared Justinia to me more. I joined her up above the high tide line.

Blackbeard had no concerns about getting his feet wet. He jumped overboard with a splash and waded toward shore. Behind him, several sets of caiman eyes submerged and the tails of the creatures left ripples in the water.

"Let's go, you lazy bastards," he said. "Get that longboat ashore."

The four men looked at each other, waiting for one of them to be the first into the water. A growl from Blackbeard spurred them to action and the four shipped oars.

"Have at it, you dogs," the biggest pirate said. He jumped in and took a position at the stern.

The others followed his lead and entered the water. One went to the bow and one to each side. They heaved and pushed and brought the ship two-thirds of the way ashore. The pirate at the stern let the transom free and smiled.

"See, you yellow curs," the big pirate said. "Nothing to it."

His derisive smile shifted to a look of surprise. Then he fell face first into the water as his feet were yanked out behind him. The lagoon exploded into a bloom of white water. Within the churn flashed glimpses of the pirate's arms and the massive leathery tails of two caimans. The pirate issued a gargled scream.

The three pirates ashore backed away from the water. No one was willing to tempt another caiman attack to help their brigand brother. Blackbeard drew his sword and stood his ground, as if begging a reptile to make a try for him. I was ready to run for the highest possible ground, but Justinia wasn't moving, so I had to follow her lead or sacrifice my claim to manhood.

The white froth in the lagoon went pink with blood, then the flailing stopped. The pirate surfaced with one caiman clamped to his legs and another to his head. The reptiles rolled in opposite directions in sync and tore the pirate's corpse in half. They swam off in opposite directions, leaving a rippling wake with the swish of their tails.

I'd seen the after effects of some terrible accidents in my medical career, men trampled by horses, victims of explosions, compound fractures where sharp bones punctured flesh. Since my kidnapping, I'd seen men killed in battle. But I'd never seen something as brutally awful as what I'd just witnessed.

I turned to Justinia. She'd seen all that I had, yet she did not appear as horrified as I was. She simply looked grim.

Blackbeard in contrast, was furious. "Goddamn Sanders. What the hell was he doing staying in the water?" He sheathed his sword and turned to the other pirates. "Secure the boat and we head inland."

The pirates went to work making sure the boat was far enough up the shore that a rising tide would not dislodge it. All the while they kept an eye on the lagoon. Blackbeard tromped past me and headed for the tree line that rose at the beach's edge.

"He certainly wastes no time mourning his crew," I said.

"Pirates die all the time," Justinia said. "And there's always more where they came from."

I remembered how, even on my ship, Blackbeard had been able to recruit a new crewman. The promise of quick riches had universal appeal.

We followed Blackbeard into the jungle that covered the island's interior. The three remaining pirates trailed behind us. Blackbeard had sheathed his sword, but those three did not. It seemed that none of them wanted to share Sanders' fate. The jungle seemed without any discernable landmarks, yet Blackbeard made his way through the scrubby undergrowth and around the palm trees as if he knew exactly where he was going. I noted to myself that it was a good thing one of us did.

As we traveled, I could not ignore the sensation that we were being watched. Then to confirm that, something occasionally skittered unseen through the undergrowth and away from our path. Having encountered the caimans, all I could imagine were some other horrid sentinels observing us and then running off to inform some larger, deadlier creature of our progress. I began to wish Blackbeard had issued me a cutlass to defend myself.

We passed by a jumble of palm tree trunks, the remnants of a stand that had no doubt been flattened long ago by some great storm. Green and black mosses coated the bark. And it was because of that growth that I did not spy the creature sitting upon one log until I was right beside it. When I did, I froze and cried out.

Outside of frightening fairy tales, I'd never seen such a beast. Over five feet long from snout to tail, a great lizard stared at me with obsidian eyes. The scaly skin was colored a mottled green and gray. A ridge of spikes ran from the crest of its head, down its spine, to the tip of its tail. Long, sharp claws tipped the toes on its feet.

A dagger whizzed by in front of me. It struck the lizard in the ribcage and pinned it to the log behind the one on which it had perched. Blood gushed from the wound. The creature squealed and thrashed its legs uselessly. The bleeding slowed, and then the lizard went limp.

Blackbeard roared with laughter. He came up from behind me and went to the toppled trees. With a quick yank, he drew the dagger from the palm bark. The impaled lizard came with it.

"Iguana," he said. "They may look fierce, but they aren't." With a flick of his wrist, he sent the iguana sliding off the dagger's blade and onto the ground. "They're good eating in a pinch."

I hoped to never be in such a pinch.

Blackbeard sheathed the dagger without wiping the iguana's blood from the blade. He turned and continued the march through the jungle.

Shortly, we arrived at a small, five-sided building at the center of a higher, sandy patch of ground. It was about twenty feet long on each side and had a peaked roof covered in palm leaf thatch. A single reinforced wooden door was the only access, save for slit-like window openings along the sides. A multitude of white, tan, and brown hues dabbled the unfinished surface of the block walls.

Blackbeard pulled a huge skeleton key from his pocket. He used it to unlock the door. As he did, I noticed the walls of this building were two feet thick.

"This is a solid building," I said.

"It's coquina," Blackbeard bragged. "The same stone the Spanish used to build their forts. It absorbs cannon balls without breaking. I had captured crews build this so I could make a last stand if I needed to."

"And those crewmen?" I asked.

Blackbeard smiled. "They made their last stand here as well."

Inside, unfinished palm logs made up the floor. A map of the island was carved into one wall. It was a duplicate of the one on Blackbeard's parchment map, even the same size, as if one had been traced from the other. Carvings around the other walls were of broad wavy arrows accompanied by numbers and dates. Other arrows hosted location names and two accompanying numbers.

I surmised that the names were locations, followed by distance and bearings. The wavy lines were currents, with speeds and dates related to their strength. Should one orient a chart on a table in the center of the room, it would be the perfect place to plan a month's worth of piracy.

Two chests sat at the base of one wall. Blackbeard popped the lids open to check the contents. Both were filled with gold and silver coins. I wondered how many people had died trying to keep those riches out of Blackbeard's hands.

"If you want this island bewitched," Justinia said, "I'll need to prepare it."

"What do you mean?"

"It takes a great deal of powerful magic to defend something as large as an island. Like sanding wood before varnishing it, the island must be prepared to accept that much magic. I need to perform a cleansing spell. I need your dagger."

Blackbeard handed her his dagger. "Do it."

Justinia went to work carving into the soft stone. Her finished symbol ended up being two feet across, a diamond shape with two wavy lines running through it. She left the hut and returned with a handful of dried, fallen palm branches. She used strands of one to bind the whole mass of them tightly together.

Then she took the dagger to her index finger and slit the tip open. I winced at the thought of the pain such a cut on a sensitive area produced, but she showed no reaction to her self-inflicted wound. Bright red blood oozed from the slash.

Justinia ran her finger along the grooves of the design, leaving a drying trail of brown in the carving. When she'd finished, she took a box of matches from a pocket in her skirt. She struck one against the wall beside the image. It exploded to life. Touching the flame to the tip of the palm branch fasces she'd fashioned, it caught fire and black smoke rose from the flames.

Justinia turned to the symbol and bowed her head. She waved the burning bundle around the symbol in a circle and chanted a spell in that strange Gypsy tongue. She repeated the spell three times during three revolutions of the symbol on the wall. Black smoke stayed in the circle she'd made, like a darkened wreath. I at first thought my eyes were playing a trick on me, but that was not so.

She touched the flaming fronds to the center of the design on the wall and uttered another incantation. The dried blood in the carving glowed bright red. Then a pulse of the same color rolled out from the design and across the room.

It struck me and set loose a flurry of visions in my mind. Dark thoughts I'd had, cruel treatment I'd endured, even horrific incidents I'd read about all came back to me, jumbled one upon the other. The experience frightened me to the core. As the wave exited my body, the visions disappeared, but they left behind a terrible knot of guilt at having conjured such images. I could also sense that the room itself had changed. The miasma of evil that permeated Justinia's cabin now poisoned the air here as well.

Justinia slumped to her knees and dropped the burning palm bundle. She leaned against the wall with one hand and hung her head. The smoking bundle rolled across the log floor to my feet. I stomped it out before it could set the floor aflame.

"Magnificent!" Blackbeard roared.

If I'd seen the horrors that unwound in my mind, I didn't want to know what visions Blackbeard had seen. The fact that he'd relished them confirmed his depravity.

I went to Justinia and knelt by her side. The scent of sulfur tinged the air. "Are you all right?"

She nodded. "I need a moment to recover, that's all."

Blackbeard ordered his crewmen to grab the two chests and take them down to the boat.

"You aren't going to bring the rest of the treasure up here?" I asked.

"No, I have the perfect place for all of it."

"Where could be better than a locked fortress like this?" I said.

Blackbeard drew his sword and gouged a big arrow in the wall across from the sign Justinia had made. "Right over there!"

I stepped over to one of the window slits and followed the direction the arrow pointed. It lined up with the extinct volcano.

CHAPTER THIRTY

Justinia and I followed Blackbeard back to the longboat. He marched ahead, seemingly unconcerned by how casting the spell had driven Justinia to her knees and how she lagged further behind as he led us to the lagoon.

I wanted to help her, give her a shoulder to lean on, an arm about her waist for support. But I was sure she would refuse, no matter how difficult walking would be for her. We got to the place where the iguana had perched on the fallen trees. The lizard's corpse still lay in the sand in a pool of dried blood. Whatever scavenger creatures the island hosted had yet to find this free meal.

Justinia touched my arm. "Bring the dead iguana back to the boat."

"Are you joking?"

"I'll need it for the spell."

In my experience, there are things naturally repugnant to human beings, a way of Nature warning us that certain things are not conducive to our health. Fire is one example. Extreme height is another. Reptiles are also firmly in that category. There is a reason the Devil took the form of a snake in the Garden of Eden.

The idea of carrying the iguana was quite distasteful. Indeed, upon closer inspection, insects already crawled across the creature's grayed skin. Medical training had prepared me for contact with all facets of the human body, but had done nothing to assuage my natural aversion to creatures such as this.

But I'd already made an embarrassing display when the lizard had startled me. I dared not lower Justinia's opinion of me further by cringing at such a simple request. I bent and scooped the iguana off the ground. It took both hands to manage the corpse and it weighed twenty pounds if it weighed an ounce. The unnatural feel of its skin and the awful stink the creature exuded did nothing to make holding it more pleasant. I cradled it in my arms while at the same time trying not to press it against my chest.

Blackbeard had not paused for a second and Justinia had continued following him as soon as she had seen me stop for the lizard corpse. As they moved through the jungle the realization that I was about to be alone in a tropical wilderness holding any scavenger's free meal occurred to me. Whatever else roamed the island, I had no intention of acting as its waiter. I began an awkward trot to catch up with the others.

We all arrived at the beach together. The pirates had already loaded the treasure chests aboard the longboat and stood by the bow with cutlasses drawn and eyes peeled for another caiman attack. One of them noticed me carrying the dead iguana and rolled his eyes.

As we closed on the boat, Justinia spoke to Blackbeard. "I need a caiman for the spell."

"An iguana is not enough?"

"Not if you want the spell powerful enough to repel even the most determined thief."

Blackbeard gave the lagoon a wary look. The eyes of several caimans broke the surface between the stern of the longboat and the pirate ship. "Why don't you cast a spell that kills one?"

"Anything tainted by magic is spoiled for use in magic."

Blackbeard pointed to one of the pirates. "Finnegan! Wade out there and bait a caiman in to shore."

The pirate's face went white. "Me, sir?"

"You can attract it alive…" Blackbeard drew his pistol and pointed it at the pirate, "…or as a floating corpse. Take your pick."

The other two pirates backed away from Finnegan, though whether to avoid a stray bullet or to keep from becoming the second caiman bait volunteer wasn't clear. Finnegan stared down the barrel of Blackbeard's pistol for a moment, and then waded out into the lagoon. He paused knee-deep in the water, with his eyes fixed on the caimans floating on the surface.

Then a set of caiman eyes disappeared beneath the waves. Finnegan shuddered and looked longingly back to Blackbeard for a reprieve. Blackbeard did not even meet his eyes. The pirate captain had all his attention focused on the lagoon. He walked down to the water's edge.

Something large sent a ripple across the water a dozen yards out. Finnegan yelped.

"Stand your damn ground!" Blackbeard leveled his pistol at the lagoon.

Finnegan fixed his eyes upon the lagoon waters. With their clarity, I knew he would certainly see the caiman coming.

Under the waves, a long, dark, cigar-shaped shadow surged for Finnegan. He saw it as well and let out a scream. Orders or no orders, he'd stood his ground long enough. With a flurry of splashes, he headed for land. But his legs moved slowly against the weight of the water, as if the lagoon itself was in league with the creature rushing to devour the poor man.

Finnegan set foot on dry ground, and glanced over his shoulder. He tripped over his own feet and tumbled down onto the sand.

Then a six-foot-long caiman burst from the water. It opened its jaws and lunged for the prone pirate. He screamed and covered his eyes.

Blackbeard's pistol boomed and obscured the Captain in a cloud of smoke. The bullet flew true and struck the caiman in the head. The caiman's tough skin was no match for the projectile. Blood erupted from the creature's head. The impact rolled the caiman to the left and its remaining forward momentum drove its open jaws into the wet sand just feet from the trembling Finnegan. The caiman's forelimbs shuddered, and then the creature expired.

Blackbeard returned the pistol to his belt. "You two! Get the caiman."

The two other pirates began a slow advance on the beached animal.

"Just the heart will be enough," Justinia said.

"My pleasure," Blackbeard said.

He headed for the caiman. The other pirates stopped and began to backtrack, apparently content that their captain could handle the job alone. Blackbeard drew his dagger.

Finnegan hadn't moved. He sat near the tip of the caiman's snout, overcome by shock. His jaw hung open. Wide eyes stared at the animal corpse, but there was no hint of comprehension behind them.

Blackbeard grabbed the leg of the caiman and flipped it belly up. Given the size and likely weight of the creature, it was an impressive feat. With a mighty downward thrust of his dagger, Blackbeard's blade speared the animal's chest. With one sideways sweep, he slit the creature the length of its belly. Steaming organs slithered out of the open cavity.

Blackbeard turned to me. "Which one is the heart?"

My first inclination was to say I was a doctor, not a veterinarian and how would I know what a caiman heart looked like. But antagonizing Blackbeard seemed like a bad idea. I set the iguana down in the sand and picked up a stick to use as a probe. I tiptoed through the growing puddle of caiman blood. The creature stank of algae and fish, plus Blackbeard's blade had nicked a bowel to add one more repugnant scent to the atmosphere.

I poked about a bit within the ribcage. Near the spine I found an organ attached to a group of arteries and veins. It was longer than a human heart, but it had four distinct chambers, though they were more side-by-side than stacked the way a human heart would be. I gave it a poke and the tissue was muscular and strong. Of all the organs in the cavity, this was the most heart-like. I rested the stick on it.

"This is it," I said to Blackbeard.

He grabbed the organ with one hand, and cut away the blood vessels and connective tissue with his dagger. With one tug, he pulled the heart free and tossed it to one of the pirates. The man caught it but lost his grip on the blood-slicked surface and the heart hit the sand. He picked it up and brushed it off.

Blackbeard turned to Finnegan. He waved a hand in front of the traumatized pirate's face. The man did not react.

"Always thought you a coward," Blackbeard said.

He traded his dagger for his sword. With a broad sweep, he sent its blade into the man's neck. Bone splintered with a crack as the blade imbedded itself in the man's spine. A fountain of blood gushed from his severed artery. His head lolled and he spat bright red blood from his lips. Blackbeard set a boot against the man's chest and yanked his sword free. Finnegan collapsed in a lifeless heap.

I balled my fists as I suppressed the rage that surged within me. Blackbeard had forced Finnegan into harm's way, then brutally executed him for a normal reaction. I was trained to have compassion for those in need, but Blackbeard displayed the exact opposite, despising the weak. Now I was glad he hadn't given me a cutlass, for in my fury I would have attacked him, and then I, too, would be lying beheaded on the beach.

I swallowed my anger. The pirates pushed the boat into the lagoon and I boarded it with everyone else. Justinia sat beside me again. She gripped her seat with both hands to steady herself as the men began to pull for the *Queen*. Soon the longboat was back at the ship, hoisted up in the davits, and level with the main deck.

Justinia and I were the last two people in the longboat. Back in the chart room, Justinia had looked tired. The trek back through the jungle had done her no favors and I'd seen her struggle to stay in her seat. By the time we bumped against the hull of the ship, Justinia's condition had worsened further. As she stood to get out, she nearly toppled over. I caught her. As proof of how exhausted she was, she did not recoil.

We stepped on the deck of the *Queen* and with my arm around her waist and her arm across my shoulder, I guided her across the deck and up the steps to the quarterdeck. When we arrived at her cabin, she pushed me away, though with all the strength of a kitten.

"Thank you," she said. "I'm going to rest."

I wanted to offer some kind of treatment, some way to use my skills to aid her recovery. But she was not battling any illness, just drained of the energy within her, like a barrel that had a hole punched in the bottom.

"Be sure to eat and drink," was all I could offer her.

She entered her cabin and closed the door without acknowledging me at all.

CHAPTER THIRTY-ONE

After the sun had set, I decided to take advantage of the moonlight and commenced a walk about the deck. With the ship at anchor, there was scarcely a crewman on duty. I settled in on the bow and took a seat over the fo'c'sle.

Anchor lines uttered a slight creak as the ship rode the lagoon's tiny swells. A breeze had picked up and brought with it sweet tropical scents from the island. The heat of the day had cooled to the most pleasant of temperatures. I closed my eyes for just a moment and forgot about the death, imprisonment, and black magic that had turned my life upside down.

"I seen him do it with my own two eyes!" a pirate said from within the fo'c'sle beneath me. "We left with four men and came back with two. What the hell do you think happened to them?"

"Aye, it's true," another voice said. "Blackbeard chopped Finnegan's head off with one blow."

I recognized these as the voices of the men who had been with me on the longboat.

A general grumbling followed the last pirate's statement. The two were apparently holding court and discussing our trip ashore.

"Finnegan wasn't the first," another man said. "Don't forget Wilkes just a bit ago. Right over the side he tossed him."

I certainly hadn't forgotten Wilkes.

"He's plenty brave protected by the witch's spell," a man said. "But when there weren't no witch aboard, he was mighty quick to kidnap another."

"What was in them chests you brought back?" one man asked.

"Gold and jewels and money," one of the pirates from our party said. "A king's ransom in each. Blackbeard said he was going to hide that and the treasure in the hold all together in one place."

"Well, if all that's buried here," a man said, "where's our share of the treasure going to come from?"

A much louder, angrier rumble of voices followed this statement. Something thumped loudly below. Though the discontent the men felt was well warranted, it still worried me. A pirate crew was by nature made of untrustworthy individuals, and also being collectively untrustworthy would be very dangerous. And an assassination of Blackbeard meant an unintended assassination of me as well.

I realized my precarious position here on the bow. If discovered, I might be seen as an eavesdropper working for the Captain, with such a transgression's penalty meted out by cutthroats desperate to ensure my silence. I hurried back aft as quickly as I could without having my footsteps arouse any curiosity.

As I returned to the quarterdeck, I noticed a lamp burning in Justinia's cabin. As a doctor, I knew that interrupting her much needed rest would be counterproductive. But as a man enamored with her, I chose to take the burning light as an invitation. I went over, knocked on her door, and announced myself. She told me to enter.

Justinia appeared much improved. The color had returned to her cheeks, her eyes looked brighter. The lamplight cast her in the kind of golden glow great artists employed for the sainted. She sat upon the edge of her bunk with the grimoire open in her lap. She closed it and stood up.

I opted to make the visit seem professional. "How is my patient recovering?"

"You were right. Food and sleep made a tremendous difference."

"I just overheard some of the crew talking. Our return with two fewer pirates in our longboat has not gone over very well."

A fly buzzed near my left ear. I turned to see a loosely tied bundle containing the caiman heart and iguana corpse sitting on the small table. Several other flies buzzed over it.

"I hope that you've found the spell you need to do what Blackbeard wants."

"I think I have, but it will take far more energy than I've ever used before."

"More than you used in the blockhouse?"

"Much more. This is a big island. I'm not sure anyone could cast a spell to outright protect it. But I can cast a spell that enlists the creatures of the island to do so. That's what I needed their hearts for. I already have the other elements onboard." A look of remorse crossed her face. "I'd promised to reverse your binding spell to Blackbeard. I wanted to do it tonight, before Blackbeard made me cast the island's protection spell. But breaking a binding spell is draining, and the one my sister cast is quite strong. If I do break your spell, I know I won't be strong enough to protect the island, if I'm even strong enough without doing that."

I was certain Blackbeard's reaction to Justinia failing to protect the island would be unbridled rage. Given his quick temper and flippant attitude about the lives of his crew, he'd be likely to kill her before he thought better of it. I could not let that happen.

"There's a way you could get stronger much more rapidly." I touched the arm of the rendering chair.

Justinia shook her head. "No. I won't have Blackbeard drag some poor soul up here for me to kill."

"You won't use a victim. You'll use a volunteer. Me."

"Do you think I'd feel any better killing you instead of a pirate stranger?"

"You don't have to kill me," I said. "You said that a witch can stop the process before that happens. You only need to drain enough from me to get you to full strength for the spell to protect the island. Then you can stop."

Justinia shook her head. "I've never cast that rendering spell before. It's completely forbidden. Even creating this abomination of a chair is considered a grave offense to our people. No. It's too risky."

"A small risk to me, maybe. But we both know what Blackbeard will do if you fail to cast that spell. He won't take the excuse that you weren't strong enough. He didn't pay any attention to how the spell in the blockhouse affected you. He'll assume you're just refusing to cast it. You'll never leave this island alive."

Justinia thought for a moment. Then she reopened the grimoire and leafed through the pages. She stopped and read one page with great intensity.

"The rendering spell and instructions are clear," she said. "And I could stop the spell at any time, I suppose."

"Do you see any other way?" I said.

Justinia frowned. "No, I guess not."

And with that, I again put my life in her hands.

CHAPTER THIRTY-TWO

"Take a seat in the chair," Justinia said.

I gave the rendering chair a wary look, then sat down. Rock hard, and poorly angled, the chair was terribly uncomfortable, and I knew that it would only get worse from here.

"This will be painful and you might not want to see what's happening. Do you want a gag, or a blindfold before we begin?"

"I think not." At the time I thought that by being able to see and speak to Justinia, I could provide any support she would need if she faltered during the ritual. Soon I would see how foolish that idea was.

Justinia raised a hand over my head and haltingly read an incantation from the grimoire. I thought I saw a flash of guilt upon her face. Then she stepped away to the chest on the floor.

As I adjusted my position, the texture of the wood changed. The unfinished surface of the armrests turned white, soft, and sticky, like they were covered in moss. I tried to lift my buttocks up from the seat, but I could not move. Something in the infernal chair had not just claimed my trousers, it somehow went through the cloth and grabbed me as well.

A slithering sound came from the sides of the chair. I looked down in time to see vines growing out from the chair's back. They crawled across my chest like a pair of snakes. Even through my clothes it felt as if hot, sharp spines punctured my skin along the vines' path. When the vines met in the middle, the two ends intertwined and cinched so tightly that they forced the air from my lungs.

The smell of sulfur seared my nostrils. Then more vines sprouted from the arms of the chair and wrapped themselves around my wrists. The pain of the vines against my skin became much more intense and I could not help but cry out, not just from agony, but from fear as well. The full memory of the horror the sailor Francois had endured now came back to me and I knew all too well what was to come.

"Are you managing?" Justinia asked.

If I'd admitted my true state of mind, I feared she'd stop this ritual that could save her life. "Yes, quite fine."

Justinia returned with the open grimoire in one hand. In the other she carried the device I'd seen Dumitra use, the slender silver shaft with what looked like lily petals at the wider end. Justinia read an incantation and the script along the side of the device glowed green. I cringed knowing what was soon to come.

A wave of dark, oppressive evil rolled across the room from the device. Being at the heart of such a sensation paralyzed me with terror. Between the vines across my chest and the clotting thickness of the air I feared imminent suffocation.

Justinia began to read an incantation. Her voice was steady, no longer stumbling over the words as it had before. Her earlier, tentative expression had become one of determination. She gave the third, last repetition of her spell a louder, faster finish. After pointing the sharp end of the silver shaft against my skin, Justinia drove it into my trachea.

An exquisite pain pierced my neck. It set my throat and then my lungs afire. I screamed but the noise came out as a raspy, strangled moan. I searched Justinia's face for compassion and hoped she could position the tube to deliver less pain. Neither outcome occurred. She stared at the open end of the device.

The tube grew hot, and my body went rigid. I could no longer move a single muscle. Justinia leaned in to the orifice.

As the air in my lungs wheezed out of the tube, I felt something much more powerful be pulled along with it. From somewhere deep within me I sensed my very essence begin to drain away. A fatigue like that which affects one's legs after a great race seemed to spread within every muscle in my body. The restraints of the chair were no longer necessary. I hadn't the strength to move if I'd wanted to.

A brilliant, white light began to glow in the tube. It lit Justinia's face and despite it all I was again taken by her amazing beauty. Snow-white smoke drifted up from the petals of the tube. Justinia inhaled and drew the smoke deep into her lungs. Much as I understood the impact this ritual was having upon me, I tried to concentrate on how the sacrifice was for her, for her future safety, and a return to her family.

Justinia's eyes began to glow a deep, emerald green, a color wholly unnatural. The look on her face shifted to euphoric pleasure and she drew another, deeper breath of the rising smoke. An animalistic growl of carnal pleasure rumbled from her.

The flow of energy from me accelerated. The draw now reached not just from my body in general, but from deep within each organ, as if tapping the reach of not just veins but down to individual capillaries to find every bit of life force that sustained me.

Justinia placed her hands on the tips of the chair's arms and leaned closer. The look on her face turned from pleasure to one of greedy lust. With a wicked smile and bared teeth, she took so deep a draw at the end of the tube that the energy pull reached all the way down to my feet. My bones ached as if the marrow within them was drying out. The world turned to shades of gray. My head swam. The cabin's thick sensation of maleficence grew and threatened to crush me. I remembered Francois' fate and knew I was about to repeat it.

"Justinia!" I could barely summon the word, so weak was my body, so empty my lungs. "Please."

The glow in her eyes blazed brighter. Her mouth opened wide and her tongue rolled out to catch the smoke of my soul upon it. Her tongue darkened, shrank, and then split into a forked tip. Justinia hissed in pleasure.

I was dying. My heart had slowed, my pulse weakened. The room felt freezing cold. The stink of sulfur burned my eyes and tears ran down my cheeks. Justinia was lost, consumed by the absolute power this spell was giving her. I would be gone before she realized what she'd done.

My right hand was a hair's width from hers. I channeled my remaining strength to it and stretched out my fingers. We touched and her hand felt white hot.

Images careened through my mind. Visions of blackened, shriveled people thrashing in a roiling sea of boiling lava. They cried out for relief to one that floated above them, a hideous winged creature, its naked skin shades of glowing green against the scarlet sky above. Pointed ears and twisted horns framed a face that could be none other than Justinia's. And it was laughing.

My fingers circled around hers. With a focus I'd never summoned before, I cried out mentally and physically, "Justinia, stop!"

The face of the flying demon fell. Its eyes widened and the vision vanished.

I was again in the chair face to face with Justinia. She yanked the tube from my throat with such violence it jerked my upper body forward. The drain of life force from my body stopped. My heart began to beat normally again. Pins and needles wracked my extremities as sensation returned. I summoned just enough strength to lean back in the chair. The vines that held me in place retracted and the chair's surface reverted to hard, unfinished wood.

"Thank you," I managed to croak.

"Oh, dear God," she whispered.

Justinia picked me up under the shoulders and dragged me over to her bed. I was too weak to offer any assistance. She laid me down and straightened my arms and legs. I could barely get her face into focus. She vanished from my sight, then returned with a damp rag she laid across my forehead.

I closed my eyes and passed out.

***

I awakened feeling as battered as a filet of tenderized meat. The sleep had done me some good and I felt much better than when I'd lost consciousness. The soul apparently had a stellar capacity for replenishment.

Oil lamps lit the cabin and I wondered how much time had passed. I sat up.

Justinia rushed over from where she'd been sitting in the rendering chair. She sat beside me and took my hand in hers. "I'm so sorry. Are you all right?"

"Yes. I'm a bit worn out, but already feel much better. How long was I asleep, by the way?"

"Over eight hours."

"Dear God!" The duration of my sleep astounded me. Then the length of my time sequestered in the cabin with Justinia concerned me. It would not go unnoticed by the crew, or by Blackbeard. Thinking I was having relations with the witch would earn me no favors among either.

Then as if reading my mind, she said "Yes, you must leave. But first, I have to apologize. I almost killed you. I don't know what came over me."

"The process seemed to take control of you."

"Yes, adding the power of another's soul to mine was unbelievable. I had the sensation of invincibility and unlimited power. It made me feel like…a god. All I could think of was taking more and more of you."

"But you stopped before you did."

"No, *you* stopped me before I did. In the midst of it all I heard your voice. I felt your mind touch mine. You made me realize what I was about to do and I took control back from whatever force of evil had taken me over."

"I saw that force of evil. A winged creature flying over a lava lake filled with the souls of the damned."

"You saw that?"

I hesitated before telling her the most awful part of the vision. "And I saw that the face on that demon was yours."

Justinia looked at the floor in shame. "Using dark magic touches the blackest side of one's personality. All the wicked impulses one has had, all the random thoughts of evil deeds one might do, even the nightmares one dreams but did not remember, all of these are released. The more dark magic one does, the less repressed that side of the witch becomes, until eventually, the good is scrubbed away and that dark version is all that is left. That winged creature was my darker half, and what the power of black magic promised I'd become. I won't let that happen."

"I'll help you. Use the magic on me. Make me as invincible as Blackbeard, and stronger."

She placed her fingertips against my cheek. "No, the price for you would be too high. You must be no part of any spells I cast. After we leave the treasure on this island, I'll burn away your binding spell and you'll be free of any trace of magic."

Justinia reached under her bed and pulled out a small wooden box. She opened it. Red velvet lined the interior. A mouse skull sat inside, along with a small leather pouch.

"I've already set aside everything I need for the spell," she said. "The mouse skull just has to be crushed and combined with the herbs in this pouch, then add the blood of both people bound together. All I'll need to do then is set it on fire as I cast the spell I showed you in the grimoire. I can do it all in moments and you will be free." She slid the box back under her bed.

I placed my hand upon her knee. "Thank you. I should go."

We walked to the cabin door together. When we got there, she placed a hand against it to bar my exit.

"I don't know what tomorrow will bring, if I will even survive casting the spell Blackbeard demands. So, I will say this now. Men shun a Gypsy witch as they would one with leprosy. I hid my true nature from my daughter's father, and even he abandoned me when he discovered it. You are the first man who knew I practiced witchcraft and still treated me with compassion."

I held her hand in both of mine. "I would treat you with much more than just compassion if you would let me. I can't deny that I am deeply in love with you."

She looked away. "But there is no future for a Romani and an outsider, no matter how you feel."

"That may be true in the Old World, but not the New. You and I and your daughter can travel to any colony, or even any country. We can go where no one knows us and start our combined life afresh."

She gave me a sad smile. "Such tender thoughts, but they're just a dream. There are too many obstacles in our way."

"We'll clear them. We'll free ourselves of Blackbeard's control, and then get off this ship. After that, there'll be no stopping us."

"You would give up everything you have for me?"

"And for no other."

I took her in my arms and held her close. My heart seemed ready to burst. But I could not ignore the sulfurous scent that rose from her clothes. I kissed her cheek anyway. She pulled away.

"Blackbeard's crew spent the day transferring the gold to the *Avarice*," she said. "He said we sail in the morning to hide it. So, go. We both need to be rested for what is to come."

I did not want to leave. I longed to stay close to her, to feel her skin upon mine, to run my fingers through her hair. But she was right. I had already been with her in her cabin for far too long.

I nodded to her and stepped out onto the quarterdeck. Night had fallen and a billion stars filled the sky. Strange sounds skipped across the water from the jungle. Bird calls, deep reptilian grunting, the buzz of nighttime insects. On the main deck, a few pirates kept a desultory watch, but they took no heed of me. No lamp burned in Blackbeard's cabin. I scurried across the deck and into my own cabin.

With the door closed behind me, I lit a lamp, and then crawled into my hammock. Physically, I was still tired to the core despite my long sleep, but my mind was wide awake and racing. The revelation that Justinia shared my feelings, the sensation of her touch, the hope for a life together after fleeing this floating Hell, all of these excited me. Just last week, I'd dreaded my future, one of being a prisoner on this pirate ship. Now, I couldn't wait for my future to arrive.

But I could not shake the foreboding driven by my experience in the rendering chair. Justinia's transformation as the dark magic took hold of her had been chilling. The vision of her as a winged predator over the boiling sea of Hell was one not soon forgotten. Were these things harbingers of what was to come, or signs to help me steer her away from that potential future?

I knew it would take a long time to sort all this out, if I ever could. Dawn was not far away, and I doubted I would sleep any before it broke over the lagoon. I rocked in the hammock and listened to the island sounds outside the ship.

A most difficult day lay ahead.

CHAPTER THIRTY-THREE

Moments later, my cabin door flew open. Blackbeard charged in. Before I could react, he was at the side of my hammock. With his left hand, he pinned me to the canvas by my throat. He stank of strong spirits sweated out through the pores. The fury on his face made me quiver. The fingers around my throat made me choke.

"I saw you leaving the witch's cabin," he said. "You're thinking of getting a bit of that sweet ass of hers?"

"No." It was as much of a rebuttal as I could choke out.

"It won't be sweet soon. I seen the magic burn a witch out before. She'll be haggard as her sister soon enough. Until then, you leave her be. She has one purpose on this ship, and that's to serve me."

With his free hand, Blackbeard drew his dagger from his belt. He put the tip of the blade inside my nostril. The reek of the gutted caiman spiked straight into my brain. The cold, sharp blade made my nose tingle.

"If she falters or her witchcraft fails because she's distracted by you, the only decision I'll need to make is whether to kill her first, or you. And if you think I'm kidding..."

With a flick of his wrist, the dagger blade sliced through the side of my nostril. His iron grip on my throat muffled the shriek of pain that tried to escape me. He gave my neck one more squeeze and then released me. I immediately grabbed my nose and felt the warm blood running from the wound.

"You aren't the one aboard this ship who's invulnerable," Blackbeard grunted. He whirled about and left my cabin. The door slammed shut.

The initial shock of the injury wore off and now the side of my nose throbbed in pain. Mashing my nostril against my face to stanch the bleeding, I hurried over to use the mirror in my medical kit. I lit my lamp, removed my hand, and grimaced at what I saw. Blackbeard's blade had left a half-inch-long gash in my nostril and the two flaps of skin fluttered with each exhalation.

I had to apply myself with great alacrity. Untreated, soon the skin would turn necrotic, and the two sides become unable to mend together. I did not want to live the rest of my life with my nose open to the septum. But that meant I was going to have to stitch my skin back together.

Every element of this scenario was set up for failure. The light was atrocious. Looking in a mirror to operate meant that I would have to work with my actions reversed. The wound being on the side of my face, only one eye would be able to see it in the mirror, and I would lose all depth perception. But the worst problem would be the pain. Running a needle through the already traumatized tissue in my nostril would be excruciating, and I'd have to keep a steady hand through the process.

But I had no choice. The procedure could not wait.

Normally I'd encourage a patient in this situation to down some alcohol to deaden the senses against the pain that was to come. Alas, I could not follow that advice myself, lest I drunkenly stitch my nose closed instead of back together.

With one hand pressed against my slashed skin, I used the other to set out a curved needle and a length of cat gut thread. I took a deep breath, let go of my nose and used both hands to thread the needle. I missed. Blood rushed down across my lips and I spat it away. The third try was the charm and I threaded the needle.

I returned the pressure to my nose to slow the bleeding. Setting the mirror up for the best view, I showed it the damaged side of my nose. I had to cut my eye hard to the left for the best view, and even that angle was poor. Time would only make the situation worse, so I committed to start. From within the medical bag, I extracted a canvas-wrapped wooden dowel I gave patients to bite down on to help alleviate the pain of some procedures. The deep tooth marks along the surface were proof that it worked. I placed the dowel between my teeth, took a deep breath, and picked up the needle. I aimed it near the top of the wound.

The point lanced my nose and I nearly bit the dowel in half. Blackbeard's slashing had put me in such terrible pain that it was hard to believe that my body could register any more, but it did. I punched the needle through the other flap of my nostril and moaned into the dowel. Now the scarlet blood coming from the wound made it difficult to see, and soon the pain made my eyes water so badly that seeing at all became impossible.

I tightened this first stitch. With no visual reference, I went by sensation, and that sensation felt like I was pulling two sheets of burning canvas together across my nose. The only plus was that the pressure slowed the bleeding.

I began a second stitch. The pain reached a level where I feared I would pass out. When a patient in surgery passed out, I thought it a godsend. The man's suffering would be temporarily over and my work much easier on an unflinching body. But if I passed out while being my own patient, in my exhausted state there was no telling how long I'd be out, or what kind of a mess my nose would be by the time I awakened. I envisioned rats scampering across the deck, attracted by the fresh blood of my wound. I kept that image front and center to help fight through the pain as I completed the second stitch.

The third stitch promised to be the worst, the tip of the nose being a most sensitive location, and I was at the end of my endurance. This last suture would have to be done with speed, or I might never finish it at all. I felt for the end of my nostril and set the tip of the needle in place. Before I could let the dread of this final stitch dissuade me, I plunged the needle in and then up again through the other side of the wound. The pain was so great the world turned white. I collapsed upon the table and sent the mirror sliding off to the floor.

Everything came back into focus. The sharp fury of the pain retreated to leave a dull, pounding ache in its place. I reached down to the floor to retrieve the mirror. The rush of blood to my head felt like an explosion in my brain. I sat back up and a wave of nausea nearly overtook me. It receded and I set the mirror back up on the table. With a gentle wipe I swept away the blood and checked my nose.

The bleeding had slowed to a trickle. The stitches were uneven, the alignment of the skin crooked. The scar would mar my features forever. But I'd had no other options. I tied off the stitches and gave myself one more round of searing pain as I fixed the knots. From my bag I pulled a small section of the fine cloth I'd been using to bandage injuries, rolled it into a tight ball, and inserted it into my nostril. It rubbed the inside of the stitches and I again bit down hard on the dowel.

I let loose the cloth and spat the dowel from my mouth. Blood and mucous would dry on this cloth pack, and removing it would be another horribly painful exercise. But that would be in the future, so I vowed to concern myself with it then. For now, I would content myself with having minimized the damage to myself.

Snoring rumbled from the other side of my cabin wall. Blackbeard was no doubt sleeping hard in an alcohol-fueled stupor. My physical pain and emotional humiliation urged me to sneak into his cabin and kill him where he slept for what he'd just done to me. My mind reminded me that his invulnerability spell was likely still working, and even if it wasn't, the binding spell meant killing him would also be committing suicide. Whatever revenge I would seek would need to wait until Justinia freed me from her sister's spell.

False dawn glowed along the island's eastern flank. Whatever fate awaited me, today's events would seal it.

CHAPTER THIRTY-FOUR

Morning brought me more misery. The rising sun seemed intent on burning my tired eyes out of my head. The throbbing in my nose created a headache that pulsed to the exact same beat. A check in the mirror in the stronger light revealed the truly shabby nature of my self-treatment. Dried blood scabbed over a crooked set of sutures. That inflamed side of my nose was half again as large as the other side. Many had considered me handsome before I set out on this trip. I doubted any would if I survived it.

If I were my own patient, I would have prescribed a day of bedrest. But I knew today would be no day for rest, for me, or for anyone else on board. I left my cabin for the quarterdeck's port railing, hoping that the freshening morning breeze might soothe me.

As soon as there was full light, the crew of the *Avarice* set about readying their ship to set sail. I thought that odd, since the treasure was to be secreted on the island. Even more odd was the men preparing the *Queen's* longboat for launch as well. Then Sneed pounded up the steps to the quarterdeck and slammed a fist against Justinia's door. He ordered her out on deck.

Justinia appeared in her doorway. She looked strong and clear-eyed. I sensed an air about her, as a trained athlete has before a match or a veteran soldier before combat. She was ready to cast Blackbeard's spell. The sacrifice of the power of my soul had not been in vain. But amidst all of that I did notice one disturbing thing. At first, I thought it a trick of the sunlight, but it was not. A streak of gray ran through Justinia's hair near the back of her head.

"Bring what you'll need," Sneed said, "and get in the longboat."

Justinia picked up a sack she'd set just inside the doorway. "Everything is here."

Sneed led her down to the main deck. Then Blackbeard exited his cabin. Bleary-eyed and disheveled, he looked worse for the wear from his bout with the bottle the previous evening. His invulnerability spell must not have extended to hangovers.

He did not acknowledge my presence as he went to the railing overlooking the main deck. He glanced over to the *Avarice*, where several limp sails had been unfurled. He grunted in approval.

He turned to look at me. "You're coming. Get down to the longboat."

I would have declined if possible. I was not interested in knowing more details about where the treasure was secreted, thereby making myself an expendable risk to its future revelation. But I couldn't hazard too far a separation from Blackbeard. Even more important, I did not want Justinia to go alone. If there was the slightest chance I could positively intervene on her behalf, I wanted to be able to exercise it.

I nodded and headed for the boat. When I arrived, Justinia gave my nose a horrified look. "What happened to you?"

Blackbeard flashed an evil smile at me.

"An accident in the dark," I said. "Lucky for me, I'm a doctor."

"You don't look very lucky."

Justinia and I boarded together, sitting in the same seats as before. The pirates lowered the boat into the water. As Blackbeard and the brigands assigned to the oars crawled down the side of the ship, I took the chance for some private words.

"Are you ready for what you must do?" I said.

"As ready as I can be. Now tell me what really happened to you."

"Blackbeard came in last night and was displeased about the amount of time we spent together last night. He's afraid I'll distract you."

"What did you tell him?"

"I assured him that you didn't fancy my type."

"So you lied."

I smiled. "This handiwork on my nose was his subtle warning to keep my distance from you."

"You should follow that order while we're still bound to this crew," she said, "and then do the exact opposite once we're free."

Her encouraging words made me want to hold her close and tell her every plan I had percolating about how we would spend our lives together, how we would create so much happiness it would obliterate the memories of this awful journey. But the descending pirates were one rung away from entering the longboat, and I dared not inspire more of Blackbeard's rage. Instead, I twisted my body for a better view of the men coming aboard. As I did, the side of my hand brushed against the side of Justinia's, and I hoped she understood the multitude of messages that motion represented.

The oarsmen took their seats and readied the oars. I recognized them as Iverson and Johnson from our previous expedition. Neither looked excited about leaving the relative safety of the *Queen Anne's Revenge* for another trip across the caiman-infested lagoon. Blackbeard again took the stern. We cast off from the *Queen* and the longboat aimed for the *Avarice*.

I got a much better look at the vessel as we approached it. The ship was smaller than the *Queen*, with two masts instead of three, and rode much lower in the water. She still carried a formidable brace of cannons and would be more than a match for any merchantmen she would come across. Such a ship would by nature have a shallower draft and be able to pursue prizes into places where the *Queen* would run aground. Blackbeard knew what he was doing when he decided which prize ships to commandeer.

After we were secured alongside the *Avarice*, the oarsman climbed up from the longboat. Blackbeard waited with Justinia and I for the longboat to be hoisted aboard in the davits. As soon as the longboat made it to the top of the davits and swung inward, Blackbeard jumped out and landed on the deck with a thud.

It seemed most of the crew was assembled on deck, though not in any remotely military fashion. At first glance, there were several major differences between this crew and the one we'd left. First off, this crew was much rattier looking. Their clothes were more worn, their hair less kempt, their physiques much leaner. It seemed the *Queen* took the pick of the litter when it came to crewmen.

Second, these men were all terrified. An epidemic of wide eyes and quaking hands infected the crew. If the depth of Blackbeard's capricious cruelty was well known on the *Queen*, it had to have been bolstered by rumors and half-truths into something resembling Jupiter's power among these men.

But it wasn't just Blackbeard that sent these men shivering in their worn-out shoes. The furtive glances they made in Justinia's direction said that they were just as much terrified of her, perhaps more so.

I realized these men had never seen a witch. The way Blackbeard had kept Dumitra sequestered in her cabin, she surely had never been to any other vessels. I could only guess at what myths that woman had inspired. And now all of them were likely transferred to Justinia.

I jumped out of the boat, and then reached a hand up to help her down. Justinia stood atop the longboat gunwale in perfect balance and reached out both hands. She chanted a short, incomprehensible spell. Her eyes flared green.

I stepped back in shock. Then she rose from the longboat, floated forward, and set down upon the main deck.

From the men on deck rose a sound that was fueled equal parts by fear and awe. As one, they backed away from where Justinia stood as far as the bulkheads and gunwale would permit. A few scrambled to belowdecks.

One man did not retreat. He stood his ground, wearing a bright red shirt over his barrel chest and the battered tri-corner hat of a French naval officer. I wondered if he'd earned it years ago, or had captured it from someone who had. From his demeanor, I ascertained he commanded the *Avarice*. Blackbeard stood before him.

"Report, Captain Tasse," Blackbeard said.

Tasse offered a deferential nod. "Awaiting your orders, sir."

Justinia strode past me, straight for the two pirates. The glow in her eyes subsided. She stopped before them.

"Have the sigils been created?" she said.

Tasse looked confused.

"The carved symbols on the ship," Blackbeard said.

"Yes," Tasse said. He pointed about the ship. "All along the gunwales and on the forward mast."

I followed where the Captain had pointed. At each location, sigils had been freshly carved, bright tan against the wood's dark exterior.

"I will need a metal bowl," Justinia said, "set at the base of the forward mast."

Tasse shouted over his shoulder at one of his crewmen to go get a bowl. The man looked relieved to have an excuse to leave the main deck, and dashed off.

"Weigh anchor," Blackbeard said. "Set a course for the waterfall."

Tasse looked across the lagoon at where the waterfall cascaded down the mountain's side. Apparently asking Blackbeard for details about his orders wasn't something he wanted to risk. He relayed the order to his first mate who set the crew to work. Men scrambled up the rigging while others went forward to raise the anchor.

Justinia took her bag forward to the mast. The crewman had already left the metal bowl and retreated to somewhere out of sight. She sat down cross-legged and rested the bowl upon her thighs. She unfolded a page that looked like it had been torn from the grimoire and set it in front of her. Then from her bag she extracted the animal parts for the spell and set them in the bowl, followed by a handful of mixed herbs and a shard of a coconut shell. Then she took a knife from her bag and cut a lock of her long hair. She sprinkled the hair into the bowl.

Wind filled the ship's sails. The pilot spun the wheel and the bow turned to point at the waterfall. Ropes creaked against the strain and the ship picked up speed. The lagoon wasn't that large. I wondered what difference it made to move the ship to the other side. From the look on Tasse's face, he seemed to be thinking the same thing.

Under the forward mast, Justinia began to chant a long incantation. The green glow returned to her eyes. The hollows beneath her cheekbones darkened. I could swear her teeth turned a brighter white.

She lit a match and dropped it into the bowl. The contents burst into flame, what I was sure was a scientific impossibility without some type of accelerant. The flames burned brighter and larger than the fuel could account for, and instead of yellow they were a sickly green. Fearful rumblings spread among the crew. Even I involuntarily stepped back to the ship's railing.

The *Avarice* gained speed and the bow sliced a V of white water across the lagoon. The pirates who weren't fearfully watching Justinia's incantation were fearfully watching the approach of the waterfall and the mountain behind it.

Tasse turned to Blackbeard. "Sir?"

"Hold your course," Blackbeard said.

Justinia spoke another incantation. It ended with a shout and she clapped her hands together three times. After the third clap, a massive green smoke cloud erupted from the bowl. Like water from a pressurized hose, it shot straight up in the air. Just as it cleared the masts, it flattened out and spread like a great emerald disc from the ship. Fast as a bolt of lightning, it raced out until it covered the island in all directions. It turned the yellow sphere of the sun into a dull olive orb and dusk fell across the land. The air turned cold.

Justinia shouted a one-word command and clapped her hands again. The cloud disk shattered like broken glass, and the bits of it rained down across the island. The sun burst forth again and re-illuminated the world in its light.

Justinia put the grimoire page back in her bag and tucked it between her and the mast. She closed her eyes and leaned back. She grinned but I could not tell if it was from relief or joy at the evil accomplishment. I did not like not knowing.

Men called out from the bow that the water was shallowing. Tasse stepped next to Blackbeard. "Sir, we're going to—"

Blackbeard whipped out his dagger and lay it hard against Tasse's neck. Through gritted teeth he said, "I said hold your goddamn course!"

At this point, no command was going to save the vessel. A freshening breeze had stretched the sails to their limits and the bow sent tall, wide waves rolling away on both sides. Timbers creaked under the strain. The tangy smell of the sea was soon overpowered by floral aromas and the scent of the freshwater falls.

The thunder of the water grew loud enough to drown out all speech. Any order to come about would literally fall on deaf ears. At yards from the pounding falls, the crew working forward broke and ran for the stern. I gripped the rail and braced for the inevitable impact. Justinia sat, eyes closed, head against the mast, unconcerned that we were all about to die.

The waterfall's mist rolled over the ship like a rainstorm and soaked me to the skin. I shielded my eyes with one hand and wondered why I was so curious to better witness the moment of my death.

The bow hit the falls themselves and tons of water pummeled the forward deck. The ship lurched bow low under the weight. Men fled the wall of water as it raced across the deck. It reached the forward mast where Justinia still sat, oblivious. It rolled over her and all I could see was white water.

The falls swallowed the ship, across the mid deck, past the hold, to the base of the quarterdeck where I cowered against the bulkhead. I wrapped both arms over my head, closed my eyes, and prayed.

Then tons of falling water slammed me into the deck. The air rushed from my lungs and I was certain that Blackbeard had killed us all.

CHAPTER THIRTY-FIVE

The pounding water ceased. I opened my eyes to see the wall of water moving behind me, across the quarterdeck and beyond the stern. Just as I realized the ship hadn't run aground, it did.

With a thunderous crack, the bow ran up onto rocks and hard aground. Pirates screamed and the impact sent me rolling forward across the soaking wet deck, aimed for the opening to the hold below. At the last second, I twisted my body to the left and missed the opening by inches. I slid to a sideways stop against a cannon carriage. Once the reality of my personal survival sank in, I used the cannon to pull myself to my feet.

The *Avarice* sat hard aground in a huge cavern, with her bow driven high upon a rocky shore. The interior of the extinct volcano was hollow, and the backsplash of the waterfall had worn a hole in the mountain that the ship had sailed through. The ceiling was high enough that the darkness overhead swallowed it, even though the waterfall edges let in enough light to see around the cavern relatively well.

I had read about extinct volcanoes in Italy and elsewhere that had similar structures. Scientists believed that retreating magma drained back into the Earth and left voids like this behind. This one was certainly larger than any I'd read about. There was room for the *Queen Anne's Revenge* to follow us in here without running aground. But I did not think Blackbeard had left orders to do so with Sneed before we left.

I checked the base of the forward mast, the last place I'd seen Justinia. She was still there, somehow unmoved by the deluge we'd passed through, or the violent grounding the ship had just endured. Her bag was still tucked between her and the mast and the metal bowl still sat in her lap. She turned the bowl upside down and poured the water out of it. Her constitution amazed me.

The crew made a groggy, sputtering return to duty as they recovered from the passage into the cavern. Tasse staggered over to where Blackbeard stood on the quarterdeck.

"You could have told me there was a cave in here."

"We needed full speed so we could be sure to ground the ship. Once the second spell is cast, we'll abandon the ship, walk out around the edge of the falls. Sneed will be there to have us board the *Queen*."

"You mean the whole crew?" Tasse said.

"We may be one short," Blackbeard said with a malicious grin.

I didn't like the way that statement rang in my ears. Of all the people on board, Blackbeard surely considered me the most dispensable. Last night he was livid at the thought of me interfering between him and Justinia. Perhaps ending my life here was why he had been so adamant about me joining the party without giving a reason for it. I grew certain he had a plot afoot against me.

"Begin the spell!" Blackbeard bellowed across the deck to Justinia.

Justinia stood and shook some of the water from herself. She opened the grimoire page again and faced the mast. She began another chant. This time her voice was very different, deep, guttural, terrifying. Were the words not coming from her lips, I would surely have attributed them to someone else.

"Tasse," Blackbeard said at a less audible level, "Have your crew draw arms. Assemble on the main deck. Quietly."

Tasse nodded and went to the main deck, where he began to pass the order among the men.

As Justinia called forth more magic, I saw small changes in her. A subtle shift in the shape of her ears, an increased prominence of her nose, a reshaping of her eyes. To my horror, she was looking more like the demonic vision I'd seen when I was in the rendering chair. I prayed such a transformation was temporary.

Many of the crew watched what Justinia was doing with great intensity as she continued to cast her spell. She placed one hand against the sigil carved into the mast. The sigil glowed a dark, forest green. The men muttered and pointed at the mast until the order reached them to go below and draw arms.

I became more concerned about being left behind, as Blackbeard had alluded to. I moved to the railing of the ship and looked down. The rocky little beach was a good twenty feet below me. A long but survivable drop. The tiny shoreline skirted the inside of the cave all the way to the waterfall's edge. I weighed the idea of jumping over and making an escape. Everyone was busy drawing arms or watching Justinia. Even Blackbeard had his attention focused on her. I could certainly be gone before they missed me.

But to what end? To hide on the island? Even if the pirates didn't find and kill me, starvation or caimans eventually would. Perhaps the option of dying with one swift blow of Blackbeard's blade would be the preferred demise after all.

Justinia continued casting her spell. She took her hands from the mast, but the sigil continued to glow. She put her arms straight out at her sides and began a slow turn as she repeated the same strange spell over and over again.

The entire ship shuddered. Pirates grabbed railing and rigging to steady themselves.

Her body made a complete revolution, but her head did not move, and she faced the ship's stern the entire time. This act was anatomically impossible, and completely horrifying. Black magic was turning this woman whom I had fallen in love with into something I doubted was even human at all.

Justinia turned faster, faster than any human being could possibly move, until she looked more like a spinning top than a woman. Through it all her eyes glowed a brighter and brighter green, and her face narrowed as if the witchcraft was desiccating her from within.

The sigils all around the ship came to life with a glow that matched the sigil on the mast. They pulsed and grew brighter and brighter as Justinia's body became a blur. She cried out one more incantation and the sigils flashed so brightly they lit the cavern like a circle of bright green suns.

Then a concussion wave emanated from the mast and rolled out across the deck of the ship. Any pirate standing was knocked off his feet as the shimmering circle expanded across the deck. Its force pushed me hard against the railing. Blackbeard gripped the ship's wheel and leaned into the force. It blew the hat from his head but he remained standing.

The wave rolled over the deck's edges and across the cavern. As it passed over the water, some kind of marine life began to boil and churn under the surface. Then the wave struck the cavern walls and the waterfall and passed right through them.

Justinia's spin came to an abrupt stop, one as impossible as the spin it had been doing. The glow in her eyes died. Her face returned to normal, though incredibly pale. She dropped to one knee and then looked across the ship at Blackbeard. The crew arrayed about the deck returned to their feet.

"The spell is complete," she said between labored breaths. "Anyone who comes to the island to take this treasure will die. The ship will repel them. Animals on land and creatures in the sea will attack them. No one could survive."

"And how long will this spell last?" Blackbeard said.

"Forever," Justinia said.

"Tasse!" Blackbeard called out.

Tasse stood beside two pirates on the main deck with his cutlass in hand. "Sir?"

"Kill the witch."

CHAPTER THIRTY-SIX

Justinia's jaw dropped.

I couldn't believe what I'd just heard. I rushed to Blackbeard's side. "You can't do that!"

Blackbeard pulled his dagger and pointed it at my chest. "Watch yourself. You can still treat the sick without a tongue in your head."

"She did what you asked. The island's safe, the treasure's safe."

"For now. Can I trust her to keep the secret? Can I trust her to not return and undo the spell? No and no. She's a loose end that needs to be cut. Pray you don't become one as well."

Tasse grabbed the two men closest to him and they made for the forward mast. Justinia tried to rise, but had to use the mast to steady herself. The three men reached her in seconds. The two pirates grabbed an arm each and held her against the mast. Tasse raised his sword over one shoulder.

"The world is about to be one witch less," he said.

Justinia growled an incantation. The green glow returned to her eyes. I could practically see strength course back through her body as she straightened up and her arms tensed. Terror swept across the faces of the pirates holding her.

Justinia swung both arms forward, taking the pirates with them. The two crashed into Tasse from both sides. Bones crunched and Tasse dropped his sword. Justinia shook her arms and the three men crumpled to the deck, moaning.

The pirate crew had been viewing this show since Blackbeard ordered Justinia's execution. The spectacle of watching another's demise had turned into the possibility of experiencing their own, and the men took a collective step back.

Justinia knelt down and pulled the silver soul tube from her bag. It seemed she'd come prepared for a double-cross after all. She drove the pointed end into Tasse's chest. She spoke some words and bent over the other end. With one deep inhalation she drew a veritable fog bank of life energy from Tasse in an instant. His body turned to dust and then blew away.

Her eyes turned a green so bright that it lit the rest of her face. Her hair went white as new-fallen snow. She stood, faced the crew, and snarled.

I ducked down behind a crate on the deck. Whatever was coming, I was certain I did not want to face it.

"What are you waiting for?" Blackbeard called out. "Avenge your captain and kill her!"

Perhaps drawing courage from their numbers or just exercising their pirate lust for blood, the crewmen shouted some kind of pirate battle cry and surged toward the forward mast with weapons brandished.

Justinia chanted a new spell and extended her arms out to her sides. Red lightning flashed from her hands and the bolts struck the cavern sides in several places. Orange sparks flew at each impact point, bright as the spray from a blacksmith's forge. The power burned the witchcraft symbol of the spiral, cross, and pentagram into the stone.

The advancing pirates stopped, stunned at the display.

Then from each sigil, burst a stream of jade-colored power. These converged on Justinia. I thought the impact would knock her down, but instead she absorbed it. The fire in her eyes brightened. Her spell appeared to have tapped into some kind of energy within the island itself.

She aimed her fingers at the terrified crew. Green lightning spat from each of her fingertips and struck ten pirates in their chests. The men shuddered and dropped to the deck with a chorused thud. Justinia surveyed the dead about her feet and then spat on the deck.

At that demonstration, the rest of the advancing crew took pause. Apparently wielding lightning like the Norse god Thor wasn't something they had expected.

"Bloody cowardly bastards," Blackbeard said.

He drew his sword and leapt to the main deck from the quarterdeck. After landing, he reared the sword back and launched it at the witch.

In retrospect, the next moments seemed to happen in slow motion, but I am certain there had been no spell cast to make that so. The big blade sailed through the air, rotating end over end, the sharpened edges flashing as they caught the light coming in from the waterfall. Justinia looked up from the dead with the sword inches away from her chest. Before she could react, the blade pierced her body and continued forward to bury itself in the mast behind her.

Justinia screamed, but it was one of fury, not pain. The glow in her eyes became so bright that it turned white. She did not try to extricate the sword. Instead, she invoked one loud incantation and then stamped her right foot.

The mast exploded just above her head. Huge wooden splinters roared through the air like shrapnel fired from a cannon. Heavy slivers struck the crate protecting me with a sound like arrows hitting wood. Other shards whizzed across the deck and peppered the pirates. Some lodged deep in eye sockets, some tore arms from torsos, some lanced abdomens and exited through the other side. Pirates jerked and spun from the impact and splatters of blood rained among them. All of them dropped.

All but Blackbeard, that is. The deadly splinters avoided him. His invulnerability spell must have still been active enough to save him, even from Justinia's own magic.

The broken mast toppled off the ship's starboard side to the sound of snapping rigging and cracking wood.

The crate I cowered behind had acted as my protection. I did not want to test its efficacy again. Whatever that creature pinned to the mast was, it was no longer Justinia. Her fury over her betrayal had driven her to tap the darkest black magic and it had transformed her into something worse than even Dumitra had been. I knew I could expect no kind treatment at her hands when she saw me alive.

Dropping the crew like a harvest of wheat had drained Justinia's strength. The fire in her eyes had dimmed to a dull green. She hung on the sword. With both hands she tried to extract it, but it didn't move.

I saw my chance. I sprang up and dashed for the railing near the fallen mast. I mounted it and leapt off the ship. Several feet down I landed in the tangled rigging. Heavy hemp rope burned my skin as I tumbled across the jumbled mess. I reached one of the sails and slid down it to land ankle deep in the water.

Invulnerability spell notwithstanding, Blackbeard opted to not press his luck against the wounded witch. He mounted the broken mast and ran straight down it to where the end rested by the cavern wall. Three other wounded survivors of the witch's wrath followed his lead. The one of them closest to Blackbeard I saw was Johnson. The other two must have been from the *Avarice*.

The four of them ran for the small, misty gap between the falls and the cavern wall. I panicked as the distance between Blackbeard and me grew, so I followed in their footsteps.

As I neared the falls, the pounding water raised such a din that it blotted out all other sound. The mist grew thick as a London fog. There was but a narrow gap between the falls and the cavern opening, scarcely wide enough for a man to slip through sideways.

I glanced back at the ship. From this vantage point I could see no details on the deck, save a low green glow from the area of the forward mast. I wondered what it would take to kill that witch.

Blackbeard faced the cavern wall and side-stepped his way between the falls and the soaking wet stone wall. Two other pirates did the same.

As the third turned to make a go of it, an enormous tentacle burst out of the water behind him. It was the size of an octopus' but was almost completely clear, with just a hint of red within it. If I did not know better, I would have said it was a jellyfish tentacle. But no jellyfish had tentacles a dozen feet long and over a foot wide.

The tentacle whipped around the pirate's midsection and then his neck. The man screeched and tried to pry himself free. He released it like the tentacle was red hot. Indeed, it seemed to be. His hands turned red and swelled. Crimson streaks sprouted from his neck and spread to cover his face. Then the tentacle yanked him back into the water.

The walls of the cavern began to vibrate. The ground and water were still, but the cavern walls crunched and grinded. Stones began to fall behind the waterfall. One the size of a cricket ball struck my shoulder a glancing blow.

Between falling stones and a killer creature in the water, I needed no more motivation to depart the cave. While the others slid through sideways, I rushed headfirst through the waterfall. The water pummeled me but fear propelled me faster than it could push me down. I burst through the other side to a brilliant, sunny day on the island. Across the lagoon the *Queen Anne's Revenge* floated at anchor.

The other three had not waited for the delayed pirate or myself. They were nowhere to be seen, but a trail of footsteps ran across the sand and around a bend in the beach.

From behind me came the roar of an avalanche. I turned to see the side of the mountain collapse in a cloud of dust and bouncing boulders. The impact sent a hailstorm of small rocks whizzing past me, and only by God's good grace did I remain unscathed. Tons of earth crashed into the lagoon and sent a twelve-foot wave heading for the *Queen*.

Warning shouts echoed across the lagoon. But there was nothing the crew could do for the anchored ship. The wall of water swelled to almost twenty feet high as it swept into a shallower part of the lagoon. It slammed into the ship broadside. The *Queen* rolled so hard to starboard that the yardarms touched the sea and I got a full view of the old ship's mossy bottom. Splashes and cries for help sounded as men were thrown into the lagoon.

Like an old lady leaving bed for the first time, the *Queen* moaned and righted herself. The soaked sails now weighed more than the rigging could stand, and booms and yardarms snapped. If Blackbeard was expecting to make a quick getaway in that ship, disappointment awaited him.

When the dust settled, the face of the mountain had retreated a great deal. The waterfall was gone, either destroyed or diverted elsewhere by the seismic activity. If there were any other brigand survivors, they were now forever buried, as was Blackbeard's treasure.

I continued down the beach. Having survived the cave in, I was now worried that the distance from Blackbeard would do me in. I rounded the corner to find Blackbeard and the two surviving pirates standing beside some palms, panting and recovering from the escape. I joined them. None of them greeted me.

"That goddamn witch tried to kill us all," Blackbeard said.

I was going to tell him she acted only after he ordered the crew to kill her, but I valued my own life too much. "Seems she's buried the treasure forever."

"Nothing's forever," Blackbeard said. "It just needs to be dug out of there. I know where it is. Even with the cavern collapsed on it, the ship will hold up. Once I get back to her, the treasure will be safe and sound in the hold."

I'd had a much better view of the avalanche than Blackbeard had. I thought his expectations far too optimistic.

In the jungle behind us, leaves swayed and branches snapped. The two pirates jumped to their feet.

An iguana crawled out onto the sand from under a palm leaf. It opened its mouth and hissed.

Blackbeard laughed. "You bunch of women! Spooked by a damn lizard, are you?"

The branches over the iguana swayed. Several other iguanas climbed up from the shadows and stared at us with unblinking eyes. Then more appeared on nearby branches, still others joined the iguana in the sand. There had to be thirty of them at least.

The first iguana hissed again. Then the group attacked.

CHAPTER THIRTY-SEVEN

The iguanas came on like a swarm, flying from branches and racing across the sand, tails held high and mouths wide open. I considered one large iguana quite fearsome. A mass of them was petrifying.

A rush of panicked energy sent me running. The others did the same, with Blackbeard leading the way. The pirate from the *Avarice* looked back, and in doing so entangled his feet together. He tripped and ended up face-first in the sand. He also ended up left behind.

The iguanas descended upon him like locusts on a field of wheat. He writhed and cried out, but the weight of the group kept him pinned. The reptiles tore bloody chunks of flesh from his body, right through his clothing. Spraying blood rained over the beasts and the bright crimson splatter made them appear even more demonic. In moments, the pirate garbled his last, weak call for assistance and went still. The voracious iguanas feasted on his corpse.

While the clumsy pirate's sacrifice had bought us time, it did not purchase an escape. The iguanas that had been denied a meal at the pirate's carcass cast ravenous eyes at our retreating assemblage, and then charged.

I was last in the group as we sprinted across the sand. The iguanas covered the beach behind me, a carpet of surging, mottled, reptile skin, punctuated with open, hissing mouths. The thirty I'd seen at first seemed to have doubled. The gap between us shrank.

Blackbeard and Johnson were to be no help. They did not even offer a backward glance to check on me. I imagined they were just glad my death would delay their own.

As my feet pounded the damp sand, I searched in vain for an escape. The jungle to my left would only slow me down. Iguanas had shown they could climb trees better than I. Could they swim? Even if a plunge into the lagoon would keep them from me, the caimans were waiting there for their next meal. Justinia had done just as Blackbeard ordered. The island's creatures were out to kill any intruders.

From the corner of my eye, I caught sight of iguanas converging on my feet, tails whipping through the air. Once one clamped its horrid teeth on my ankle, the added weight would send me tumbling down, and I'd suffer the same cruel fate as the previous pirate.

A boom sounded on the lagoon. A cannonball screamed past my ear and buried itself in the sand just behind me. It exploded and the beach erupted in smoke and flames. The shockwave lifted me off my feet and threw me down the beach. I landed with a splash at the water's edge.

The iguanas fared far worse. The force shredded the reptiles it did not obliterate on impact. A puree of blood and limbs rained down all around me. An iguana head landed inches before my eyes.

The iguanas left alive lay about, stunned by the blast, some half-covered in sand and blood. They twitched and began to pull themselves from the sand.

The noise of the exploding shell had sent my ears ringing, but I heard another muffled cannon report from the lagoon. A second cannonball sailed over my head and landed just inside the jungle down the beach. Its detonation sent palm trees and ground cover skyward in a cloud of dirt. The crew of the *Queen* were covering our retreat.

I raised myself from the water and saw they were doing more than that. A longboat with two pirates rowing splashed its way toward the shore a hundred yards down the beach. Blackbeard and the surviving pirate waved to them. I didn't want to miss this final chance for rescue. I staggered down the beach in their direction, and arrived as the boat nosed onto the sand. Again, Blackbeard took no notice, focused solely on his own survival.

"It's about damn time," Blackbeard said to the oarsmen. "I'll have Sneed's hide for leaving me ashore this long."

I guessed there would be no credit given to his first mate for the cannon fire that had saved our lives from the iguanas.

Blackbeard and Johnson climbed aboard into the stern. I pushed the boat backwards and then climbed into the bow. The oarsmen spun the boat around and headed for the *Queen*.

As the brigands pulled hard for the ship, one of them could not contain his curiosity. He wasn't about to ask Blackbeard, but the other pirate survivor was fair game.

"So, mate, what the hell happened in there?"

"The witch," Johnson said. "She went berserk, she did. Started throwing lightning bolts, killed everyone, then buried the boat and herself in the mountain."

"I knew she was crazy."

"It was all okay until we were ordered to—"

"Pipe down!" Blackbeard ordered. "If you can waste breath talking, you must not be rowing hard enough. I'll have the lot of you lashed when we get back aboard."

Johnson practically shriveled in his seat. The oarsmen shut up, put their backs into it, and dug the oars deep into the water. Looking past them, I spied something ominous astern. Several sets of caiman eyes had surfaced. All were headed for the longboat.

"Caimans coming up astern!" I said.

Blackbeard and Johnson turned about just as another caiman joined the first two. They were swimming faster than we were moving. A cannonball from the *Queen* to save us from these creatures would surely kill us as well.

"Goddamn animals," Blackbeard said. "Row, you useless bastards."

The oarsmen needed no threats. They'd started rowing faster as soon as I'd called out the caimans' approach. I checked the distance to the *Queen*. We were hundreds of yards away. The caimans would catch us long before we arrived.

Muffled shouted orders came from the ship. Several pirates appeared at the railing and aimed muskets in our direction. I thanked God we were still out of range. I had no faith that these untrained ruffians were accurate enough with their aim to strike the caimans and not us.

The caimans closed on us. They were over a dozen feet long each. Their tails swept faster until they moved so quickly that the eyes cut wakes across the water. They split one on either side of the longboat and raced up the sides.

When they were amidship, the caimans burst from the water. Each clamped a massive set of jaws around an oar. The shafts shattered and the caimans dove back into the water. The startled oarsmen dropped the stubs left in their hands and they rolled onto the floor of the boat.

The third caiman approached the rear and turned sideways to the boat. Then it sent its tail crashing against the stern. The rudder shattered and left Blackbeard holding the severed tiller in one hand. The stern of the boat buckled. The impact was so great it launched the boat forward. I gripped my seat to keep from falling against the oarsmen.

"Mount the other oars!" Blackbeard ordered. "Get me to my ship."

The men pulled the second set of oars from under the seats, nearly striking each other in their haste. They set them in the oarlocks.

"If they chew these up, we'll never get back," one of them said.

"Then we should distract them." Blackbeard rose and drew his dagger from his belt. He plunged it into Johnson's chest. The man screamed and Blackbeard shoved him over the stern.

"Now row, you bastards," Blackbeard said.

Oars plunged into the water. The betrayed and wounded pirate surfaced, sputtering and crying for help. In a moment, he was far behind the longboat.

The man's splashing acted like a caiman dinner bell. The caimans broke away from the longboat and headed for the foundering man from three different directions. They struck simultaneously and the water around Johnson transformed into a frothing explosion of white water tinged pink with blood. Human limbs and caiman tails surfaced amid the melee. The oarsmen pulled harder under a torrent of Blackbeard's unnecessary threats.

The sea behind us calmed down and a red stain was the only hint that Johnson had ever floated there. Three sets of caiman eyes surfaced around the blotch, turned toward the longboat, and renewed their pursuit.

But the man's death had purchased us precious time. With two more strokes the nose of the longboat nudged against the *Queen's* side. I grabbed one of the ropes the crew had dropped along the hull. The pirates shipped oars and did not wait for the longboat to be recovered. They grabbed other ropes and began to scale the hull. Even Blackbeard knew our time was short, and climbed out as well. I followed their examples.

The longboat drifted away from the ship. A second later, the three caimans struck it from all sides. The hull collapsed. In a flash it sank beneath the water.

The three pirates were onboard long before my tired muscles delivered me to the deck. I rolled over the gunwale and collapsed on my back. Not only had no one helped me get aboard, even now no one acknowledged my presence. The attention of all was directed at Blackbeard dressing down Sneed for leaving him ashore so long. The two pirates who'd rowed us back stood to one side, unsure of what to do but appearing like they were more than ready to blend back into the rest of the crew.

I wondered if Blackbeard was as furious as he presented himself to be. He *had* just been rescued. Perhaps this was all feigned fury, an attempt to intimidate and divert attention, like his skeleton flag did to merchantmen. This plan of his had been a disaster. The treasure was entombed. He'd lost one vessel and its entire crew, and now the remaining ship was without the protection of a witch's spells. Perhaps he did not want the crew mulling that over.

He'd also just sacrificed a crewman to the caimans, and in full view of the crew of the *Queen*. The pirates had already been grumbling about his heartless disregard for them. That act would be more fuel to the fire. Perhaps his histrionics now were to keep the men from dwelling upon that murder, as well.

Then I thought more about that action he took in the stern of the longboat. We were close enough to the ship that we might have made it to safety, or at least to killing range for the musket men, once the pirates started using the second set of oars. Blackbeard was far too quick to kill and dump Johnson. He must have planned to do so before the caimans attacked.

My conclusion made perfect sense. That surviving pirate was another "loose end" Blackbeard did not need. Without his testimony, Blackbeard's story of what transpired in the cavern was the ultimate truth. No one would know he lost control of the witch and no one would know that he provoked her by double-crossing her.

That meant the only person alive who could contradict the pirate captain was me.

I needed to convince Blackbeard that I never would.

CHAPTER THIRTY-EIGHT

Blackbeard gave the lagoon a glance and then ordered Sneed to weigh anchor and leave the island.

"We'll need to check the rigging first," Sneed said. "That wave from the mountain collapse nearly rolled us over. We also sprung leaks along the keel. Men are pumping the water out and caulking the hull right now."

Blackbeard's cheeks went red with wrath. "Goddamn it, did I ask for an excuse? Get this ship underway or I'll order it myself and leave you here with the caimans."

I checked the lagoon and indeed the caimans were all about the ship, swimming back and forth, the way a begging dog paces about the floor waiting for food to fall from a table. I wondered if they could work together and damage the *Queen* so badly that we would all be stranded here. Having seen them sink the longboat, I wasn't about to dismiss the idea.

Sneed seemed to know that Blackbeard had reached the limits of his already limited patience. He began to issue orders to the crew to get underway and the men scrambled about the ship. Blackbeard mounted the steps to the quarterdeck and went to his cabin.

I decided the best place to be was my cabin, out of the crew's way and out of Blackbeard's line of sight. Perhaps he hadn't considered me a threat to his telling of what happened on the island yet. The less he saw of me, the less likely the idea would come to him.

I mounted the steps to the quarterdeck near Justinia's cabin. The excitement I'd felt spending time with her in there made me so much sadder knowing that would never happen again. The tragedy of her succumbing to the addiction of dark magic was quite depressing. The sight of her transformed from a beautiful vision into a creature horrific and repulsive broke my heart.

I paused and touched her cabin door. The signature evil still pulsed from the room. The reek of gangrene often permeated an operating room long after the patient had been removed. Perhaps the black magic practiced in this cabin had done the same thing. My heart longed for that to be true, otherwise the evil within was still an active force to be feared.

I returned to my cabin and shut the door behind me. Barren and uncomfortable as this miserable room was, I was quite glad to be back. As I'd cheated Death several times over the last day, my return to this stinking, sad example of quarters was an event to be celebrated.

My celebration was short lived. The door opened to reveal Blackbeard standing in the opening. My stomach sank. The same dagger with which he'd dispatched Johnson still hung from his belt, and it still carried that man's blood. This would be the perfect opportunity for the pirate captain to add my blood to that blade. Blackbeard stepped in and closed the door. He approached me and drew the dagger.

"I'm thinking my need for a doctor aboard may now be at an end," he said.

I was quite sure this wasn't his opening line to proclaim my emancipation. I hid my fear. "It's actually quite the opposite."

"How so?"

"A witch's invulnerability spell only lasts so long. Once it wears off, you can be injured as easily as the next man. You'll want medicine on your side when that happens."

Blackbeard seemed to ponder that.

"You already burned through some of it," I said. "That exploding mast killed most of the crew, but you were unscathed."

Blackbeard rubbed his chin and then pointed at me. "As were you spared."

"Because I was cowering behind a box. You were out in the open. I watched splinters stop an inch from you and fall to the ground." I opted to play the loyal minion at this point. "She specifically tried to kill you. You knew she couldn't be trusted. If you hadn't put that sword through her chest, she'd have killed everyone in there, then finished off the *Queen* and her crew."

Blackbeard nodded. "I knew it would always come down to her or me."

"And it ended up being her who lost. If the other crew had been more wary of her, they might have met a better fate. You tried your best to save them."

"We're all better off with her dead." The pirate gave his beard a thoughtful stroke. "But why were the animals under her spell attacking me after the cavern collapse? This is my goddamn island!"

That did seem strange until I remembered Justinia's exact words. "Justinia said the creatures would attack anyone who wanted to remove the treasure. Anyone would include you."

"The bitch of a witch! She was always plotting to double-cross me, make it so that only she could return and take my treasure."

"Now, no one will," I said. "Between the island creatures and a ship's tomb made up of thousands of tons of rock, no one will ever see that gold again."

Anger flushed Blackbeard's face. He clenched hard his dagger and I feared he was about to kill the messenger bringing bad news. Instead, he stabbed the wall beside him as he cursed Justinia's name in no uncertain terms.

"She may be dead," Blackbeard said, "but that doesn't mean she won't pay for this treachery."

Blackbeard stormed out. I'd managed to avoid his planned assassination. I wasn't at all sure what retribution Blackbeard could deal to a dead witch.

I considered my survival of all that had happened. The tentacle in the cavern had dragged that pirate to his death, but it just as easily could have been me. Then when the iguanas charged us, and some of them had overtaken me to the side, they did not attack me. They were still running forward, heading for the greedy pirates. Perhaps it wasn't chance that had spared me from death, but the fact that I was the only one who harbored no desire to take the gold in the *Avarice*. The spell only targeted anyone who wanted to take the treasure away.

Perhaps Justinia had been more clever in creating the spell than I had imagined. Not only did she make sure that even Blackbeard himself could not return for the treasure, any people who innocently chanced upon the island in the future would not be attacked.

Whatever she had been forced to become in the end, she had started out being something special.

CHAPTER THIRTY-NINE

It was impossible to imagine a more precarious situation than where I now found myself. I'd never believed that Blackbeard placed much value on my life. I was now certain of that. On a whim or in a fit of paranoia, he'd not think twice about slitting my throat.

I was also certain that while I did not know when, at some point his invulnerability spell would wear off. If it happened before he went into battle, he'd suffer a painful death by blade or bullet, and moments later, so would I. My life was in grave danger whether Blackbeard lived or died.

As we sailed north, back to Carolina, the weather turned quite poor. Rain lashed the deck and the daytime sky was nearly dark as night. A strong wind gave us speed, but it also woke the sea from its placid slumber. The *Queen* alternated between charging up and down waves like a mountain goat and crashing into them like a bull through a locked gate. The unholy ride made me wonder if the sea would dispatch my soul to Heaven before Blackbeard had a chance to. Seasickness plagued me.

The *Queen* fared the passage no better than I did. Even with my limited maritime experiences, I could tell the ship had become unsound since the wave strike in the lagoon. The masts and rigging bent and moaned with every gust of wind. Each time the ship struck a wave, a shiver ran through the deck and an awful groan emanated from deep within the hull. Every pump had been manned to keep the vessel afloat. Sneed snapped off orders to the crew on deck, sometimes the next countermanding the last, as he tried to keep the storm from plucking the masts from the deck.

Despite all the imminent peril about me, I continued to feel the need to leave the relative safety of my cabin. From the moment I'd awakened that morning, the desire to go to Justinia's cabin had lodged itself in my mind. I did not know what I was supposed to do or find in there, but the urge remained undeniable. The desire was even stranger given the aura of evil that still permeated the location.

During the raging storm was both the worst time to cross the quarterdeck and the best. The worst because there was the very real chance that I'd lose my footing and slide into the sea. The best because with Sneed working the crew and Blackbeard holed up against the weather, I could make the visit and remain unobserved. So strong was the call that it overwhelmed my sense of self-preservation, and I had no choice but to heed it.

I opened my cabin door and was rewarded by a lashing from the cold rain. Heavy drops beat against the still-raw incision on my nose and sent a sharp pain that drove all the way through my skull. The quarterdeck was unoccupied and Blackbeard's hatches battened down. I shielded my tender nose with one hand and steadied myself against the doorway with the other. As soon as the ship heeled to starboard to help me travel in the right direction, I sprinted for Justinia's door.

In an instant, my feet slid out from under me. I landed on my back and pinwheeled across the deck. The rough deck boards scraped my shoulders and I choked against the rain that now forced its way down my throat. I slammed shoulder-first into the bulkhead beside her door. Even in the storm I sensed the maleficence that lurked within the cabin, as if tendrils of it reached out through the wall and wrapped themselves around my chest.

Even that did not abate my compulsion to enter the cabin. Before the ship could roll back to port and send me across the deck again, I rose and grabbed the door handle. It was unlocked, likely because the idea of any pirate voluntarily entering hadn't crossed Blackbeard or Sneed's minds. I entered and slammed the door behind me.

With the hatches closed and the sunless sky gray as lead, the room was nearly pitch black. The air smelled of sulfur. I knew the cabin to be unoccupied, but I did not in the least feel alone. A presence filled the space, a malicious force that prowled the cabin, like a caged animal desperate to break free and escape. I had not felt this presence before, perhaps because I was in here when Dumitra or Justinia had been present, and the darkness that lurked within had already found a conduit into our world.

I felt my way along the wall to where one of the lamps hung from the ceiling. I lit the lamp and a yellow glow illuminated the cabin. The swaying light cast shadows that waxed and waned with each roll of the ship, and everything in the room seemed alive and in motion. The light confirmed that I was indeed alone, but my sensation of being stalked did not diminish.

The cabin was as I'd remembered it last. Justinia's few personal items were still as she had left them, more proof of two things: she had planned on returning, and it was likely no one else had set foot in here since she'd left. The grimoire rested on the rendering chair. It may have been my imagination, but the evil in the room had an epicenter, and the book on that chair was it.

A violent wave struck the ship and gave it a sudden lurch. The action sent me against the dreaded chair. My hands grabbed both armrests to arrest my fall. The touch of the wood brought forth all the memories of Justinia sucking the life force from my body. The terror of that moment returned as if the event was now happening. I imagined the chair's arms coming back to life and sending out new vines to lock me in place.

The ship rolled back to level and I pushed myself upright. I staggered back to the bunk and collapsed upon it. Whatever had compelled me to enter now kept me from fleeing in the face of the cabin's still strong malevolent force.

The boat continued to thrash about in the storm. The room's growing and shrinking shadows made the evil chair seem to be walking from one side of the cabin to the other. I felt that if I spent another minute here, the dread and fear would drive me into madness.

Then on the cabin's far side, a form appeared. White and milky it was, wispy and insubstantial, like a cloud in the shape of a person. Though everything else in this cabin oozed a sensation of bad intent, this ethereal form did not. In fact, it did just the opposite.

Could this be Justinia's spirt come back, piercing the veil to speak to me? Though the face, as it was, had no features, the height and general shape were a match. The very idea that something of Justinia remained, something of the good and decent woman that I'd fallen in love with, excited me no end. Add to that she'd sought me out and all the malicious intent of the rest of the cabin could not compel my retreat.

The specter moved to the bed and pointed to a box beneath it. That jogged my memory of Justinia telling me she'd filled the box with elements for the spell to break my connection to Blackbeard. That reminder shined a brief glimmer of hope into my hopeless situation, but reality extinguished it.

"A carriage with no horse to pull it," I said. "The elements are there without the spell to make them work."

The specter floated over to the chair. She placed her hands above the grimoire and the book opened. Pages flipped by. They stopped on the page headed by the symbol Dumitra had inked into my chest, the page Justinia had said contained the counter-spell to break my bond to the pirate captain. I examined the page more closely. A list of items in Justinia's strange tongue ran down beside the diagram, then below it were two separate paragraphs. The grimoire layout resembled nothing as much as a cookbook.

The specter's hand moved to the bottom of the page. The black ink of the final paragraph turned a glowing green. This was the key to open the lock. Justinia had shown me the spell to free me of the pirate captain.

"But there's no witch to cast the spell," I said. "And I can't imagine the next one Blackbeard kidnaps to give a whit about my disposition here."

Justinia's spirit waved one finger, and then pointed it at me.

"Me? I can't cast the spell." I remembered Dumitra dismissing my ability to survive using the grimoire. "I am no witch."

She pointed to me again and then vanished.

The book lay open to the incantation that would set me free. I stepped closer to get a better look. Another lurch of the cabin sent the lamp swinging over the pages again. The spell was in the ancestral tongue of Justinia's family. I did not understand it, but if Justinia's spirit was to be believed I must not have had to. The words looked easy to pronounce. Perhaps as long as I said them with the right intent and a firm conviction, the spell would work.

The spiteful sensation of the cabin grew stronger again. The thought occurred that this could all have been a deception. The power behind the black magic had compelled me to enter the cabin, then created a false specter to convince me to practice the dark arts. This passage I was to read was unintelligible. Was I going to set myself free of the binding spell, or was I committing my soul to Hell and consecrating myself to the practice of witchcraft? I did not know, and worse, there was no way I could.

And if I did cast a spell, what would happen to me afterwards? The power the magic tapped was all-consuming. I'd seen it pull Justinia down to its sub-human level, and she had been schooled to resist it from an early age. If I touched that shadowy force, what hope would I have of that absolute power not consuming me absolutely?

But I *had* felt Justinia's presence, the shining goodness that was her before the magic had destroyed her. That was all the proof I needed that casting the spell was possible.

Unless it was all a trick. Would it not be cleverer for the awful to hide behind the mask of the good to gain my trust before betraying me? Then, like water once the stopper is pulled in a filled sink, I would be sucked down into darkness.

The ship crashed down upon another huge wave and the deck timbers flexed beneath my feet. I skidded back against the cabin door. Now I was convinced this had all been a deception, the darkness trying to draw me out from under the light. The sooner I got away from its source, the sooner I would feel clean again. I blew out the lamp and threw open the door.

A blast of cold rain struck me in the face. It acted like a slap to restore my senses. A flash of lightning was followed by a crack of overhead thunder. The ship heeled over to port, and I ran for my cabin. Justinia's cabin door slammed behind me. It could have been because of the angle of the ship, but it more seemed to be an act of frustration by the evil within that had failed to seduce me.

Once back in my cabin, I shook the rain from my clothing as best I could. I was chilled to the bone, though whether from the rain or the brush with dark magic, I could not tell.

The door to freedom Justinia had promised to open for me a few days ago had been a sure thing. Now it was locked and sealed forever. I feared that I would spend the rest of my days as a prisoner aboard this pirate ship.

CHAPTER FORTY

The storm abated later that night, but I could not sleep. Overtired is what we called it during long days at medical school. Add in my soaked and chilled state, and nothing short of a blazing fireplace and a snifter of fine brandy could have stopped my shivering. As the sun rose, I prayed that it would bring a warm day with it.

Later, as I stood upon the quarterdeck like a lizard basking in the sunlight for warmth, I took stock of the ship's condition. It was not good. The roll in the lagoon, the makeshift repairs, and the pummeling of the storm had taken their toll. Men continuously manned the bilge pumps and sent an alarming amount of water over the side and back into the sea. The ship also made a cacophony of noises as she sailed. Pops and creaks and moans accompanied even the slightest shift in the breeze. Every pirate who had to climb aloft to trim a sail, did so with a look of fear upon his face. If the crew no longer trusted the ship to stay afloat, I did not know how I could.

I wondered if the spell Dumitra had cast to protect the ship in combat had protected it from decay as well. Now that that spell had worn off, was the *Queen Anne's Revenge* showing her true age? Offering up prayers to God that a pirate ship could make a safe journey seemed a blasphemous request of the Almighty, so I opted not to.

Eventually we reached the Outer Banks of the Carolina colony. A thousand yards off the port side, breakers rolled in against a long sandy beach. Thoughts of my potential escape surfaced, but my binding spell to Blackbeard pushed them back down.

"Sail ho!" called the lookout from the crow's nest. "Starboard bow."

My initial worried thought was that a Royal Navy vessel had been lying in wait for us. Such an interception now would be a catastrophe. *Queen Anne's Revenge* was in no shape for combat against a true warship and I had no desire to be on the receiving end of His Majesty's cannon fire. I went to that side of the deck for a better look. A single-masted ship floated near the horizon. That was a relief. Even if the smaller ship was a Royal Navy vessel, she would run before engaging the *Queen*.

Sneed arrived at the railing beside me and raised a spyglass to his eye. "Well, what do you know? Dawson actually followed orders."

Blackbeard left his quarters and came pounding across the deck. "What is it?"

"The *Ravenous* actually made it to the rendezvous point, sir. I didn't think Dawson had the necessary seamanship."

Blackbeard grinned. "Signal her to follow us through the channel. Get us into cannon range of Big Pine Point and anchor."

I remembered that as the name of the town where Blackbeard had kidnapped Justinia.

"You want to bombard the city?" Sneed's question was pregnant with concern.

"Only if they don't give us what we need. We're short-handed by one witch and they need to provide us another."

If he thought one of Justinia's relatives would fit the bill and be in the area, I knew he was to be disappointed. Justinia had made it clear that her aged parents were her only nearby family.

"Are you sure the town has another witch?" Sneed said.

"If they don't," Blackbeard said, "we took the sister of our first witch as a replacement, and we can always take the daughter of our second to replace her."

My heart sank. Justinia's daughter was too young to be forced to cast black magic spells. If the spell's power could seduce and destroy Justinia, who was trained to be on guard against it, I shuddered as I comprehended what that power would do to a young girl unfamiliar with what she'd be unleashing.

"Aye, aye." Sneed shouted orders to the crew and the men moved about the ship. Sneed checked the *Ravenous* through his spyglass again. "Captain, the *Ravenous* is flying the danger signal flags."

"Dawson can be a pusillanimous bastard," Blackbeard said. "Come alongside her, and let's see what he's afraid of."

The *Queen* closed on the other vessel and took up a station on the ship's starboard side. The vessels paced each other. Aboard the sloop, a pirate I assumed was the maligned Captain Dawson stood facing us from the ship's stern.

"What the hell are you afraid of here?" Blackbeard called to Dawson.

"We was in the lagoon yesterday and got word that the governor of Virginia sent a pair of ships under a Lieutenant Maynard to hunt us down. I took the ship offshore to give us some fighting room."

"Or more likely give him some running room," Blackbeard said to himself. Then he called back to Dawson, "This is Carolina, not Virginia. Screw the governor and the toy boats he sends against us. Follow us in and we anchor off Big Pine Point."

Dawson's face went white, though I wasn't sure if that was because he was afraid to get into combat with real sailors or if it was because he was sure he'd soon be facing Blackbeard's wrath. Personally, I thought a quick death under British cannon fire would be preferable.

"Aye, aye," Dawson replied.

The *Queen* took the lead passing through the channel between the barrier islands. I recognized the crude lookout tower that stood about twenty feet above the sand on pine log feet. As the ship passed, the man in the tower offered a wave.

We headed south between the barrier islands and the Carolina shore. The calmer sea did not seem to make the ship sail quieter. All about me an unnatural amount of moaning and creaking of the timbers occurred when the wind filled her sails. Just as Big Pine Point came into view ahead, a great crack sounded from the stern of the ship. The ship swung to port and headed straight for the barrier island.

"What the hell?" Blackbeard said.

The panicked helmsman looked up at Sneed from the ship's wheel. "Rudder's broken! I have no control."

Sneed shouted orders for the men to drop the sails, but before they could respond the *Queen* ran hard aground. The impact threw me forward and only the railing along the quarterdeck saved me from falling to the main deck. Several pirates aloft in the rigging lost their grip and were thrown into the sea. They did not surface.

From below came the sound of snapping timbers and the cries of scared men. Pirates ran up from below deck, some carrying injured comrades. One shouted that the keel had broken.

Blackbeard let fly a string of curses and gripped his sword like he was ready to take his frustration out on the first thing he found. I stepped back to the furthest part of the quarterdeck.

"Sir," Sneed said. "Look north."

A plume of white smoke rose from the Outer Banks lookout post.

"That's the lookout's signal," Sneed said. "The Virginian ships have arrived."

CHAPTER FORTY-ONE

At what should have been bad news, Blackbeard's demeanor shifted from dismayed to delighted. His eyes lit up at the idea of approaching combat.

"My luck is unmatched," he said. "This ship is lost and the Virginians deliver us a new prize to take her place."

With a ship sinking beneath my feet, I questioned Blackbeard's definition of lucky. The only person this calamity had favored was Justinia's daughter, who at least for now was still safe from pirate hands.

The *Ravenous* came up alongside our broken vessel. Its crew tossed lines to ours and the men pulled the ships hull to hull.

"Transfer our gunners to the *Ravenous*," Blackbeard ordered Sneed. "We sail to capture the Virginians."

"And the rest of the crew?" Sneed said.

"Would slow the ship down. They stay."

The ship was slowly settling to one side. The deck had already separated from the gunwale amidships.

"The *Ravenous* can't take on a fleet, sir. Even using our gunners."

"I'm protected by the witch's spell," Blackbeard said. "If they can't kill me, they can't kill my ship."

I was absolutely certain that was not how the spell worked. The look on Sneed's face at Blackbeard's statement said he was aware of the same thing.

"The *Queen's* breaking up," Sneed said. "The men will be thrown into the sea. The ones who survive the sharks will be hanged as pirates when rescued off the beach."

"They won't be the first to die so."

Sneed squared his shoulders. "I can't leave them to that fate."

Fury twisted Blackbeard's face. "Then you won't have to."

Blackbeard drew his sword and plunged it deep into Sneed's gut. The tip exited through his back and bright red blood spurted out of the wound. Sneed looked shocked, taken unaware by Blackbeard's attack. He reached down for the hilt of the sword in slow motion, as if still disbelieving what had happened.

But Blackbeard yanked the sword back out with one pull. Sneed collapsed on the deck in a widening pool of blood. I needed no close examination to know that he was dead.

Those sailors on the main deck who'd had a good view of what had just happened trembled in fear as Blackbeard approached the railing. I could hear a chorus of whispers saying "He's killed Mr. Sneed." Captain Dawson had seen it all from his ship and appeared to be quaking.

"Gunners, board the *Ravenous*," Blackbeard called out. "Dawson, have your men run through anyone else who tries to board."

At this point any loyalty between pirates was sacrificed on the altar of self-preservation. The *Queen's* gunners raced for the other vessel. The *Ravenous'* crew took positions along the railing with brandished weapons. Blood still dripped from Blackbeard's sword as he headed for the other ship. The men doomed to remain aboard the broken *Queen* skittered out of his way.

My invitation to depart hadn't been issued, but my binding spell meant I had no choice but to pretend I had one. But there was one thing I could not abandon aboard the sinking ship.

I ran for Justinia's cabin. Bursting in, I spied the box beneath the bed, the repository for the elements that could free me from Blackbeard should I ever encounter a witch skilled enough to cast the spell. I pulled it out and stuffed the contents into my pockets.

I was almost out of the cabin when I realized that whatever witch I recruited would not know the proper counter-spell to cast. That was in the grimoire.

I turned to the rendering chair. The grimoire sat upon it, still opened to the page the specter had shown me on that stormy night. I was still undecided if its message was intended to bring on my salvation or damnation, but without the spell, the elements in my pockets were useless.

I bent and touched the page in the book. A horrific sensation engulfed me. I remembered the visions of a transformed Justinia, of the demons dancing in the sea of lava, of the death that had surrounded me since I'd come onboard. Touching this book showed me all of it, as if it was bragging of its accomplishments.

I quickly tore the page with my spell from its binding and stepped away. The vision receded, but the paper itself felt unnatural, the surface slimy instead of dry, and it seemed to move between my fingers, the way a worm wriggles when above ground. I quickly folded it into as tight a packet as I could and buried it deep in my pocket.

I longed for my freedom, but felt sorry for the witch who would have to touch this page to give it to me. I promised myself to reward her greatly.

Then I left the cabin and I followed Blackbeard. Having been at the Captain's side so often, none of the crew looked at this as odd. Blackbeard didn't object, so I counted myself lucky. He must have thought I would have some future use to his new crew and vessel, or more likely his new quest for glory had him uncaring about my presence one way or another.

Blackbeard's expert gunners brushed aside the *Ravenous'* gunners and took over their cannons. The other gunners did not object. Indeed, from the way they voluntarily transferred to the foundering *Queen*, they were eager to be further from the action when the cannonballs began to fly.

The *Ravenous* cast off from the dying *Queen* and sailed north. Dawson took the position of first mate as Blackbeard took command. Off in the distance, the sails of two sloops passed through the channel into the lagoon.

"Full sail, Mr. Dawson. Set a course to cross those ships' bows."

There was no denying that now Blackbeard saw the world through a madman's view. He'd made none of the usual calculations he'd made in the past before battle. Instead, he was sailing to strike at two ships with one, uncaring of how many guns those other ships carried. A lunatic's fire burned in his eyes, and none of the crew seemed willing to question his commands. I could not fault them, as they'd just seen the awful fate Blackbeard meted out to a rebellious Sneed.

We closed on the other two ships. They were both sloop-rigged and measured the same length as the *Ravenous*. The pirate ship carried only eight guns with three in each broadside. Even if each of the colonial vessels had only two-thirds our cannon, together they would still outgun us.

On the deck, the transferred gunners scrambled about like a kicked colony of ants. The cannons' powder, ball, and tools were differently organized than on the *Queen*, and the gunners who knew where everything was had abandoned ship. The cannons were mismatched, likely transferred from captured vessels. They were of varying calibers, and nothing about the battery was universal. This only added to the confusion and cursing that rose from the gundeck.

The distance between our ship and the Virginians shrank to where I could make out their colonial flag at the stern, and the Captain beside it watching us with a spyglass. To my dismay, a brace of three cannons peered from gunports along the side. That meant the one vessel alone was at parity with our ship. Unless the second was unarmed, we sailed into combat with the odds against us.

Then the odds became much worse. The helmsman had set a course to cross the first ship's bow. But it was clear that the wind did not favor us to do so. In addition to being unable to travel the preferred course, this other vessel was faster than ours. By the time we closed the gap to the Virginian lead, instead of crossing the T and bringing all our cannons to bear broadside against the ship's lightly armed bow, we'd be exchanging broadsides at our disadvantage. If our gunners ever managed to load the cannons, that was.

I began to wonder if Blackbeard had forgotten that he wasn't captaining the more powerful *Queen Anne's Revenge*, or if he'd become enchanted by his own perception of invulnerability. The option that I preferred not to entertain was that the loss of his treasure and his ship had been more than he could bear, and he'd become suicidal, with no compunction about taking the rest of us with him on that final journey.

The Virginian ships began the engagement. The lead ship fired a cannon in our direction. The ball fell far short of the ship and sent up a plume of white spray. The men on deck laughed at the poor marksmanship of the rival gunners. I thought the Captain was just giving us a warning, the opportunity to surrender or at least show them our stern and head back to sea.

If that was the colonial captain's plan, it failed. Blackbeard whooped at the short round, dashed down to the gundeck, and returned with a host of burning fuses sticking out from his beard. Excitement sparkled in his eyes and he cried, "Show them some iron, men!"

His display kindled the crew's fighting spirit. A cheer rose up from the *Queen's* gunners. The remaining *Ravenous* men could not help but be caught up in the rising enthusiasm.

Then the fuses in Blackbeard's beard sputtered out and died. The rousing spirit of the men seemed to die along with them. Sailors are a superstitious lot, and none could deny this as being anything but an ill omen.

With Blackbeard declining the Virginians' invitation to surrender, the lead ship let loose a full broadside. Fire spat from the cannons along its hull and a cloud of white smoke enveloped the ship's gundeck.

Cannonballs came screaming in our direction. I could track the balls as they flew through the air. This time, the gunners knew their range. Two balls punctured our mainsail. The others missed the canvas and its rigging by inches and then plunged into the sea behind us.

Blackbeard ordered a course correction so we would parallel the first ship's course. Then he shouted down to the gunners to fire at will.

The men had managed to get two of the cannons loaded. Fuses flared and then the guns fired a split-second apart. The acrid stink of burnt gunpowder stung my nose as a wave of smoke rolled over me.

The balls struck the sloop amidships and sent splinters and one of the cannons into the air. The inexperienced colonial crew fell about the ship in panic. Sails flapped and the ship veered away.

Blackbeard shouted in triumph. He ordered a course change for deeper water and the ship swung away from the shore.

I noticed several inexplicable spots of blood on Blackbeard's tunic. But there were no accompanying holes in the cloth where anything had pierced him, and it could not have been blood splatter from anyone around him.

My pondering of this medical puzzle was cut short by the sound of a volley of musket fire from the damaged sloop. I looked over to see several sharpshooters on the retreating sloop's deck who apparently had wanted one more crack at the pirate ship.

The marksmen knew what they were after. Musket balls struck our mast and severed a halyard. Our jib sail came crashing down onto the deck, smothering several men. With the ship mid-turn, the loss of this critical sail cut down our speed and our helm control. Instead of a sharp, speedy tack, the ship wallowed through a lazy turn, and came out of it practically becalmed.

The second Virginian sloop now bore down on us like a fox on an injured squirrel. At the stern I could see their Lieutenant Maynard shouting orders. What I did not see were any cannons on deck. This sloop was unarmed. What it carried instead was a healthy contingent of soldiers, formed in line of battle upon the deck, with pistols in their belts and muskets at the ready. It seemed Lieutenant Maynard's plan had been to have the first vessel disable us so the men of the second ship could board and subdue us. It appeared he wasn't going to let the failure of the first part of his plan keep him from executing the second part.

"She's unarmed!" Blackbeard said. "Keep her coming about! Canister broadside at close quarters."

I could see what his plan was. He'd come about to a course heading for the second sloop. When the ships passed, he'd blast it with shrapnel and shred the soldiers to bits. One can't defeat cannon fire with Minie balls.

Lieutenant Maynard must not have sensed the trap. He continued to shout orders to his men. A few scurried along the deck in front of the soldiers by the gunwale. I hoped they were pre-positioning bandages. They were going to need them.

By now, the gunners on our vessel were organized. The port side would be facing the sloop and the men quickly readied the guns with canisters of iron pellets. Any trepidation they'd felt at the start of battle seemed to have been replaced with murderous glee.

Blackbeard, however, looked even worse. The red stains on his shirt had spread. Blood ran down one arm and dripped off his elbow and onto the deck.

Sharp pains pricked my chest. I looked down to see blood had stained my shirt as well. I pulled my shirt away to see several wounds like bullet holes had erupted on my chest.

Then I watched a wound open up along the side of Blackbeard's neck, as if an invisible knife blade had slashed across his skin. Suddenly, I sensed the slash of cold steel against my own. I placed a hand against my neck and felt a bleeding wound that matched the one that had just appeared on Blackbeard.

To my horror, I realized what was happening. The protective spells the witches had cast over him were losing their potency. Even worse, all the wounds that they had protected Blackbeard from enduring were now showing themselves. The avoided effects of every bounced bullet, every deflected sword thrust, and every shed bit of shrapnel were appearing. Blackbeard was too engorged on bloodlust to feel it, the rest of the crew too preoccupied to see it.

Dumitra's binding spell meant that I'd experience every one of those wounds as well. Even if we slaughtered the Virginia crew and Blackbeard survived this attack, one of those returning wounds, or at least the combination of them, would likely prove fatal. My own time on Earth was running out as fast as Blackbeard's.

My binding spell to Blackbeard had to be broken, or I would certainly die alongside him.

In my pockets I still held the elements needed to cast the decoupling spell. With no chance to have a witch cast the spell, I had no choice but to attempt it. Doing so might kill me, but Blackbeard's demise would do just the same thing.

The sloop came broadside to us and within cannon range.

"Fire!" Blackbeard ordered.

The cannons boomed in unison. Smoke and flame belched from our ship and obscured the view of the sloop. When it cleared there wasn't a man left standing. Shredded sails flapped in the breeze and it stopped making headway. Soldiers lay about the deck like a fireplace's scattered ashes. We continued past the ship.

The pirate crew let out a roar of approval.

I moved to the lee of a bulkhead, pulled a mouse's skull from my pocket, and pressed it between my palms. I ground and ground until it was little more than dust. Holding that in one hand, I pulled the leather pouch of herbs from my pocket with the other. I opened the top and sifted the mouse skull bits into the pouch.

Blackbeard shouted commands to bring the ship around and board the enemy vessel. The glee on his face said he felt his dream of re-forming his little personal navy coming true. Then he moaned and swayed on his feet. He looked down in confusion to his right boot. The leather had swollen to twice the size of his left.

Pain shot from my right foot. I leaned against the bulkhead to favor it. I diagnosed Blackbeard's decaying spell had delivered the two of us an earlier avoided fracture or at best a severe sprain.

But the *Ravenous* approached the enemy ship and took Blackbeard's attention back to the battle. He favored that foot as he hobbled over to the starboard side where the crew would be boarding the ship filled with Virginian dead.

I needed blood to complete the elements for the spell. A drop of mine and more importantly, a drop of Blackbeard's. My sympathetic wounds made getting the sample of mine simple. I dripped some blood from the tip of my finger into the pouch. Now came the hard part.

Finding the pirate captain's blood would be easy. By now, I'd suffered at least a dozen wounds that had opened up on Blackbeard's body and my own. The edge of his hat was saturated from an erupted scalp wound. Some parts of his shirt were soddened to the point where one could think its initial color had been red. His face had the ghastly, pale pallor I'd seen on accident victims with severed arteries. I imagined that by now my face looked much the same.

I certainly felt these wounds' effects. I was becoming lightheaded and my knees were weak. Yet Blackbeard still commanded the crew with vigor, but where he got that reserve of strength was beyond me. What I was sure of was that he could not draw on it forever. Neither of us could long survive the culminated wounds Blackbeard was presenting. My time to cast this spell was quite short.

I went to Blackbeard's side, only gaining his notice as I touched his arm with my left hand. I held the leather pouch open in my right, just below his dripping elbow. I dared not look down to see if it was aligned to best catch the blood. His head snapped around and he looked at me with fury on his face, the way a lion would look at a pestering hyena distracting it from its kill.

Though it felt like staring into the sun, I locked my eyes on his. I needed his attention on my face, and not my actions. "Captain, you're wounded. Let me treat you."

"Get away from me before I strap you to a cannon barrel." He yanked his arm from my grasp and then used it to backhand me so hard that I went tumbling across the deck. I clenched the leather pouch tight in my hand. My head struck a railing and I became dizzy.

Blackbeard returned his focus to combat. The *Ravenous* coasted to a stop up alongside the sloop. Men heaved grappling hooks onto the other ship and pulled them tight. The two hulls crashed together to the moan and scrape of heavy timbers.

Blackbeard limped down to the main deck. "Board that ship!"

All the gunners who'd transferred from the *Queen Anne's Revenge* responded with a cheer. Then to a man, they drew cutlasses and swarmed onto the enemy ship. Blackbeard led their way.

The brigands crossed over the bodies of the dead and paused at the center of the colonial ship's deck. The pirate foray seemed to sputter out, as if they realized the same thing I had, that the ship was unnaturally calm. The broadside from our vessel could not have killed everyone at once.

Then Virginian soldiers came surging from the fore and aft stairways to the hold. They fell upon the intruders from both sides with a blaze of pistol fire. Pirates spun and dropped. The soldiers kept coming and soon the pirates were outnumbered two to one. Shoulder to shoulder, step by step, they beat a retreat to their own ship.

Then the dead rose. Most of the soldiers believed slaughtered in the shrapnel storm stood, pistols at the ready. The soldiers on deck had been but a fraction of the crew, and it appeared they had ducked down behind the gunwale, which I could now see had been reinforced with untrimmed logs. The layers of wood had absorbed the shrapnel while the men had feigned death. Virginia's Lieutenant Maynard had been the one setting a trap, and Blackbeard had stepped fully into it.

And now Blackbeard was ensnared. He and the boarding party were surrounded. Swords and knives crashed and banged in a solid ring around the pirate party. Their circle of defense kept contracting around the main mast.

The original crew of the *Ravenous* did not rush to their comrades' rescue. Perhaps they were untested in battle and shunned it, perhaps they were happy to have the boastful men of the *Queen* receive a comeuppance. They looked up to Captain Dawson, standing by the wheel. The look of dread on their faces said they prayed he would not order them across the gunwale.

He did not. He just watched the melee.

If I did not try to cast this spell now, in moments I'd share the fate about to befall the pirate captain.

The pouch had droplets of fresh blood around the opening. If none had fallen within as well, all my effort would be for naught. I closed the bag, whipped the grimoire page from my pocket, and unfolded it. The sensation of it between my fingers still repulsed me, so I pressed it against the deck with the sole of my shoe.

Lieutenant Maynard emerged from the sloop's hold and jumped up onto a crate on deck. He scanned the crowd until he saw Blackbeard just a few yards away.

I tore open my shirt. With a swipe across the deck, I set a match ablaze and read the phrase Justinia's spirit had shown me on the grimoire page. The place where Dumitra had tattooed me turned red. Then I touched the match to the pouch.

It came ablaze more powerfully than could be expected. I repeated the incantation in case I'd missed a syllable the first time, and then slammed the burning pouch against the tattoo's location on my chest.

"Blackbeard!" Lieutenant Maynard shouted. "Justice is served."

He aimed a pistol at the pirate's head. At that range, he would not miss.

My body caught fire with a breadth and intensity far beyond what the flames could do. The released power of the witchcraft surfaced the tattoo and set it aglow. Every nerve in my body screamed. Whatever I'd unleashed did not feel good, did not feel like it was dissolving the unnatural bond I had with Blackbeard. Instead, it felt like it was killing me, exacting revenge for daring to practice a dark art I had not mastered, nor even fully believed in.

Just as I accepted that my attempt had been a failure, the Lieutenant pulled the trigger of his pistol. The bullet crossed the deck and struck Blackbeard square in the heart. He staggered back until he hit the mast. Then he slid down to the ground.

As he lay dying, the world around me grew dark. My last thought as I entered a silent, lightless, dreamless void, was that I would never see my sister and niece again.

CHAPTER FORTY-TWO

A sharp poke to my side awakened me. I moaned and shielded my eyes from the sun.

"This one's still alive." One of the Virginian soldiers stood over me with his bayonet pressed hard against my rib. His tone was one of disappointment, rather than the elation one in my profession would have displayed upon discovering a survivor.

I felt as if I'd been baked like a shepherd's pie. I could name each muscle in the human body, and every one of mine felt like they'd been roasted from the inside. A film of ash and sulfur coated my mouth and I longed for a way to wash it out.

I realized that I had survived Blackbeard's death. I pulled back my tattered shirt and saw that the re-surfaced tattoo was gone. In its place was a purple, circular scar, such as I'd seen on burn victims. A quick inspection found no other burns on my body, despite the sensation that I'd been set afire. With great effort, I pulled myself up by the railing to survey the ship.

I couldn't tell by the sun how long I'd been asleep, but a lot had transpired during that time. The two ships were still lashed together by Blackbeard's grappling hooks, but the soldiers from Virginia had ended up being the ones to use them to their advantage. Apparently after Blackbeard's demise, they had leveraged their momentum and boarded the *Ravenous*.

The crew that had no stomach for saving their pirate admiral seemed to also have had no stomach for saving their own ship. These bullies were only brave when attacking the weak. No dead dotted the deck. Instead, what looked like the whole crew sat huddled by the bow under the watchful eyes of several soldiers. Other soldiers delivered new additions from around the ship, like shepherds herding scattered sheep. As hanging was the punishment for piracy, these sheep were being led to slaughter.

Lieutenant Maynard approached me. He stopped and looked me over head to toe.

"I haven't captured a lot of pirates in my day," he said, "but you certainly don't look like one."

My attire, though dirty and torn from my time as Blackbeard's guest, seemed to still be presentable enough to differentiate me from the rest of the pirate crew. I drew myself up and tried to stand straight on my broiled muscles.

"I am Doctor Baxter Whitcomb. Several months ago, I was taken prisoner from the passenger ship *Maureen Lavelle* by Blackbeard."

"I'm inclined to believe you," Lieutenant Maynard said. "Few still practice piracy at your age."

I hadn't seemed much older than the men onboard this ship and bristled at the insult. But so relieved was I about being alive, I chalked his assessment up to the dirt and gunpowder that caked my skin, and my wildly astray hair.

"I trust you can give me passage to the mainland," I said, "in different quarters than the prisoners. I have had my fill of pirates for a while."

"You may board my ship, Doctor. We'll tow the pirate ship home with its crew secured aboard it. Take care crossing between vessels. One of my soldiers will help you if needed."

I was embarrassed to be so unsteady on my feet, but relieved that it would be naturally attributed to the stress of the battle, rather than me having to explain my supernatural exercises.

I made my way to the other ship. I dared not look at the bow of the *Ravenous*, lest I catch the eye of any of the captured pirates. I did not want it thought I was lording my freedom over them. This crew's surrender likely saved my life, for had there been a pitched battle, there was no telling what might have befallen my sleeping body. I fervently desired to put this whole awful experience behind me as quickly as possible.

The Virginians had set some planks between the ships and I made my way across one with as much speed as my exhausted body could muster. At the other ship, one of the crew offered a hand to help me down onto the deck. I accepted it and was thrilled to finally set foot on a vessel that was not a prison.

"There you go, Gramps," the soldier said with a laugh, and then he walked away.

Such a clear insult was not something a man in my station of life should accept from a common soldier, especially a Colonial. I raised a finger to admonish him and noticed how wrinkled and spotted my skin appeared. A check of my other hand revealed the same.

I touched my face. My beard felt coarse, my skin like aged leather. Deep wrinkles creased the corners of my eyes.

A polished brass plaque on a bulkhead contained the name and launch date of this sloop. I dashed over to it and buffed one section to a better shine with the sleeve of my shirt. I peered at my reflection and recoiled in shock.

In appearance, my age had doubled. My hair and beard were white, my face wrinkled, my skin had the transparency of old age. I had passed out a while ago as a young man, and awakened now as a septuagenarian.

My disbelief of the situation vanished as I remembered Justinia's admonition. *All magic has a price.* She had been trained to perform it, practiced on small spells to allow her body to grow strong enough to withstand the power. Even with that, the mystic power had taken its toll on her. In my case, it had ravaged my uninitiated body.

Magic had saved my life, but taken most of it back as its fee.

CHAPTER FORTY-THREE

We were halfway to Big Pine Point when Lieutenant Maynard ordered Blackbeard's body brought to the bow of his ship. Blackbeard's hat, shirt and trousers had been removed, likely shredded and passed out as souvenirs to the soldiers. His body contained at least two dozen punctures and slashes, not including the ragged hole Maynard's bullet had made in his chest. I could hear crewmen marvel at how he could have survived so many gashes. Only I knew the true source of all those wounds.

The men dropped the corpse back-first onto the deck. Lieutenant Maynard stepped up to Blackbeard with his sword drawn, and spat on his corpse. Then he raised his sword over his head and with one mighty stroke severed Blackbeard's head. It rolled to one side.

"Put that on a pike," he ordered, "and then display it on the bow. Let any in this town who harbored pirates know that this is the fate pirates earn, as will those who support them."

Several soldiers took to this task with ghoulish zeal. By the time we reached the dock, Blackbeard's milky eyes stared out from the bowsprit.

The other Virginian sloop had already docked, remaining seaworthy despite its battle damage. We cast off the captured pirate ship. One of our men dropped its anchor and prepared its longboats to ferry in the prisoners.

We tied up to one of the docks and received a hero's welcome from the townspeople. The crowd along the wharf were thrilled that the pirate scourge had ended, or at least were adamant that they be seen feeling that way if they'd had any previous pirate loyalties.

Setting foot on land was a more disconcerting experience than I was prepared for. The human constitution adapts to its environment, and when at sea it learns to compensate for the constant motion of the vessel. Now ashore after so many months, my body could not comprehend having stable ground under my feet. Bouts of dizziness came and went as my equilibrium compensated for motion that was no longer present. Perhaps many of the staggering sailors I'd seen in English streets had not been quite as drunk as I'd assumed.

So here I was in Big Pine Point, a stranger in the New World with nothing but the tattered clothes upon my back. The mayor, who'd been so quick to appease the pirates in exchange for bribes, greeted the Virginians with effusive praise for ridding the coast of the brigand scum, and decried how their own corrupt governor had let them run wild. The man's hypocrisy disgusted me.

Blackbeard's impaled head upon the bow wasn't greeted with the revulsion such a display would have aroused in my London neighborhood. The people responded with anything from a morbid fascination to a vengeful spitting on the head.

I overheard many conversations in the crowd. The story of the battle had just been relayed by Lieutenant Maynard, but already the versions repeated by listeners were wildly embellished and sometimes outright wrong. The size of Blackbeard's boat doubled. The number of dead pirates tripled. There was treasure aboard the captured boat.

The rumors that churned my stomach were the ones where Justinia was reported to be a willing accomplice to the pirates, and had made spells to help Blackbeard plunder the innocent. These were always followed by a lengthy disparagement of the Gypsy people.

Being a stranger on an arriving ship full of strangers from Virginia, no one took any special notice of my arrival. The soldiers milled about, accepting praise and offerings of food and drink. But I declined and stepped away. I had something here I needed to do.

I left the dock and made my way through town. The streets were less familiar in the daylight, and my recall of events I'd experienced under Blackbeard's reign of terror were not the clearest. But eventually I found my way to the house where Justinia had entrusted her daughter to her grandparents. I knew myself to be an awful sight, but I had no way to make myself more presentable, and I could not delay telling the family the truth about Justinia.

I went to knock on the door and it opened before I raised my hand. A disheveled old man blocked the doorway. Dark half-moons hung under his bloodshot eyes. He gripped a large hunting knife in one hand.

"Damn you all! I told you if another one of you set foot on my property, I'd split you wide open."

I stepped back off the porch, wishing to appear unaggressive and also wanting to stay out of his reach in case I didn't.

He squinted and looked me over. "You're not from around here. What do you want?"

In my new, aged state, he did not recognize me as one of the party who had kidnapped Justinia. There was one positive outcome from the price magic had extracted from me.

"I was a captive aboard Blackbeard's pirate vessel, just liberated by the Virginians."

Before I could say any more, Justinia's daughter Abigail stepped in front of her grandfather. Her face had an eerily calm expression. "It's okay, Pop Pop. Mommy sent him."

The girl's statement wasn't true, but it wasn't exactly untrue either. Had Justinia sent me? Perhaps indirectly she had. My bigger question was how did this girl know? Since the grandfather didn't flinch at the comment, Abigail and her mother must have had some mystic Gypsy connection that I didn't understand.

The grandfather stepped aside. "Come in if you don't mind people seeing you enter a Roma house."

"I hope they all see it."

I stepped in and he closed the door behind us. The house had but one room, sparsely furnished. There were two large beds and one smaller one I assumed was for Justinia's daughter.

"I was onboard the ship with Justinia," I said. "There are already rumors around about her helping Blackbeard. I can tell you that none of them are true. She only went with him to protect all of you from retribution if she didn't. Once she was onboard, she consistently worked against Blackbeard every chance she had."

"Was she killed when the Virginians captured the pirate ship?" the grandfather said.

I had to relate the sad story of Justinia being forced to protect the pirate treasure and her betrayal. The grandfather nodded in approval when I described the vengeance Justinia wrought upon her attackers and was definitely pleased that Blackbeard had been forever cut off from all his ill-gotten gains. Abigail just listened with the same impassive look on her face.

At the end of the story, I told them I would pray for Justinia's soul. I may have started my voyage to America as an indifferent practitioner of religious faith, but I arrived with a changed outlook on both the spiritual and supernatural. My sister would have been proud.

But the grandfather just shook his head with sadness. "Your prayers will make no difference. Dying like that, with so much anger, entombed in that rock, her spirit will never rest."

The little girl pulled something on a chain around her neck from within her shirt. It was the missing part of the medallion Justinia had worn.

"Your mother never took her part of that medallion off," I said.

"She promised we would reunite the pieces in the future," Abigail said, "and we will. We will find her."

"You were there," the grandfather said. "Where is this island?"

"I am a physician, not a seaman. I couldn't say where I'd been during any of my enforced voyage. Blackbeard had a map of the island and its location, but I can't say if that scroll of parchment survived the grounding of the *Queen Anne's Revenge* or the battle with the *Ravenous*."

"That's okay. As of now, this is a Roma family matter, no longer any of your concern. Thank you for telling us the true story."

I opened the door to leave. "My condolences for your loss. Justinia was a fine, brave woman."

It would have been horribly inappropriate to mention my personal feelings for her, or the similar ones I am sure she returned. I was content to keep that my special secret. Writing this memoir is the first time I've shared it with anyone. But she is gone, and since the magic robbed many years from me, I fear that soon I will be gone as well, so I thought it best to leave a record of my devotion here. My love is another tribute to refute any wild rumors about such a fine woman.

As for me, I was a penniless stranger in a strange land. The only people I knew were over a thousand miles of wildlands away in Boston. My prospects were so bleak that making any kind of plan seemed pointless.

Then as if to validate my new-found religious interest, Divine Providence shined upon me. The mayor approached me as I walked through town. He said he'd heard from the pirates that I was a doctor. He said the town, and the sailors on the ships that stopped here, were in need of one. He begged me to set up practice here instead of whatever my original destination had been. In my elation, I nearly kissed the man for his offer. Big Pine Point became my new home.

In time, I was able to send a letter to my sister and give her a shorter, sanitized version of my adventure with Blackbeard. She replied with heartfelt joy and demanded that I book passage to Boston at her expense for a permanent reunion.

But I could not. My body felt worn and weak, now being twice its chronological age, and a long journey was not in the cards. I did not want to admit it, but I was also now deathly afraid of sea travel. In addition, my practice here was quite robust, and these people needed me.

But the main reason, one that no one would ever know, was that I wanted to spend my final few years watching Abigail grow up. She was all I had left of Justinia.

And it seems that end is coming close. The downside of being a physician is that you can diagnose all your own ills with great accuracy, as you intimately know all the patient's symptoms. My self-diagnoses have been rather grim recently.

I've left two copies of this memoir. One will be entrusted to my sister, Elizabeth, who deserves to know the whole story. The other will go to Abigail, so she and all her descendants will know the truth about the time I and Justinia were forced to sail under the skeleton flag.

The End

AFTERWORD

When is a prequel not a prequel? When it is *Under the Skeleton Flag*.

I wrote the second installation of the Rick and Rose Sinclair Adventures series called *Voyage to Blackbeard's Island*. Rick and Rose are antiques dealers in 1938 who discover an apparently authentic map to the island where Blackbeard was said to have hidden his treasure. Rick convinces Rose to go. There are a lot of twists and turns as they fight off giant caimans, huge iguanas, and a horde of sea wasps. They eventually find a pirate treasure ship buried inside an extinct volcano. They also discover the angry spirit of a witch named Justinia who wants all trespassers dead. I'll let you read the whole novella yourself for all the details and the ending.

The more I wrote of that manuscript, the more interesting the backstory of how that ship got there became. I made myself a lot of notes, but the bulk of them could not be incorporated into *Voyage* because they didn't drive the plot forward, and most of all because no one alive in 1938 would know all the details about what had happened in 1718.

Unwilling to let a good story go to waste, I finished the first draft of *Voyage* and then plunged right into what would become *Under the Skeleton Flag*. Though it is in a completely different style, written more in the 18th century language and structure, I think it is a good complementary read to *Voyage*, and vice versa.

In this book, I'm afraid I've played fast and loose with some of the details around Blackbeard's last voyages, but most of the main events really happened, though I compressed the timeline.

Likely born as Edward Teach (location in dispute), the future Blackbeard acquired a taste for plunder as a privateer for England during Queen Anne's War. At the end of the war, his legal commission to plunder expired, but he just kept at it.

He commanded his own ship for the first time in 1717. He rechristened the captured ship *Queen Anne's Revenge* and it had a crew of approximately 300 men and between 30 and 40 cannons, depending on the source material. He and his men sailed the Caribbean and the Atlantic coast of North America. He was able to make present day North Carolina a base of operations by bribing the governor to look the other way.

Blackbeard knew that a fearsome image could tip the battle in his favor, and cultivated one of being a bloodthirsty, crazed pirate. He did indeed wrap slow-burning, lighted fuses in his long hair and beard to intimidate his victims. As in the story, he did have a reputation for inhuman strength and for invincibility, but there was never any claim that witchcraft was the source of either.

The pirate blockade of Charleston actually happened and medical supplies were part of the ransom Blackbeard demanded. Medical care was scarce anywhere, but more so on pirate ships. Even with that, there is a good collection of medical devices that have been excavated from the wreck of the *Queen* and on display at the North Carolina Maritime Museum.

By 1718, Blackbeard had amassed a personal fleet of four captured vessels. At this point, the governor of Virginia decided if the Carolina colony wasn't going to stop this pirate, he would, and he dispatched Lieutenant Maynard and two Virginian vessels, the *Ranger* and another sloop, to take out Blackbeard. By now, The *Queen Anne's Revenge* had been run aground and abandoned on a sand bar off the North Carolina coast and Blackbeard's fleet was down one other vessel.

In real life, there was a large amount of time between the loss of the *Queen* and the arrival of the Virginian ships, not the same day like in my story. By all accounts, the battle played out as depicted here, with the Virginians ambushing the pirates as they tried to board their ship. In the ensuing battle, Blackbeard suffered twenty-five stab wounds and five gunshots before succumbing to his injuries. As in the story, he was decapitated, and his head hung on the victorious *Ranger's* bowsprit as it sailed back into port.

While there has always been talk about Blackbeard's treasure, it is very unlikely that there ever was any. Blackbeard's crew split the spoils after raids, and pirates were not known to be thrifty or to put a few doubloons away for a rainy day.

In 1996, a private salvage company discovered the wreck of the *Queen Anne's Revenge*. A lot of the artifacts have been salvaged and conserved. There's a splendid display of them at the North Carolina Maritime Museum in Beaufort, and anyone interested in seeing some up close and personal pirate gear should check the museum out. I've made pictures I took during my visit available on my website www.russellrjames.com.

The skeleton and heart flag described was one actually flown from Blackbeard's ship. One of the earliest pirate flags used, it depicted a heart dripping blood and a skeleton holding an hourglass and spear. The hope was that the sight of it would intimidate ships to surrender, and it did just that. And while this symbol was the real thing, the witch symbols used throughout the book are straight from my imagination.

All of the Roma witchcraft is just as fictional, although the Roma people do have a very rich culture with ties to mysticism.

To make the doctor's practices and procedures as accurate as possible, I did a bit of research into 18th century medical practices. There's an entire horror story ready to be written just about those. What were considered scientific facts and sound practices at the time were supported more by myth and wishful thinking than the use of any scientific method. There was little concept of the cause of infection and "laudable pus" oozing from a wound was considered a good sign. Manufactured medicines were a rarity and the few that existed frequently contained poisons like mercury. Blood-letting was a common treatment for practically anything. I so wanted the doctor to be seen as conscientious and concerned, but given the practices in use at the time, it's likely he came across as some quack butcher. So please cut him some slack as he uses some, at best, questionable practices. He honestly meant well.

In the first chapter, the doctor refers to the eleven colonies in North America. Before you send me angry emails that there were thirteen, that number is historically accurate. North and South Carolina were not legally separated by the king into two colonies at the time, and Georgia, the thirteenth colony, wasn't founded until well after 1718.

Thanks go out to Donna Fitzpatrick, Deb DeAlteriis, and Lucille Bransfield for judicious Beta reading of the typo-ridden first draft. You are all amazing!

I hope you enjoyed this historical thriller and it inspires you to check out *Voyage to Blackbeard's Island* if you already haven't, as well as the other Rick and Rose Sinclair Adventures. Feel free to drop me a line at rrj@russellrjames.com or through Twitter via @rrjames14 or on Facebook as Russell R James or Russell James – Author. Your purchase of this book has helped make my dream of being an author come true, and from the bottom of my heart I say thank you.

-*Russell James*

www.ingramcontent.com/pod-product-compliance
Lightning Source LLC
Chambersburg PA
CBHW061235170626
46809CB00007B/2692